D0593534

Honestly Dearest, You're Dead

ALSO BY JACK FREDRICKSON

A Safe Place for Dying

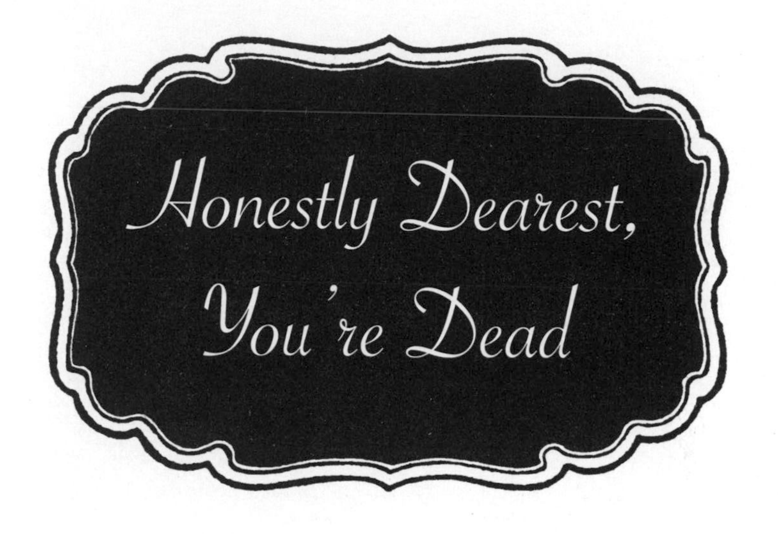

Jack Fredrickson

MINOTAUR BOOKS
NEW YORK

This is a work of fiction. All of the characters, organizations, and events portrayed in this novel are either products of the author's imagination or are used fictitiously.

A THOMAS DUNNE BOOK FOR MINOTAUR BOOKS.
An imprint of St. Martin's Publishing Group.

 Printed in the United States of America. For information, address St. Martin's Press, 175 Fifth Avenue, New York, N.Y. 10010.

www.thomasdunnebooks.com
www.minotaurbooks.com

Library of Congress Cataloging-in-Publication Data

Fredrickson, Jack.
Honestly dearest, you're dead / Jack Fredrickson.—1st ed.
p. cm.
ISBN-13: 978-0-312-38092-2
ISBN-10: 0-312-38092-5
1. Private investigators—Illinois—Chicago—Fiction. 2. Chicago (Ill.)—Fiction. 3. Murder—Investigation—Fiction. I. Title.
PS3606.R437H66 2009
813'.6—dc22 2008030429

First Edition: January 2009

10 9 8 7 6 5 4 3 2 1

For Jack and for Lori

ACKNOWLEDGMENTS

Once again, Missy Lyda, Eric Frisch, Mary Anne Bigane, and Joseph Bigane III worked at more than the words.

Once again, Kate Scherler worked at more than direction.

Once again, Patrick Riley worked at more than the Web site.

Once again, Marcia Markland and Diana Szu worked at more than keeping everything moving forward, and once again India Cooper smoothed over everything I missed, and some of the things I should have.

And once again, as she has for forever, Susan . . .

Lucky me.

Honestly Dearest, You're Dead

Prologue

She wouldn't have heard the back door glass being punched out, not in those winds. Later, the blueberry cop would say the *Gazette* reported they gusted up to fifty miles an hour, and that was in Kalamazoo, safer inland. Where she was, close to Lake Michigan, they would have raged louder. Hawking across the ice cliffs at the shore, building their furies as they screamed across the frozen fields, sucking the red branches of the lifeless blueberry bushes into grotesque tendrils, like twists of frozen blood, the winds could have hit her narrow little cottage at sixty, seventy miles an hour. Shingles clattering, windows banging, her place must have sounded like a cheap pine coffin being beat on by a hundred angry hands. She wouldn't have heard the glass break.

Nor would she have felt the sudden chill. Her thermostat was set down to a frugal sixty degrees, and there were gaps in the siding a fat man could stick his thumb through. There was no knowing what the inside temperature was that night—if it even was night—because nobody came by for days. By then the frigid air blowing through the three broken windows—the one on the kitchen door, broken carefully inward; the other two, larger, smashed out in panic, spraying bloody glass all over the snow-packed drive—had chilled the house to freezing.

She'd fought. In her frenzy and her fear, she'd thrown herself at those two big windows. Each time, she'd been grabbed and dragged back, dripping bloody shards onto the frayed living room rug. I tried to step around them, but they were everywhere, crunching under my feet like bits of old bones.

There was blood in the bedroom, too, frozen little droplets on the faded floral wallpaper, the oak table, the bare plank floor. On the knurled wheel that turned the rubber platen of the ancient black Underwood typewriter.

I stopped, took a breath, like always when I saw one of those old Underwoods. A long time ago, I'd known a girl who owned a typewriter like that, a blond girl with a boy's name. I was with her when she bought it, helped carry it home, watched as she turned it upside down to scratch her initials on it to make it her own.

Outside, in the dimming light, the wind rustled, restless, waiting. I eased the old typewriter over and bent to look for marks made long ago. My eyes stung, wet. From the cold of the cottage, I told myself. From the horror of the butchery that had happened there.

It had nothing to do with the past.

One

Three days earlier, I was up on a ladder.

February is the wrong month to be outside on a ladder in Rivertown. It's especially wrong when it is twenty degrees outside, the wind blowing up the Willahock River is strong, and the ladder, bought too well used from the widow of a housepainter who'd died in a fall, swayed like Katharine Hepburn sashaying through an old movie. But I had no choice. A pigeon, apparently still distraught from being evicted from the stone turret he'd spent a lifetime marking with excrement, the place I now called home, had killed himself smashing in the glass on one of my second-floor slit windows. That in turn sent what little heat I'd managed to trap blowing out that shattered window like smoke up a flue, and me up a ladder on a day when I should have been inside, bemoaning the fact that I didn't have central heating.

I'd just gotten to the top of the ladder with a piece of plywood and was hugging the top rung like life itself, waiting for the swaying to stop, when my cell phone rang down below.

"Mr. Elstrom's office," Leo Brumsky said, on the ground. He'd insisted on coming over to hold the ladder. He's a highly regarded provenance specialist, makes upwards of four hundred thousand dollars a year authenticating items for the major auction houses in New York, Chicago, and Los Angeles, and has been my friend since grammar school. As a counterweight to my swaying ladder, though, his five feet six inches and one hundred and forty pounds was worthless. Carefully, so as not to excite the ladder, I looked down at the world shifting beneath me.

"Who may I say is calling?" In the frigid air, Leo's words made white puffs under the chartreuse knitted acrylic hat, topped with a purple pom, that he told me he'd bought for fifty-nine cents. He'd also told me the hat was new, but I didn't believe it. The way the acrylic drooped below the fur of Leo's black eyebrows suggested there'd been a previous owner, somebody with an enormous head. Either that or that the hat had been stretched, for years, over a basketball.

"I'll try to catch him as he's coming down." Tilting his head back to grin, preening with his wit, he covered the mouthpiece between two mittened hands, chartreuse to match, and waved the cell phone high, like Muhammad Ali back in the day, after a victory.

"Is this necessary?" I called down.

"How many business calls do you get?"

He had a point: I hadn't gotten a client call in five weeks. I undulated down to the frozen snow, set the plywood against the ladder, and took the phone.

"Dek Elstrom," I said.

"Vlodek Elstrom, of Rivertown, Illinois?" a man's voice asked.

"How may I help?" Unless the guy was offering unbreakable windows, installed free, I wasn't interested. I was cold.

"My name is William Aggert. I'm an attorney in West Haven, Michigan. A client of mine, Louise Thomas, has passed away."

He paused so I could mumble the appropriate regrets.

"Never heard of her," I said.

"Never heard of Louise Thomas?" I learned long ago that lawyers like to repeat themselves. It doubles their billable hours.

"Never," I said, switching phone hands and jamming the cold one in the pocket of my surplus store pea coat. One doesn't risk gloves when clinging to life aboard a moving ladder.

"Never heard—"

It was too damned cold. "Are you going to try to bill me for this?"

"Miss Thomas named you executor of her estate," he said.

"If I don't know Miss Thomas, how can I be her executor?"

"You've never heard of Louise—?"

I stomped my feet, switched hands again, thought this time of plunging the cold one under Leo's hat. There was plenty of room between his bald head and the acrylic.

"Happens all the time," he said.

"Misidentifying an executor?"

He gave a lawyerly laugh, dry and uncomprehending. "Executors being named by people they don't know."

Leo pulled the basketball warmer down to his chin and started to dance around, stomping his feet to keep warm. In the orange traffic officer's jacket he'd gotten at the same place he'd bought the hat, he looked like a fire hydrant with rhythm.

"My obligation is to inform you of her passing, and to provide you with the necessary instruments for you to fulfill your responsibilities," Aggert said.

"To be executor."

"Exactly."

"How much would that cost me?"

Aggert made a clicking sound. It could have been a loose tooth, or it could have been a breath mint. "Ms. Thomas gave me money to be escrowed for your fee."

"How much?" I asked, perked up like a falcon sighting a field mouse.

"Seven hundred dollars."

"Seven hundred dollars to close out the estate of someone I don't know?"

"Exactly," he said.

"When did she pass?"

"Recently."

"How recently?"

"How flexible is your schedule?" he clicked. No doubt, he was working on a breath mint. "West Haven's just a couple of hours from you."

I didn't tell him I had no appointments scheduled, for anything. "I can rearrange things, be up there on Monday."

"Morning, then?"

"What's the rush?"

"I try to close out estates quickly. I like things nice and tidy."

"Afternoon," I said. It wouldn't hurt to create the impression I had other things to do besides rehabbing a limestone turret to sell, should Rivertown ever become fashionable.

"One o'clock," he said and started to say good-bye.

"Wait," I said. "Who inherits?"

"It's an odd will, Mr. Elstrom. Yours is the only name stated."

"No one is named a beneficiary?"

"You merely execute, Mr. Elstrom."

"I don't understand."

"I look forward to meeting you on Monday," Aggert said and hung up.

Next to me, Leo was still stomping, his hat down over his chin. I tapped his hand with the phone in case the chartreuse had been too noisy for him to hear.

"That sounded intriguing," he said, proving me wrong. He lifted his knitted veil.

I handed him the phone, picked up the plywood, and swayed back up the ladder.

A half hour later, we were on that half of the second floor that I call my office, because it's where I keep my card table desk, the electric blue La-Z-Boy recliner I bought for twelve bucks, thirdhand, and the cartons of files from the days when I had a healthy business, chasing down information for law firms and insurance companies.

Leo, huddled in the white plastic chair and still bundled in orange and chartreuse, waved a mitten at the curved limestone walls. "What is it with you and inheritances?"

I'd inherited my grandfather's five-story turret, the only part of his dream castle he ever got built, from an aunt who hadn't liked me much. At the time I'd scoffed—it had come plastered with decades of pigeon poop, old tax liens, and a zoning classification that made it unsalable. Then my business and reputation got trashed, my bank account vaporized, and my marriage collapsed. My perspective got altered. I moved into the pigeon-scented turret prepared to shovel my way to a new life.

"It didn't turn out so bad," I said to the limestone walls.

Leo pulled the chartreuse another inch down his head.

"Besides," I went on, "I'm not inheriting this time; I'm merely executing."

"The estate of somebody you've never heard of." He pulled the chair closer to the oil space heater I drag around in the winter. It won't heat the whole room, but it keeps the coffee from icing over.

I switched off the computer, ending a quick Internet search for Louise Thomas, L. Thomas, Lou Thomas. There were hundreds, but none listed near West Haven, Michigan. "All I can figure is that she worked for a client," I said, pointing to the boxes of old files. Nowadays, all that got added to the cartons was dust.

"I've got to get out of this igloo." Leo stomped his feet as he stood up. Jamming his mittens into his traffic jacket, he angled his purple-pommed head toward the huge stone fireplace. There was one on every floor, each large enough to roast Paul Bunyan and his ox. "Don't you ever want to build a fire?"

"It would take a cord of firewood just to get it going."

"But jeez," he said, tapping the space heater with the toe of his boot, "how long will that little thing take to warm up this pile?"

Central heating was several thousands of dollars away.

"Come July, this place will be toasty," I said.

Sunday afternoon, Amanda Phelps stood behind the lectern on the stage of Fullerton Hall in the Art Institute of Chicago, her face owlish in the yellow glow above the little hooded lamp. She is round-faced and beautiful, and she is my ex-wife.

She snapped off the display from the overhead projector, ending her presentation. "Immediately following the concert, we will meet at the top of the Grand Staircase for a short tour to view Jean-Baptiste Joseph Wicar's *Virgil Reading the Aeneid to Augustus, Octavia, and Livia,* 1790 to 1793, Pompeo Batoni's *Peace and War,* 1776, and Antonio Canova's *Bust of Paris,* 1809."

Of such came excitement—hers, not mine, although I did let myself hope that the name of the last piece, Canova's, promised something akin to presenting Dolly Parton as the Bust of Pigeon Forge, Tennessee.

Amanda introduced the brass quintet, lit the hall with a dazzling smile, and left the stage to sincere applause.

She'd gotten me a center seat in the second row. "To keep an eye on me, to make sure I'm paying attention," I accused. "To fully appreciate the interplay of the trumpets, trombone, French horn, and tuba," she said, shaking her head. "To make it impossible for me to sleep discreetly," I said. Winters, I get drowsy when exposed to heat. She smiled and said nothing more.

The five hornists, or whatever they're called, materialized in suits dark enough to enthuse funeral directors and arranged themselves on the stage in a semicircle, trumpets at the outside, tuba fellow at the base. Amanda had carted me to enough performances at Chicago's Symphony Center to learn to distinguish a violin from a drum, but never had I sat so close to the horns. For the first part of what the program called Hellendaal's Centone No. 10, all went well enough. Then the group stopped, and the trombonist and the French horn player slid curved pieces off their instruments and began shaking them vigorously, as though they'd discovered cockroaches dancing inside their horns. It wasn't bugs they were shaking out, though—it was spit, lots of it, glistening as it cascaded onto the hardwood floor. Incredibly, no one laughed; the audience sat patiently and silently, as though what they were witnessing was normal behavior.

The trumpeters got into the spirit of the event after the second part of the Centone, and removed their own bits of brass for a solid shake and spray. The performance became complete at the end of the third part, when the tuba player, a bald, genial-looking fellow who could have passed for a television weatherman, lifted the tuba above his head and began shaking it as if he were summoning Zeus to send down the rains. His face went purple as, indeed, the rains did come. Great gobs of spit pelted the floor like a summer thunderstorm. So it went, to the end of the program. It was wet work for sure, and at last I understood why, in full orchestras, the horn players are kept at the back of the stage.

Afterward, I followed the audience up the Grand Staircase to join Amanda for the gallery tour. I stayed with the group for fifteen or twenty minutes as Amanda explained some of the nuances in the works she'd presented during her slide presentation, though once I'd ascertained that Canova's *Bust of Paris* had nothing in common with Dolly Parton, I lost interest and hung back as the group followed Amanda through the galleries. When it was over, I waited downstairs in the marble foyer.

She came down in a hooded black wool coat that matched her hair and was only one shade darker than her eyes. "What did you think of the performance?" she asked, slipping her arm through mine.

"Drainage," I said, holding the door open for her.

"Hopeless," she said as we went out.

We ate at the little trattoria where I'd proposed, two years before. Even though we were divorced, we were still trying, and it was still our place.

She tore a piece of Italian bread and dipped it in olive oil. "Tell me more about this mysterious phone call."

"I've been named executor of a will written by a person I don't know."

"No clue?"

"None. I'm guessing Louise Thomas is someone I brushed against when my business was healthy."

"But you'll be paid?" She was looking at me intently, inspecting my eyes for visions of dancing sugarplums. Amanda likes it when I'm solidly grounded.

"Seven hundred clams," I said, before she could test the point. "The lawyer told me lots of executors are not personally acquainted with their decedents."

"What's to do if there are no beneficiaries?"

"I'm guessing the estate has just enough money to pay all the outstanding bills. Should be a quick seven hundred."

"You didn't really discuss what's involved with the lawyer, did you, Dek?" Her eyes sparkled from the candle burning atop the wine bottle.

"Just the important part: the seven-hundred-dollar fee. I'll drive up tomorrow morning, and then the rest will be known."

She smiled at my foolishness, and we talked of other things. Afterward, we went back to her condominium on Lake Shore Drive. That was still one of our places, too.

Two

I set off for Michigan at ten the next morning. The sky was low, and a light snow was falling, but it was not enough to slow the Illinois Tollway. By February, toll road pilots are a brazen lot. With months of winter driving behind them, they blow through whiteouts and icy patches, balancing coffees, croissants, and cell phones, with barely a twitch of a thumb on their steering wheels. I breezed to the state line.

Things slowed, though, in Indiana. Winter grows potholes along its northernmost interstate the way summer grows weeds in its fields. My Jeep is nine years old, its shock absorbers and springs long retired, and I had to back off on my speed to keep my teeth in the places I was accustomed to finding them.

Slowing things, too, were the billboards picturing surgically perfected women with come-hither pouts, who danced naked at gentlemen's clubs. So many of them smiled under banners proclaiming that truckers were especially welcome that I began to wonder how long it took long-haul drivers to pass through that part of Indiana. If a gentleman trucker stopped at even a third of the clubs where he was sure to be welcomed, it might take months. I left Indiana understanding why over-the-road shipping had become so expensive.

. . .

West Haven was right on Lake Michigan, two miles due west of a Wal-Mart. It was an old resort town of ice cream parlors, beachwear shops, and sandal stores, set on a main street that sloped down to a shore lined with curled ice cliffs of waves that looked flash frozen, as if by an instant's touch of an ice goddess's wand. Everything was white and shiny—the sky, the lake, the beach—except for a small red lighthouse at the end of a pier that stood like a crimson exclamation point against the vanished horizon.

I parked the Jeep in an angled space and walked along the sidewalk. Most of the shops were closed, their bright awnings rolled up tight against the gray of February. Attorney Aggert's name was lettered in gold leaf on a second-floor window in the next block, above a lit-up discount store named Fizzy's. The discounter's window featured a display of black hydraulic automobile jacks nestled on a scattering of fluffed striped beach towels—everything one would need for a festive day of tire changing at the beach. SHOP EARLY, the banner exclaimed. I accepted the universality of that, even though I had never thought to combine beach time with auto repair, for never had I seen a banner proclaiming SHOP LATE.

I had an hour before my appointment with Aggert, so I opted for lunch in an exposed-brick-and-fern place across the street. I enjoy opting for lunch, though it's not something I can afford to do often. But today was a special day. I was about to come into seven hundred dollars for very little work.

The hostess smoking a cigarette at the little table by the door appeared to have undergone the same flash freezing that had trapped the waves along the shore, right down to the curl of smoke that hung suspended in the air above her head. I made a polite cough and she looked up, crushed out her cigarette in a black Bakelite ashtray, and told me I could sit anywhere I wanted. She lit another cigarette as I headed to a booth against the wall.

There was only one other diner in the place, a blond fellow frowning at the stock market pages of the *Wall Street Journal* like a man reading his own obituary. He was about my age, too young to be wearing a red-checked shirt with a blue necktie and blue suspenders.

I was hungry but ordered responsibly—only a Diet Coke and vegetables consisting of a Cobb salad and the house specialty, a foot of fried onion rings, stacked on a pole. While I waited, I sipped the Coke and studied the old photographs on the wall. They were from the days when ships carrying commerce used to float over from Chicago. In the century that had passed, shipping had gone high speed, but I wondered if goods from Chicago might have arrived faster in those old days, given the proliferation of gentlemen's clubs slowing trucks in Indiana. Still, I allowed there might have been ladies in high-button shoes, feather hats, and little else back in those old days, too, dancing along the shore in Indiana, pouting at the ship captains. Indiana might always have been that kind of place.

The salad was excellent. So, too, were the onion rings, served twelve inches high as advertised. At five to one, I paid the bill and tiptoed away, careful not to disturb the hostess nodding by the smoldering ashtray at the front door.

I popped Tic Tacs, climbing the stairs next to the discount store, so I'd arrive smelling like a candy cane. The frosted glass door at the top opened right into Aggert's office, and there sat the man in the red-checked shirt and blue suspenders I'd seen in the restaurant, still reading his *Wall Street Journal.* He set down his newspaper and stood up, and we shook hands across his desk. He was chewing breath mints, as well—Altoids—from a little red and white tin centered on his desk. He motioned for me to sit in one of the visitor's chairs.

He ground up a last fragment of Altoid and handed me a tan envelope. "Ms. Thomas's will, and her keys. The estate doesn't appear to be very large. It shouldn't require much of your time."

I opened the envelope. Inside was a folded single sheet of paper and a key ring. I unfolded the sheet of paper. "LAST WILL," it read, in slightly uneven manual-typewriter letters. "I, KNOWN AS LOUISE THOMAS, BEING OF SOUND MIND, HEREBY LEAVE ALL MY ACCOUNTS, POSSESSIONS, 1983 DODGE, CONTENTS IN THE HOUSE

ON COUNTY ROAD 12, RAMBLING, MICHIGAN, AND ANY OTHER ITEMS AS MAY BE OF VALUE TO MY EXECUTOR, VLODEK ELSTROM, OF RIVERTOWN, ILLINOIS, TO DISPERSE AS HE SEES FIT IN THE RESOLUTION OF ANY MATTERS RESULTING FROM MY DEATH." Her signature was at the bottom. Aggert and somebody else had signed on the two witness lines.

I looked across the desk at the lawyer. "Odd sort of will, counselor."

He shifted in his chair. "I didn't draft it. She brought it in the morning of New Year's Eve. All she wanted was for me to witness it."

"Just witness?"

"That, and hold it for her. After I signed, we walked downstairs to get one of the clerks at Fizzy's to be the other witness."

"She didn't ask you to look it over or offer advice?"

"She didn't even want a photocopy. It was very strange."

I looked at the document again. "The wording seems odd: 'I, Known as Louise Thomas.' "

"Sounded to me like she was just trying to lawyer it up. People do that sometimes, to make it sound more legal."

"Known as? Sounds like she's admitting it's a fake name."

He shrugged.

"What did she look like?"

"I don't know."

"Surely you must—"

He held up a palm to stop me. "She came in with her coat collar up, a wool beret pulled down low on her forehead, a scarf around her mouth. I wondered if she was sick, because she never took off the hat or the scarf. It was bitterly cold that week, lots of wind."

"Could you at least tell if she was young or old?"

"She was only in here a few minutes, and she wore those glasses that get darker in the light—"

"Twenty or sixty?"

He shook his head. "Somewhere in between."

I picked up the little ring of keys. "And these?" There were two Chrysler-logo keys and a standard house key.

"For the car and the house, I imagine."

"Did she give you a list of assets as part of the will?"

"No, and that's what's needed. It's called an inventory, and I have to file it with her will in the probate court. As executor, it's your responsibility to provide me with an accounting of everything she had that's worth something."

"Lockbox?"

"Again, your responsibility." He shrugged. "I have no authority to contact the local banks. I'm hoping that, if she had a box, you'll find a key among her effects."

"When did she die?"

He looked away, as if he were trying to read the fine print on one of the degrees framed on the opposite wall.

"There's some dispute about that," he said after a minute.

Something greasy worked its way down my throat, but it could have been the last inches of the foot of onion rings. I cleared my throat, prompting.

He turned to face me. "You sure you didn't know Louise Thomas?" he asked, leaning forward in his chair. He smelled of mint and spring.

"Not by that name."

"Think, Mr. Elstrom."

"I knew a lot of people through my business."

He gestured at the laptop computer on the credenza behind him. "You got quite a lot of notoriety through that business as well."

He'd done an Internet search on me. He might have been a resort-town lawyer, but he knew how to do homework.

"I was cleared," I said.

Aggert nodded, accepting, and eased back in his chair. "It took some time to discover her body," he said, coming around to my question.

The onion rings started to dance. "No neighbors noticed she wasn't around, or the mail piling up? Nobody at work thought to report her missing?"

"I don't know where she worked."

"And people aren't neighborly in Rambling?"

"It's a blueberry town. Not many people. Just blueberry bushes, picked mechanically or by seasonal workers. Nobody much is left except for some back-to-the-earth nuts, folks who need to live out where they can't see other house lights at night."

"How did the cops know to contact you?"

"They must have found my card in her house. I didn't think to ask."

"Did you tell the cops she'd just been in to give you her will?"

He opened his little tin of Altoids, slipped one in his mouth. "That has to be coincidence."

"Coincidence?" Suddenly, I didn't like William Aggert very much. He was a man who asked too few questions.

"It happens," he said, scenting the air with the fresh Altoid. "Somebody gets the urge to write a will and dies right afterward."

I jangled the keys. "What am I supposed to do? Go out to Rambling, inventory her stuff, and then give it away?"

"And call around to the banks, see if there's a lockbox. I don't imagine there'll be much to inventory. Nobody who has anything lives in Rambling." He opened the center drawer of his desk and pulled out his check for seven hundred dollars, made out to me.

I stood up.

"You'll get on this right away?" he said.

"I'll drive out there now."

"As her attorney, I need to be kept informed, every day."

His phone hadn't rung since I'd been there, his desktop was empty, except for the Altoids, and he didn't have a secretary. He was looking for something to do.

"I'll do what I can. I have other obligations," I said with a straight face. I started to turn for the door.

"One more thing," he said. He handed me a scrap of paper with a name and phone number on it. "Miss Thomas's landlady, a Mrs. Sturrow. She wants to know when the house will be available to rent out."

"How far in advance did Louise pay up?"

"Mrs. Sturrow said until the end of May," he said.

"Tell her the executor says the end of May," I said and walked out.

Downstairs, in Fizzy's, a smiling man was pulling a watch from a case marked $5.95 to show to a woman wearing a mended fleece coat.

"Are you sure it'll keep good time?" the woman asked, squinting at the watch. She could have been sixty or she could have been forty; her face was weathered and deeply lined. I guessed she was from a surrounding farm town and had cut those lines working days in the sun and sweating nights about rain and crop prices and interest rates. Skin gets furrowed just like dirt in farm towns.

"Fine quartz movement," the man said, smiling at the watch in the woman's hand.

The woman rubbed the shiny silver on the watchband, testing to see if it would come off under her thumb. "I'll think on it, Mr. Fizzeldorf," she said, handing it back. And then she walked out.

Fizzy Fizzeldorf glanced over at me, then quickly put the watch back in the display case. I took no offense that he suspected I was not to be trusted around a six dollar watch.

"Got maps of Michigan?" I asked.

His smile reappeared. He rootled under the counter and came up with a folded map that had been stained with a coffee cup ring. "You're in luck," he said. "This is the last one left." The map had an out-of-business oil company logo beneath faded red letters announcing that it was ALL NEW FOR 1984.

"That'll be two dollars," he said.

A stained old map for two bucks seemed like a wrong value, considering that four dollars more could get me a whole chrome watch, but I didn't make the point. "I'll buy it if it's got Rambling on it," I said.

He smiled, unfolded the map, and laid a thick forefinger on a spot an inch northeast of West Haven. "Thar she blows," he said.

I gave him the two bucks.

The asphalt crumbling on the road to Rambling was the same bleached gray as the sky, and one slight shade darker than the snow lying wind-rutted on the fields. Only the branches of the blueberry bushes, blood red and gnarled, as though contorting to wrench themselves out of the ground, gave any color to the landscape at all. I made the eighteen miles to Rambling in twenty minutes because there were no other cars on the road to slow me down.

Aggert had been right: Rambling in winter was indeed a blueberry town, populated only by bushes. There'd been a drugstore with an ice-cream-cone-shaped sign, a café, and a resale shop. They were vacant, offering nothing now but sun-faded FOR RENT signs propped in their dirty windows. A fourth building that had once been a food store was no longer anything. It had burned, and snow covered what remained of its roof, lying on the ground inside its walls. Rambling looked to be a ghost town, abandoned even by its ghosts.

I followed Fizzy's map and continued east. County Road 12 was a mile past the frenzy of downtown Rambling, a whispery road, more dirt than gravel. I stopped at the intersection, looked both ways. There were no houses visible in either direction. I turned right and drove south through more acres of twisted red blueberry bushes. The first sign of life was two miles down, a cluster of three cottages set close to the road. HAPPY FARMS, a wood sign read. The occupants must have been away, being happy elsewhere, because the snow on the single drive heading up to the houses was unmarked by tire tracks, and there was moss showing on the roofs where the snow had melted off. I kept driving south until I came to the town limits of the next metropolis, a place named Tadesville. It looked to be no more affluent than Rambling. I swung around and headed back the way I'd come.

I crossed the West Haven road, this time heading north. A mile up, I came to an asbestos-shingled faded green cottage, set in a clearing surrounded by spindly trees. It was a skinny place, no bigger than a house trailer, with a glassed-in front porch. I bounced onto the ruts of the driveway and cut the engine.

Ripped plastic sheeting billowed in and out from the two large side windows facing the drive, catching the wind like sails on a sloop. Dark splotches of moss and mildew spotted the siding where the wind had torn off the green shingling. The cottage looked like it had been abandoned for years, except for the tire tracks in the snow on the drive. There were plenty of those—and they were new since the last snowfall.

I got out and went up the two front steps to knock on the front porch glass. I waited a minute, knocked again, then stepped down. Nobody would live in such a house, not with torn sheeting slapping against broken windows, fanning in the cold.

I started toward the back of the house. Beneath the plastic-sheeted windows, my shoes crunched on bits of broken glass. They lay everywhere across the driveway, sparkling like strewn diamonds, even though the day was overcast.

At the rear, more plastic sheeting had been duct-taped to the back door window.

A carriage-sized garage leaned at the end of the drive. Its swing-out doors were bowed, sunk in the middle, but arcs had been swept in the snow in front of them. They'd been opened recently. With a lift and a tug, the left door opened easily.

An old metallic-blue Dodge Aries sedan was parked inside. Big, irregular spots of rust marred the roof, hood, and trunk, as though acid had been spilled on the car and eaten the paint. There was no license plate on the rear bumper.

The driver's door was unlocked. I pulled out the ring of Louise Thomas's keys and slid in. Even in the cold, the interior smelled of damp and must. The first auto key slipped easily into the ignition. I gave it a turn. The engine fired instantly. I looked at the gauges; the gas tank was full, the battery was charging. I shut off the engine.

The fit of the car key confirmed it: I'd found Château Louise Thomas.

The dome light showed a car interior that was immaculate. There was no clutter on the upholstery or floor. The glove box was empty. I felt under the front seat, touched metal and a thin plastic. I pulled out a supermarket bag containing a screwdriver, a license plate—white and green and orange, from Florida—and two shiny screws. The plate had a renewal sticker that would not expire until October.

I got out and walked around to the back of the car. The paint on the vinyl bumper where the license attached was clean. Louise Thomas had recently removed the plate I'd found under the front seat. I used the other car key to open the trunk, but there was nothing in there except a well-worn spare tire. I closed the trunk, locked and shut the driver's door, and walked back up the drive, crunching glass as if I were walking on granola.

The third key turned the porch door lock easily. I opened the door, stepped inside.

I saw blood.

Three

There wasn't much of it, just a dozen rust-colored splotches, the size of dimes, spread far apart on the walls and across the scuffed gray-painted floor. Four more drops had dried on the square windowpanes that faced County Road 12. Combined, it wasn't enough to indicate a slaughter, but as I moved around the tiny porch, the few spots of dried blood chilled me more than if I'd found great, caked puddles of it. The splatter pattern, sprayed so wide, showed panic. Fast, frantic panic.

The only furniture was a wicker sofa, backed against the wall that separated the porch from the rest of the house. I got down on my knees to look closely at the small dark specks on the faded foam cushion. It was mildew, not more blood.

The porch key also unlocked the white-painted door that led inside. The living room was cold, colder than outside, and dim in the gauzy light wavering through the opaque plastic sheets undulating against the broken windows. I felt for a light switch next to the door, flipped it, but nothing came on. The power had been shut off.

As my eyes adjusted to the gloom, dark furniture shapes, lying at wrong angles, began to materialize in the middle of the room: a small sofa, a tipped-over reading chair, a lamp, and a table lying next to it. I stepped all the way in. My shoes ground bits of glass into the carpet.

The room had been attacked. As on the driveway, shards of broken glass glinted in the dim light. Dozens of sheets of newspapers lay everywhere, on the floor and across the tilted sofa and overturned reading chair—strewn about by the wind from the shattered windows. Or by someone in a hurry.

A sliver of daylight showed from an almost-closed door to my right. I stepped carefully through the rubble and pushed it open.

The bedroom had been savaged like the living room. White bedsheets and a blue blanket lay balled in one corner, a mattress and box spring had been dropped back askew onto the wrought-iron bed frame. Against the far wall, the drawers had been jerked from a dresser and upended onto the floor, spilling out proper, no-frilled white panties and bras, some dark sweaters, and a couple of sweatshirts. Scattered over it all, as in the living room, were dozens more sheets of newspapers. In the bedroom, though, the windows were tightly shut; the wind hadn't blown the newspapers around.

There was blood, another dozen of the dime-sized spots, on the floral wallpaper and the bare plank floor.

Looking strangely untouched, a small, old oak library table with a pedestal base sat under the window. On it was an ancient manual typewriter, an Underwood.

I knew a girl once, a blond girl with a boy's name, who had an old Underwood Number Five, just like the one on the table. I'd been with her when she bought it. I helped carry it home, watched as she scratched her initials on the bottom of it with a fork, to make it her own.

For a time, years ago, I'd hunted those typewriters. I'd prowled antique stores, resale shops, scrap metal dealers, anyplace I could think of, looking for an old black Underwood like the one that sat on the table. I'd given it up, finally, but I'd never quite healed. Even now, years later, my breath still caught every time I came across one.

I reached to touch it, but stopped. There was one obscene drop of blood on the knurled wheel that turned the platen.

Blood on the porch. Blood in the bedroom. Aggert had said nothing about a crime. I wanted to leave that house; lock it up and hurry away. But I would wonder. Every night, for the rest of my life, I would wonder.

I eased the typewriter onto its side. The rails underneath the machine were smooth, the black paint shiny. Mercifully, they were unmarked. I turned it back over, right side up.

My teeth started to chatter. It was the cold in the house, I tried to tell my head. The cold, and the blood. But my head wasn't buying: The cold went deeper than that, deeper than my skin, my muscle, and my bones. It was the cold of an old memory.

I buttoned my coat all the way up, kicked at the newspapers littering the floor as I left the bedroom, and crossed through the living room. I didn't care where I stepped. What happened in that frozen little house was for cops, not me. I'd been hired only to execute a will.

The kitchen at the back of the cottage had been trashed, too. Metal cabinet doors, blue-enameled but chipped, and worn to bare metal around the pulls, yawned open, their contents swept out. Pots and a pan, silverware, and two shattered mugs lay on the green linoleum floor, on top of spilled flour and sugar and the oozing contents of a dozen opened cans of mixed green and orange vegetables, sliced peaches, and what looked like chunks of pineapple. There were sealed cans lying in the mess, too; dozens of them with generic labels. In the middle of it all lay an impossibly yellow box of Cheerios and a black banana, a breakfast for a dead woman. If the house hadn't been as cold as a refrigerator, it would have stunk to hell.

The bathroom was next to the damaged back door. A stand-up fiberglass shower, a tiny porcelain sink set in the corner, and a toilet had been jammed into a space no bigger than a modest closet. The mirrored door hung by one hinge from the medicine cabinet. An opaque glass jar of cold cream and a lavender toothbrush lay on the floor, mixed in with the shattered pieces of the porcelain toilet lid. I didn't go in to look for blood. I'd been hired to execute a will.

A sudden breeze rattled the tiny bare window above the kitchen sink. I looked out. At the back of the lot, scraggly trees were swaying. In the fading light, they looked like skeletons dancing, waving their spindly arms.

I didn't want to be within ten miles of the death in that house when the last of the daylight had fled. I hurried through the living room, trying to shut out the sounds of the glass crunching beneath my feet, the whip-snapping of the ripped plastic against the windows, the moan of the wind. I locked the two doors and stepped down to the ground.

A pair of headlights cut the dusk a few hundred yards down County Road 12, growing larger as they approached the cottage. When they flashed on the red of the Jeep, they stopped abruptly. For a second the car idled, frozen. Then it swung around, sweeping its lights across the fields, and raced back the way it had come. A minute later, its taillamps disappeared into the dusk.

I got into the Jeep and goosed the engine until the heater kicked in and I could hold my hands to the dash vents. I felt like I'd been cold for years.

And like I'd been had.

I called Aggert. "You said nothing about her being killed."

"You might not have gone out there."

"What happens if I just walk away?"

"The estate reverts to the state," he said in lawyerly English, "and you return the seven hundred dollars."

"There isn't much here. Her stuff, even with the car, can't be worth a few hundred dollars. Her killer trashed her house. If she had anything, it's gone. You don't need an executor for what's left, you need a guy with garbage bags and a shovel."

"You don't know that yet. Look for her files, brokerage statements, savings accounts."

"Have you been out here? I doubt the woman owned a whole roll of postage stamps."

"She had to have had something."

"Perhaps, but her killer got it. Whatever she had is gone."

"Ms. Thomas must have had some reason for trusting you, Mr. Elstrom," he said, tossing the guilt card onto the table, faceup.

"I didn't know the woman."

"So you say."

I looked out the tape-free part of the Jeep's side window. A mailbox was set on a post by the road. Its little red flag was down. "Hold on," I said, dropping the cell phone on the passenger seat. I got out, crossed the yard, and opened the mailbox. The reclining little flag was right: There was no mail.

"What about your fee?" I asked, back in the Jeep.

Aggert chuckled. "You don't need to worry about that."

"Did you send her a bill?"

"Why do you ask, Mr. Elstrom?"

"Because I want to be a very good executor," I smarmed, "and because I'm curious why there's no mail piling up in her mailbox. Did you mail her a bill?"

"She paid me when she came in."

"Do you know if someone stopped her mail delivery?"

"I don't know. Maybe she had a post office box. Or maybe she had her bills sent to a bank. As executor, you should check around for both."

"What did the cops say about Louise's death?"

"She died during a break-in. Let them worry about that. Our job is to file an inventory of her assets and liabilities with the probate court."

The last of the light was disappearing across the frozen flats to the west, dissolving the shadows of the bones of the trees that surrounded Louise's cottage.

"I'll call you tomorrow," I said.

"You can't leave," he said quickly.

"I'm going back to Rivertown. I'll get on the Internet, make up a list of banks and post offices near Rambling, and start sending out some letters, asking if they have anything for Louise Thomas."

"They might take months to respond. Better you visit them in person, right now. I'll make up a list; you can pick it up tomorrow, begin knocking on doors."

"I like the U.S. Postal Service."

"Respect the dead woman's wishes, Elstrom. She counted on you to settle her estate properly. You can be done and out of here in a day or two."

The mailbox was almost invisible now in the dark. He was right, but he was sitting in a warm office, not outside the cottage where Louise

Thomas had been killed. I had only forty-five dollars in cash, and no clean underwear.

"I'll give it a day. Have the list ready for me tomorrow," I said and hung up.

I have a theory that, when the apocalypse comes, everyone already will be living inside Wal-Marts and won't learn that the outside world has ended for at least a generation or two, and then only because the Oreos run out. For by then, the last of the cities and towns will have long since crumbled away, obsolete as buffalo skin tents, as dozens of generations will have been born, lived entire lives, died, and been recycled into puppy food inside huge, windowless Wal-Domes.

They will be the size of villages, these new habitats, and will contain thousands of tiered Wal-Apartments circling miles of display shelving. Aisle thoroughfares will be wide enough for thousands of extended families—great-grandpa and great-grandma, stuffed inside shopping carts, drooling on the chrome, being pushed by tottering grandparents as the kids, grandkids, and great-grandkids, all of them slack-jawed and glassy-eyed, shuffle along behind, under the glow of the fluorescents, admiring the end displays, marveling at the grinning happy-face signs announcing that, once again, prices have been rolled back. No one will miss the sun, or notice that there's no longer rain. No one will remember them because they won't be relevant. Only things, things that can be outsourced and price-reduced, will matter. It will be a safe world, that Wal-World, a place where there's no worry, where there's nothing left to do but roam the acres of aisles and shop.

It will end, of course; everything ends. It will come by meteor or toxic explosion, a flame-out of the sun or a superheating of some forgotten nuclear bomb dump, left to molder in a used-to-be country that had been too small even to have issued its own postage stamps. When the end does come, word will be sent first to corporate headquarters, to an emergency buying meeting hastily convened in a bunker buried deep in the Arkansas hills: "I think we better stock up on Oreos," the corporate cookie buyer will say. "Why's that?" Sam the Eighth, or Twelfth, will ask. "Well, with the world ending and all, people might get curious if there's no Oreos on the shelves." Sam will nod, finger the cuff of the flannel shirt he'd just bought for thirty-nine Wal-Cents. "Good thinking; tell the factory"—for by then Wal-Mart will own all the factories, including the crown jewel, the Oreo plant, operating belowground, beneath what used to be the Pentagon—"to ship a few million metric tons of the double-stuffed ones to the Wal-Domes ASAP." Thus disaster, the realization of it, and therefore the reality of it, will be deferred. Another generation or two will be born in the aisles before the creamy white center of the last Oreo is licked and mankind is forced at last to confront its own end.

These thoughts were on my mind as I walked into the Wal-Mart on the outskirts of West Haven. It was cheerier than thinking about what must have happened to Louise Thomas.

After being greeted by a man old enough to have sailed with Columbus, I bought a three-pack of underwear, toiletries, an orange knit shirt that was being dumped for three bucks, a box of garbage bags, and, after the briefest of pauses, a family-sized bag of Oreos, because it never hurts to plan for the end of the world. Even after buying all that, I still had twenty-eight dollars left from my forty-five.

Fortified, I drove across the street to a blue and turquoise cinderblock motel with an empty parking lot and a lit-up sign saying they had cable television. The desk clerk, a lad of about seventeen, told me a room would be thirty dollars, including color television. "But no cable," he said.

"The sign says you have cable."

"We drop our subscription in the winter. We get one regular channel, though, out of Grand Rapids."

"It'll do," I said and gave him my credit card.

My room had a nice view of two perfectly matched Dumpsters, and if that got boring, there was indeed the color television set that the desk clerk had promised. There was also a Bible with its cover torn off and a phone book for the whole area, including Rambling. I looked under the government section at the front of the directory, but there was no listing for a Rambling police station.

I walked back across the highway to the Wal-Mart and sat in a molded brown plastic booth. I had the nacho platter for dinner. It, too, looked to have been molded, though in a different color. Afterward, I passed the rest of the night in my motel room, watching a *Starsky and Hutch* retrospective on Grand Rapids television and eating Oreos. At midnight, I set the bedside alarm for six thirty and turned out the light. It was too early for the Oreos; they wanted to stay up for a while and play with the nachos, so I lay in the dark and listened to the trucks rumbling by on the interstate, wondering what kind of woman would want to live on a humanity-forsaken, dry bit of ground in Rambling. It didn't seem like anybody I'd ever known.

Sometime around two in the morning, I said, "Who are you, Louise?" for the hundredth time to the darkness and fell asleep.

Four

Without caffeine, my brain is mush. Since my thirty-dollar room didn't come with a coffeemaker, nor even brownish powder that could be added to tap water, I hurried through my shower and shave and had my hand on the doorknob in a fast twelve minutes, telling what was left of the Oreos they had until that evening to survive.

I sped across the road to the Wal-Mart and got a large coffee and a Wal-Doughnut with yellow sprinkles on it. As I drove northeast to Rambling, I wondered if I was obsessing too much about Wal-Marts, but it was impossible not to marvel at their efficiency. I'd heard that eighty percent of Wal-Mart's goods came from eight thousand factories in China. Yet even getting their goods from that far away, they still managed to deliver their coffee hot and their doughnuts moist. It was no wonder that the merchants on Main Street U.S.A. were getting creamed.

I was savoring the last of the yellow sprinkles stuck between my teeth when Aggert called.

"When are you stopping by?" he asked.

"It's only seven thirty; I didn't figure you to be at work yet. I'm on my way to Rambling to bag up Louise's stuff."

"If you're sure there's nothing there, let the landlady clean it up. Better you should start on the banks and post offices."

"Maybe the cops will want to examine her stuff again for clues."

"The cops are done. Come by my office, pick up that list of banks and post offices."

"I'm going to bag her stuff; she's owed that." I told him I'd stop by later.

A huge dark blue SUV, the kind of monster that squeezes a mile, maybe two, out of a gallon of gasoline, was parked at the end of Louise's drive. The garage doors were open, and inside, a man was leaning into the open driver's door of the Dodge. I'd meant to lock the car the previous day but must have forgotten.

When he heard me bounce up the ruts, he straightened up and came out. He wore jeans and a quilted black parka and moved easily, with his shoulders square, arms loose and ready at his sides. Gray-haired, he was older than me, maybe fifty, but he was physically fit, probably a weight lifter, not the type to be crunching nachos at Wal-Mart. He looked like a cop.

"How you doing?" he asked. He spoke softly, but there was an underlying tone of insistence in his voice, as if he were used to people doing what he said. Right away.

"That depends," I said. "I'm here because I have legal authority. You look like you're trespassing, maybe even breaking into a vehicle over which I have control." It was a lot of strong words, but I'd been energized by the yellow sugar sprinkles on the doughnut.

"Fair enough." Grinning, he reached into his pocket and handed me a business card with a logo and a cluster of blueberries on it. "I'm John Reynolds. I do security for some of the growers." He smiled wider, but it didn't reach his eyes. "And you are?"

"Watching empty fields and picking machines extends to this cottage?"

The smile went away. "I could tell you that's part of it, watching the neighborhood. And I could tell you that watching those empty fields and frozen picking machines occasionally gets boring." He shook his head. "The real reason is that I think someone should try to find out what exactly happened here."

"Dek Elstrom," I said. "Louise Thomas's executor."

"Got anything to back that up?"

I handed him my driver's license and Louise Thomas's will.

"You knew her?" he asked, studying my driver's license photo. I had to crouch when they took the picture, and it made my face look like it had more chins than federal buildings have steps.

"I don't know. I may have met her through my records research business, perhaps years ago."

He nodded. "How may I help?" he asked, handing back my license and the will.

I got out of the Jeep. "Tell me what happened."

"I'll give you the guesswork tour."

We started up the drive, but he surprised me by stopping almost right away, at the back door. He pointed at the ground beneath the square of plastic that had been taped over the broken glass. "See anything?"

I looked at the ground, then up at him. "No."

He nodded and motioned for me to follow him. Halfway up the drive, he again stopped, this time right under the two large windows at the side of the house. The ripped plastic sheets billowed softly in the morning air.

He pointed to the ground. "See anything?"

The thousand bits of glass I'd seen the day before glinted in the snow. "The window on the back door was broken inward; no glass left outside on the ground. But these," I said, pointing up at the two large plastic-sheeted windows, "were shattered from the inside out. And with great impact."

He grinned. "My guess, too. Now the tour continues inside." He started to reach to pull himself through a rip in the plastic.

I jangled the ring of keys. "We can use the door, like invited guests," I said.

He followed me to the front, waited as I unlocked the two doors, then stepped ahead to go in first. Pulling a small flashlight from his jacket pocket, he switched it on and pointed the beam at the floor beneath the two shattered windows. Glass crystals winked back from the carpet.

"Some glass was dragged back in," I said.

"Hell of a struggle." He raised the beam toward the back of the room. "You've seen the kitchen?"

"Yesterday."

"It's been cold enough inside here for the food on the floor not to have spoiled, so I don't imagine they can pinpoint a time of death." He started walking through the living room to the back.

"Who's 'they'?"

"State police, or the county."

"What are they telling you?"

"Nothing. They left a message, telling me of the death and saying I should keep an eye on the place for vandals when I'm passing by."

"Nothing else?"

"Mr. Elstrom, they don't have the resources to work full-time on a home invasion gone bad. The way it works is that sometime in the future, some small-time greaseball will offer up something he heard in exchange for leniency on his own case."

"Nobody's doing anything to catch the killer?"

He started walking to the kitchen. "You mean, did anybody comb the area, ask all the neighbors when was the last time they'd seen Ms. Thomas?" He stopped at the window over the sink and gestured at the skinny trees and the empty fields beyond them.

I looked out at nothing. "Nobody is close enough to have seen anything."

"You got it." He pointed at the green linoleum floor beneath the back door window. "The intruder was very careful at first. He tapped out the glass, pulled the pieces outside and tossed them in the bushes, then reached in to unlock the door."

"To be silent?"

He nodded.

I looked down at the floor. Something had changed. The black banana and the yellow box of Cheerios still lay on top of the spilled flour and sugar, but the only cans that remained were the ones that had been opened. The full tins of vegetables and fruit were gone. At least one pot, a big two-quart aluminum thing, had disappeared as well.

We walked through the living room to the door to the bedroom.

"She was struck high on the back of the head, which I think means that she was seated at that table, maybe typing," he said, pointing at the old Underwood on the table across the room.

"The blood spatter shows that," I said.

"He knocked her out," he went on, "then started rummaging through everything." He gestured at the pulled-out drawers, the clothes mingled with the newspapers that littered every inch of the tiny room.

"A robbery."

"I want to think that, but something bothers me."

I went for the obvious: "Why break into a shack like this looking for valuables?"

"Not that," he said. "Some of the people around here will steal for chump change." He walked over to the worktable, and tapped the old Underwood. "She fell forward, over this. We can assume that because there's blood spatter on the side of the typewriter, and on the wall behind the table." He turned around. "But there was no paper in the typewriter, no ribbon, either. In fact, I couldn't find one sheet of anything typed in the whole place."

"The cops took whatever she was typing as evidence?"

"Could be." He said it vaguely and then looked down at the typewriter on the table, as though hoping it would speak.

I waited.

"Or the killer took whatever she was working on out of the typewriter and still searched the rest of the house," he said.

"Looking for something more that she'd written?"

"Or to make sure he grabbed everything that would point to his identity."

"What about all these newspapers?"

"That I can't figure." He looked at me with unblinking eyes. "You must have known her, if she named you executor."

"I don't remember her. She might have worked for one of my past clients."

We walked into the living room and stopped to look again at the two shattered windows.

"I figure she came to while he was searching the house," he said. "She tried to escape by throwing herself through those windows."

"Multiple impacts. He kept grabbing her, dragging her back."

"Jesus," he said.

We walked out onto the porch.

I pointed to the dime-sized spots of blood. "You saw the blood in here as well?"

He nodded, looking where I was pointing. "She fought here, too, poor thing."

"This was no ordinary home invasion gone bad," I said. "Not with the paper missing from the typewriter."

"And no other paper, blank or otherwise, anywhere else."

"Damned shame, nobody investigating."

He paused at the porch door. "I've got no pull with the sheriff. I do what I can, but it's just a couple hours a week. That's what I was doing when you pulled up, checking her car. I've stopped at all the occupied houses in Rambling, which is about ten. Nobody knew Louise Thomas."

"Her lawyer told me she'd just started renting this place."

"She showed up last spring, paid a year's rent up front. The landlady can't remember if she paid by check or not."

"That means Louise paid with cash."

"You bet," he said, grinning as he stepped down onto the ground.

"Any idea where she banked, or where she worked?"

"I don't know anything about her."

We walked back to his SUV. The sun was high enough now to be bright on the snow.

"What are you going to do?" he asked.

"Sort out what can be given away and what's trash. Should take me a day," I said. "Then I'll call the sheriff, see what he knows."

He paused by his driver's side door. "I've been doing what I can. Any more, I could lose my job."

"I'll take a look at my records. Maybe they'll jog my memory."

He turned to look back at the shabby little cottage. "Nobody should die so . . ." His voice trailed off as he hunted for the right word.

"Anonymously?" I offered.

He nodded as he opened his car door. "Crappy way to die."

There was nothing to say to that.

Five

With a spatula picked off the kitchen floor, I began poking through the spilled, opened tins that had been swept from the refrigerator. Louise Thomas had liked canned fruit—pineapple chunks and sliced peaches and fruit cocktail were mixed in among the peas, corn, and salmon. She ate frugally, saving partial cans, and she ate nutritiously. I imagined her to have been a slender woman.

I stood up, certain. The tins on the floor had all been opened. The full cans I'd seen the day before were gone.

For one crazy second, I thought about picking up the few metal spoons, forks, knives, the plastic plates, the saucepan, and dropping them into the sink. The water had been shut off, though, and executors, even seven-hundred-dollar ones like myself, weren't responsible for cleaning up, especially when the executor himself disdained metal utensils and used only what plasticware he could grab from fast-food restaurants. Still, for a moment, the mess on the floor nagged. It wasn't about cleaning up for the landlady; it was about respect. I was beginning to shape Louise into a woman of propriety, someone who'd be troubled at leaving disorder behind.

I looked inside the few cabinets. Every one was empty. That fit with the stolen canned goods. Rambling was poor, and the rips in the plastic sheeting were wide. It wasn't like the dead woman would need the food. Someone in that worn town had seen an opportunity and had taken it.

Outside, automobile tires crunched on the driveway. A second later a car door slammed and heavy feet pounded up the two wood stairs to the porch.

I hurried through the living room and got to the porch just as a short, stout, gray-haired woman wearing a long greasy red coat was raising a key to the porch door lock. Behind her, a Ford station wagon, loaded with empty cardboard boxes, had been backed into the drive. I put on a neighborly face and opened the door.

"Name's Sturrow," the woman said, trying to push her way in. "I own this place."

Amanda tells me I'm too quick to form dislikes, but that's usually when she's conned me into taking her to unfathomable places, like sushi restaurants or opera performances. Still, there was no doubt it was happening now, with Mrs. Sturrow. I disliked her pushiness instantly and was eager to dislike more.

I stood in the doorway, blocking her entry. "I'm Elstrom, court-nominated executor," I said, fumbling with the lint in my pocket as though looking for a business card.

She wasn't impressed. "I own this place," she said again, pressing her bulk between my right side and the doorjamb.

I stood my ground, being a full head taller and ballasted by more Oreos than she could ever eat. "I can't let you in," I said, pressing back. "In addition to being a crime scene, this is a court-nominated site of executing, and I'm here to protect the interests of the judicial system."

I had no idea what I'd just said, nor did she, but it was enough to make her pull an inch of her bulldog bulk back. Or perhaps she'd merely recognized my superior weight advantage.

"Well, what the hell am I supposed to do?" she asked.

"About what?"

"About the mess in there," she said. "I got prospective tenants wanting to rent this place."

I looked past her, at the empty boxes in the Ford, and knew who'd cleared out the kitchen. It must have been her headlights I'd seen the previous evening. She'd lurked someplace, waiting until I left, then emptied the place of the undamaged canned goods. And who knew what else.

"I'm sorry," I said, "but no one gets in until everything has been inventoried."

She rolled her eyes. "Inventoried for what?"

"Surely you knew Ms. Thomas was an heir to the great Thomas fortune?" I summoned as straight a face as I could muster.

"The what?" Mrs. Sturrow pressed forward again, suddenly aquiver at the word "fortune." A foot below my chin, a little gray whisker sprouted from a mole on her cheek.

"Though eccentric, Louise was quite a wealthy woman." I looked around as if I were making sure no one could hear. "As a court-nominated executor, I can tell you the court will be quite generous to those who have eased our work in this inventory."

Her small eyes grew wide.

I gestured at the Ford full of empty cartons. "You've not taken . . . ?" I made a delicate cough.

"Of course not!"

"No clothes, no personal items, no radio or television?"

She scrunched up her face, trying for indignant, but it only made her look like she was suffering from irregularity.

"As soon as I locate those Krugerrands—little one-ounce gold coins, you know—I can turn over the place to you . . ." I paused, then added, "Appreciatively."

She wet her lips. "You mean like a reward?"

"What did she look like, your Louise Thomas?"

Her eyes narrowed. "You mean you don't know what she looks like?"

"Just verifying we're talking about the same woman," I said, as greasy as a griddle cook's nose.

Mrs. Sturrow pursed her lips. "Can't quite say. She wore a scarf wrapped around her neck and mouth, even though it was warm that day. She had on a big trench coat, though I had the impression she was skinny."

"Last May?"

"How much of a reward?"

"What do you remember about Louise's height, or the color of her eyes?"

Mrs. Sturrow's eyes narrowed further in suspicion.

"In matters of high net worth, especially when there will be substantial rewards for information, it's vital that I verify each claimant's information."

"Five five in height," she said quickly. "Don't know about the eyes; she wore sunglasses, even indoors. How big did you say that reward was?"

"Did she pay the rent with a bank check?"

"I don't remember."

"Month by month?"

"A year in advance, with utilities." She shook her head almost mournfully. "When do you pay the reward?"

"As soon as we find the gold." I expelled the sigh of a true bureaucrat. "Problem is, those little gold coins are so very easy to hide. And like many rich women, Louise was very, very clever. Can you believe I found a can-sealing device? I believe she actually could have hidden the gold in cans of food, if you can imagine. Alas, I've not found any sealed canned goods, so I'll just have to keep searching."

If she'd had a functioning brain, one not clouded by greed, she would have smelled manure.

"I won't keep you," she said, bustling down the two steps. "Take all the time you need." She strode to the Ford, fired it up, and shot out of the driveway.

I watched her speed away, thinking she'd have all of Louise's canned goods opened within ten minutes of getting home. Once she realized there was no gold inside, she would eat as much as she could of the filched fruit, rather than let it all go to waste. It was another kind of greed.

"Let us hope her bathroom has wide pipes, Louise," I said to the porch ceiling.

I began in Louise's bedroom because there was sun and I didn't want to be in that room if it turned cloudy. It was her most intimate room, the place where she slept, the place where she was most defenseless. The place, if Reynolds was right, where she was first attacked.

I started by picking up the newspapers. I'd almost filled one garbage bag before I realized I wasn't picking up whole newspapers, pulled apart, but rather single sheets of different editions, some going back at least a year. All seemed to feature astrological forecasts, crossword puzzles, and advice columns.

Bagging her clothes was quick. What she had would have fit inside one large suitcase, had one been around. Everything was sensible. Her underpants were high and white, her bras serious and small. She had two pairs of black jeans and one pair of khaki slacks, a few knit tops in blacks and beiges, a light fleece jacket, a thick black wool sweater, and a couple of plain sweatshirts, one a faint green, one a faint yellow. Eights and thirty-twos and smalls and petites, the labels from JCPenney and Sears. She'd dressed in dark or muted colors, the frugal Louise, in clothes not meant to be noticed. I put them all in one bag, next to the bag of newspapers.

All that remained in the bedroom now was the old Underwood Number Five, but I wanted nothing to do with that. I carried the two bags to the porch and labeled the clothes with masking tape as donations for the Salvation Army or the Goodwill box. Anonymous clothes from an anonymous woman.

I'd emptied her bedroom, that most intimate room, in less than fifteen minutes. It didn't seem right, to be able to empty such a room so quickly.

The living room was quick work as well. As in the bedroom, I started with the newspapers. This time I filled two bags with the tabloid-sized sheets. I took them to the porch, then came back in to drop the cushions back onto the sofa, right the red upholstered reading chair, and set the white plastic lamp on the chipped brown end table. Restored, the living room didn't look much better than when it had been trashed.

In the corner, beneath a fresh-looking nick in the plaster, the pieces of a small green glass ashtray lay on the worn sculpted rug. Mixed in were three cigarette butts and a tablespoon of cigarette ash. I bent to pick up one of the cigarettes. It was a Salem, smoked down to the filter. I dropped it back on the floor for Mrs. Sturrow.

On my way out of the cottage, I grabbed a half dozen newspaper sheets from one of the bags. By now, it was eleven thirty, and I hadn't had any nutrition since the Wal-Doughnut earlier that morning. I drove to the exposed-brick-and-fern place in West Haven. Again I took a booth against the wall. Again I turned up my nose to the evils of a cheeseburger with French fries, ordering vegetables, though this time I selected a large chicken Caesar salad to accompany the foot of onion rings on a pole.

Five of the newspaper sheets had come from the *Southwest Michigan Intelligencer*, a shopping advertiser, but one went back over a year and had been pulled from a shopping rag on Windward Island, in Florida. All six contained variations of usual middle-newspaper filler: crossword puzzles, astrology columns, ads for groceries and women's clothing, some cartoons. All, though, shared one identical item. Each contained an advice column, headlined in capital letters, called "HONESTLY, DEAREST."

The waitress came then with the salad and the foot of onion rings. I moved the salad out of the way and began eating as I read on.

There was no picture of the advice columnist, nor a name. Each column ran two or three responses to reader letters. "Dear Honestly Dearest," each began, "I'm a. . . ." Then the letter reported the quandary. The first ones I read were from a fourteen-year-old girl miserable about the breakup with her boyfriend, a midforties man married to a woman who'd lost interest in him sexually, and a twenty-one-year-old woman whose new husband wouldn't help address the thank-you notes from their wedding.

I assumed the columnist was a woman. In every case, her voice was respectful. To the fourteen-year-old, she wrote, "Honestly, Dearest, this will pass. You will love again, and again after that, and twenty years from now . . ." To the midforties man, "Honestly, Dearest, perhaps you might begin by talking, *really talking*, about how things are going for her. You've said she's a terrific mother . . ." To the young woman beginning her married life with a man who wouldn't address thank-you notes: "Honestly, Dearest, surely some compromise over such a minor, first disagreement can be reached? Perhaps you could suggest you'd be happy to address those to your side of the family, but for those to his side. . . . well, perhaps that's when you put on your sexiest smile, and . . . wake him up!"

Honestly Dearest wrote ordinary advice to ordinary people, but she had fun with it. She did it with a clever business touch, too. From the Honestly Dearest column heading, through the Honestly, Dearest salutation beginning each response, to signing off with yet another Honestly Dearest, she was drumming the column's identity into her readers' brains. She was building Honestly Dearest into a brand name.

I finished the last onion ring and folded up the newspaper sheets. The waitress handed me my untouched salad in a box, and I walked out into the cold wondering whether, on one of the newspaper sheets I'd stuffed into a garbage bag, there was printed a letter from Louise Thomas, because she'd had no one else to talk to.

Aggert was in. Today's checked shirt was blue, the suspenders and tie green. Joining the rectangular red and white tin of Altoids on his desk was a prim little stack of white sheets of paper. The additional clutter must have been driving him crazy. I parked myself in his guest chair.

"I've made two lists of banks and post offices," he said, pushing the sheets to my edge of the desk. "The first is those within a half hour's drive of her cottage. The second lists towns an hour away. I didn't go farther, thinking that would have made it too long a drive. I didn't figure she'd want to spend the gasoline."

I picked up the sheets. There weren't very many towns with banks and post offices, and a couple of big ones were missing.

"Kalamazoo? Grand Rapids?"

"I skipped them. Too much city congestion and hubbub."

"You've got a sharp eye, counselor. All that from her one visit."

He opened the tin of Altoids and popped a little white tablet into his mouth. Instantly, the scent of spring touched the air. "You ought to be able to check out a couple of others besides West Haven yet today," he said in the fresh breeze.

I shook my head. "If I have no luck here, I'll do them tomorrow. The rest of the afternoon, I'll be at her cottage, finishing up."

He ground the Altoid with his back teeth. "I told you: That's a waste of time. Let Mrs. Sturrow get rid of the stuff."

"What's the rush?"

Aggert pointed at his desktop, blessedly bare now except for the tin of Altoids. "I like things neat and tidy."

"I met Mrs. Sturrow," I said, standing up. "For seven hundred bucks, Louise Thomas gets the full-respect treatment. That includes privacy from Mrs. Sturrow's pawing little hands. I'll dispose of Louise's things myself."

"Waste of time," Aggert said again.

"I like things nice and tidy," I said, reaching for the doorknob.

The assistant branch manager of the bank next to the shuttered beachwear shop shook his head. "Not one of ours," he said, handing back Louise's will.

"You're the closest bank to Rambling?"

"Us and First National, one block over."

The customer service manager at First National said Louise didn't bank there either.

Down the street, the postmaster scrutinized Louise's will, then went to the back. He returned in five minutes. "We have no mail holds for anyone in Rambling. Most of the people there have moved away."

"How about mail being held general delivery for Louise Thomas?"

He shook his head. "I checked that, too."

"You are the nearest post office to Rambling?"

"Your Miss Thomas could have rented a post office box anywhere."

"There would be no reason for that, would there?"

"People are funny," he said.

Leo called as I was driving back to Rambling. "Want to have dinner tonight? Endora's working late, and Ma's having her friends over for late-night cable. Even listening to you blather about executing a will would be preferable to a blow-by-blow—you'll pardon the pun—running commentary about cable sex, in Polish, by septuagenarians."

Two years before, Leo had bought his mother a big-screen television. It hadn't taken her but a day to discover late-night soft porn on the premium channels, and only one more day to tell her friends. They'd flocked to her, in the late evenings, like lemmings.

"You don't speak Polish," I said.

"Even through the floor, I get the gist from the giggles, the sharp intakes of breath, and then the long silences. Mrs. Roshiska bounces her walker when the action gets really interesting."

"I'm still in Michigan."

"The estate is that complicated?"

"Do you want the short answer or the long answer?"

"Give me both; I'm desperate for diversion."

"Here's the short: Louise Thomas was killed during a home invasion."

"Random burglary?"

"So it would appear, though burglars who kill are rare."

"What's the long answer?"

"Nobody's interested, except a security guy who works for some fruit growers. Louise Thomas's lawyer just wants to be rid of the matter."

"She wasn't wealthy enough for real attention?"

"For sure."

"And?" Since we were kids, Leo's been able to read my mind as if my thoughts were playing on a movie screen. He knew there was more.

"She lived in a shingled cottage the size of a small house trailer, drove an old Dodge, had very few clothes, no friends, and read advice columns just for the human contact."

"At least now you know why there was no named beneficiary: There was nothing of value to leave." He said it like a question. He was still prompting.

"Why hire an executor?" I said, before he could.

"Exactly. You've got yourself a riddle."

"Nobody even knows when she died, except that it was in the last couple of weeks. Apparently, the house was too cold for them to accurately determine time of death."

"Nobody missed her, reported her missing from work?"

"Her lawyer doesn't even know if she worked. I still have to talk to the cops."

"You need to do that?"

"Do you want the short answer or the long answer?"

He laughed. "I told you: both."

"The short answer is, I pack up her things, drop whatever she has in clothes in the Goodwill box, toss the rest. Stamp 'paid' on an unfortunate life, try to forget why she needed me as her executor."

"What's the long answer?" he asked.

"I'm not sure when I'll be back," I said.

Six

The sun was two feet off the horizon when I got back to Louise's cottage. That meant maybe an hour and a half before it got dark, enough time to finish up.

As I carried out the three bags of crumpled newspaper pages to leave by the garage, I thought of Louise's nimble-fingered landlady. The Honestly Dearest columns were the only traces I'd found of any contact Louise Thomas had sought with her world. Maybe those columns were all that had touched her heart. I turned around on the drive and put the bags into the back of the Jeep. Tossing them in the Dumpster behind the motel would be a minor gesture, but one that would guarantee they'd never be touched by Mrs. Sturrow.

I went back inside. With her sheets of newspaper gone and her sensible clothes in a bag on the porch, Louise's tiny house had the stale air of a place closing in on itself. That was my imagination working, of course. Perhaps she'd never really occupied that house; perhaps she'd merely drifted between its three rooms for a time, careful to leave nothing of herself behind. I walked through the mess in the kitchen to look a last time for anything left of Louise Thomas.

In the tiny bathroom, there was a bar of Ivory soap in the fiberglass shower enclosure, another on the corner sink. One white bath towel hung on a hook; a second had been thrown to the floor. A jar of cold cream also lay on the linoleum floor, upside down, a foot from a tube of toothpaste, rolled carefully up from its bottom, and a scuffed-down purple toothbrush. There was no aspirin, no cough syrup, no thermometer. Whatever pain or fever she'd known, she'd managed it without help.

I picked up the jar of cold cream. Deep finger gouges raked the inside, as though someone had been searching for something buried in it. The cold cream smelled of roses. My fingers began to cramp; I'd begun squeezing the jar too hard. I'd known a girl once who'd smelled of roses and of Ivory soap. Lots of girls, lots of women smell of roses and Ivory soap. There was nothing in the bathroom. Nothing at all.

The sunlight was fading quickly in the living room now, the light behind the plastic sheets deepening into gray. I took another look around the room. There'd been nothing personal there, no photo albums or whiskey, no old records or CDs. If Louise Thomas had owned a television or a radio, they'd been taken by the intruder or by Mrs. Sturrow. Something, though, perhaps just an overworked fancy in a darkening cottage, made me allow the possibility that Louise Thomas had lived without television or radio or books. I wondered what kind of woman could manage the nights, in such a desolate place, with only the wind to keep her company.

The bedroom, too, demanded little more than a fast, final glance. I went to the empty closet, this time thinking to feel along the top shelf. My fingers touched a small box in the farthest corner. It was a new black typewriter ribbon, marked for Underwood models like the Number Five on the oak table. I put it in my coat pocket.

I had to pass the oak table on my way out of the room. From habit, I started to reach for the typewriter.

We bent to look at what she'd just cut into the paint on the underside. M.M.'S FUTURE MACHINE, *she'd scratched, with the fork. She smiled, pleased by our scrutiny. "I'm going to write my way out of this town," she said.*

I pulled my hand back. It was just an old reflex. I didn't need to turn over the machine. I'd already checked. There was nothing there.

I felt in my pockets for Louise's keys. It was almost dark.

Something glinted faintly as I reached to close the living room door. I stepped back inside. It was the brass knob on a closet door, caught just right by the last of the daylight. I'd never noticed that closet; it had always been hidden by the opened living room door. I turned the knob.

Two wire hangers dangled empty on a metal pipe rod. There was no jacket, no coat, no hats to protect from the cold or the sun. On the floor was a woman's pair of gray running shoes, size eight. I grabbed the clothes bag from the porch, dropped in the shoes, locked both doors, and left.

Jeep Wranglers have no trunks, and the shelf of a backseat is comfortable only for people with removable legs. Since the car was already crammed with three bags of newspaper sheets, it was tempting to leave the clothes behind.

But they might fetch a few bucks for Mrs. Sturrow at a resale shop.

"Let her eat fruit," I said to the bag of clothes. Smug with pettiness, I jammed it in the back of the Jeep. I'd find a Salvation Army bin in West Haven.

I got behind the wheel, twisted the key in the ignition—and then I sat, stalled by a hazy mix of old memories and new questions. The engine seemed to grow louder and louder, as if impatient with my indecision. Finally, I could not stand it. I shut it off, ran to the dark house, and unlocked the doors. By now, the living room was almost black, the bedroom barely lighter. Even in the cold, I was sure there was a scent of roses and Ivory soap.

I grabbed the Underwood. The heavy old black steel was frigid under my grip as I relocked the doors and hurried to set it on my passenger's seat. I fired the engine and drove away.

The road to West Haven was deserted, the snow on the fields a pale blue blanket lit softly by a rising quarter moon. Past the broad turn a couple of miles west of Louise's place, something flashed red a few hundred yards behind me. It could have been the quick tap of brake lights of a car following without headlights, or it, too, could have been my imagination.

. . .

Setting down the bags of newspaper sheets to unlock my motel room door, I made a bargain to shut up the little bean adder that crabs around inside my head: I'd spend only the seven hundred Louise had earmarked for me to be her executor, and not one dime more. Whatever questions remained when the seven hundred ran out would have to stay unanswered.

The little bean adder snorted in disbelief: You don't have any other money, he said. Ah, but I have a credit card, I almost said, but I didn't. It isn't seemly to argue with oneself aloud, even when one is within earshot of only twin Dumpsters.

Inside, I called Reynolds's cell phone and left a message asking him to call. Then I dumped the bags of crumpled Honestly Dearest columns onto the bed and began sorting them by date. It would have been boring work, but I'd switched on Grand Rapids television. Its *Starsky and Hutch* retrospective was still going strong, and though the plot of each episode was identical, the names of the distressed damsels and the colors of the villains' cars varied enough to keep me enthralled. Time almost flew.

The Honestly Dearest columns went back over a year. As I'd noticed at lunch, the oldest were from the *Gulf Watcher*, a shopping tabloid from Windward Island in Florida. More recent were a couple of sheets from Georgia and Ohio papers. The newest, and the largest batch by far, came from the *Southwest Michigan Intelligencer*, beginning the previous May.

As Starsky and Hutch traded witticisms about women and cars, and cars and women, I nibbled at my salad from lunch and what was left of the Oreos and read Honestly, Dearest columns. To victims of faithless marriages, teenage insecurities, bad-smelling coworkers, a peeping pizza delivery man, and a college lad who objected to his roommate having sex with a girlfriend while he was trying to study not five feet away—all of them ordinary people, sadly at their most ordinary—she offered up respect and common sense.

However, none of the letters appeared to have been written by a frightened, lonely woman living in an isolated cottage. And none had been spotted with blood. The newspapers had been scattered by the intruder, after he killed her.

No blood, no trail to Louise. I didn't know what that meant.

I'd fallen asleep rereading some of the newer columns, notwithstanding Starsky and Hutch being mirthful in the background, when Reynolds called. It was eleven twenty.

"Who's got Louise Thomas's purse?" I asked.

"Why do you want to know that?"

"I'd like to notify next of kin. She might have had wallet pictures, letters, something else that can help me trace them down." It sounded better than trying to justify a growing obsession.

"Most likely, the intruder took the purse for the cash and the credit cards."

"We don't know that for sure."

"All I know for sure is I got a message on my cell phone saying there'd been a home invasion and a death on Twelve, and to keep an eye peeled for vandals."

"Who left the message?"

"Some woman with the county. I didn't write down her name."

"So you wouldn't know where they took her?"

"Whichever funeral home they use as county morgue?"

"I want to find out where her purse is, and if she was wearing a coat."

"A coat?"

"There was no coat in her house. Maybe the landlady swiped it, but maybe Louise was wearing a coat when she was killed—it was cold in that house—and the sheriff has it."

"How is that important?"

"You're going to love this."

"Tell me."

"I want to know if she had cigarettes in her coat pocket, or in her purse."

"Now you're really confusing me. Cigarettes?"

"I think she smoked. Too much fresh air was blowing in through the plastic to smell it, but I found a broken ashtray with three Salem butts spilled out of it. There were no other cigarettes in the place."

"I still don't understand."

"Ever know a cigarette smoker who didn't have a backup pack in a drawer? Especially somebody who lived way out in the tulies, miles from a gas station or a convenience store?"

Reynolds exhaled slowly into the phone. "Look, my job is to watch warehouses and fruit fields. In the winter, that might not seem like much, but in the summer, it's plenty. There's a population then, some stealing from each other, some stealing from the growers. And that's when I'm on the phone with the sheriff's office, all the time. I've got to be careful with that relationship. I can't bother them with some bright idea about a missing pack of cigarettes."

"So nobody investigates."

"Not true. I'm sure the county is keeping the file open. And I'm doing what I can."

"That old Dodge in the garage has a Florida license plate. Do you know anybody who can trace it backward, get me her previous addresses? Maybe I can find a relative that way."

"I had a buddy run that Florida plate. The guy who purchased that Dodge new sold it to some young woman some years ago." He paused, then said, "She never retitled the car in her own name."

"She left it in the previous owner's name for all those years?"

"Apparently."

"How did she get a license plate?"

"She learned ways of circumventing the law," he said.

I saw her then, in my mind: huddled in a long coat, a wool beret pulled down low, a scarf and dark glasses hiding her face, coming out of the narrow little cottage.

"She owned nothing but a few things that could be packed quickly." I spoke fast, anxious to get the words out so I could understand. "She drove up here in a car she never titled in her own name, paid a year's rent up front, with cash. She arranged to have her mail diverted, kept nothing in that cottage she couldn't walk away from."

"Indeed," he said. He already had it figured.

She hurried the few steps from the back door to the garage, clutching her coat to her thin body, against the wind, against the world.

"The back bumper, where the license attached, was clean," I went on, "because she kept the plate under the front seat, screwed it on only when she went out, so she wouldn't get pulled over by a cop. Otherwise, the plate was off the car."

She knelt at the back of the Dodge, attaching the plate.

"So no one creeping around the cottage could trace her from the license, find out where she was from," I said.

"Paranoid to the extreme," he added.

Louise straightened, moved to the driver's door.

"Or extremely careful," I said.

She started the car.

"Every minute, she was running scared," I continued. "Not just in Rambling, but down in Florida, too, because she never retitled the car. For years, she was running scared."

"What does this mean?" he asked.

"I don't know."

Louise backed out along the rutted drive. As she passed, in the center of my mind, I could not see her face.

I awoke in the dark. The red letters on the alarm clock read 3:45. I lay still for a few minutes, trying to pretend nothing had nagged me awake. But I knew.

I gave it up. I got out of bed, slipped on Nikes, jeans, and my pea coat, and padded down the outside stairs to the Jeep, to lug the frozen old metal back up to the room. I wouldn't be able to sleep until I made sure. Again.

I balanced the typewriter upside down on the bathroom sink, because that's where the light was brightest. The metal undercarriage shone back, black and smooth. Nothing had been cut into the bottom of the front rail.

To be certain, I looked at it from different angles, front to back, side to side. It was then that my eye caught the small piece, high up in the undercarriage, that was blacker and shinier than the rest. I felt for it with my fingers, touched a rounded surface with a hole cut into the center of one end.

I turned the typewriter over and began working the odd shape with my fingers. It didn't move. When I withdrew my hand, bits of black paint came back stuck to my finger. Old factory paint didn't come loose that easily.

I hustled down again to the Jeep for the little rolled pouch of small tools, prudence for driving a heap as old as mine. Upstairs, I worked the blade of a small screwdriver under the piece of curved metal. After a minute, it began to move. Then it clattered loose and fell into the sink.

A flat key, stamped with the number 81.

Seven

The key I'd discovered probably weighed an ounce, but it dragged like a thousand pounds. She'd painted it to make it blend in, then epoxied it too high and too tight inside the typewriter to be gotten at easily. Whatever the key unlocked, she hadn't planned on accessing it for some time.

Or maybe forever.

I didn't figure the key worked anything in West Haven. It was too close to Rambling for such a secretive woman. Besides, I had already checked out the banks and the post office. They'd had nothing for Louise Thomas.

So I started across the street from my motel, for fortification for a road trip. At seven thirty, the Wal-Mart parking lot was already half-filled, no doubt by people there to buy Oreos for breakfast. Not me. I strutted right past the end display of the dark, round dunkers—sugar and flour, fat and sin—and exited clutching only a huge foam cup of coffee and a lone doughnut, this one barely dusted with green sprinkles, and even those were the precise color of broccoli. It's always best to begin a challenging day with a sense of moral superiority.

I'd drawn two concentric circles on Fizzy's map, to correspond to Aggert's list of towns a thirty-minute, and then a full hour's, drive from Rambling. I was guessing the numbered key would fit something in one of the four post offices or eight banks in the closest circle. I didn't figure a woman afraid of leaving a license plate on her automobile for fear of being discovered would want to be on the road for very long.

Santha, Michigan, population 3,012, was thirteen miles of tree orchards north of West Haven. Wood signs stuck in the frozen dirt said the lifeless trees I was seeing produced peaches and apples, and if I happened to be around in late summer, I could pick them myself. It seemed a world apart from chasing the trail of a key hidden by a dead woman.

The flat key didn't fit box 81 at the Santha post office, and the man at the window said there were no mail holds for a Louise Thomas. Oddly, for such a small town, Santha had two banks on the two blocks of its main street. Both were branches of banks, one in Detroit, one in Lansing. Louise was not a customer of either one.

Grand Plain was straight east through seventeen more miles of fruit trees. It appeared never to have had a post office, though it did have a gas station with two pumps. Grand Plain had recently had a branch of a bank, too, though a new-looking sign in the window said it was closed and referred customers to the main location in Kalamazoo. I wondered if intense competition from the two-bank metropolis of Santha, population 3,012, had been responsible.

Woodton was fourteen miles southeast of Grand Plain. A bank and the post office filled one side of the block-long main street. I walked into the post office lobby at twelve fifteen. Though it was lunchtime, I was the only customer, and my running shoes made loud squeegee noises as I crossed the polished marble floor to the small wall of brass postal boxes. Their numbers stopped at 75, six short of my number 81. I went over to show Louise's will to the young girl in the service window.

"Do you have any mail holds for this woman, Louise Thomas?"

"No, we sure don't," she said right off. Then she stopped, pursed her lips, and turned to open a small wooden box. A second later, she produced a three-by-five index card. "Leastways, we're not getting any mail addressed to Louise Thomas. But a person of that name did fill out a hold request last year. We do that for people who are gone a lot." She smiled a good, white-toothed smile of youth, told me she'd be right back, and disappeared through a door at the back of the mail sorting room.

Five minutes later, the interior door to the lobby opened and a thin, sour-looking fellow emerged. His narrow face was pinched and wrinkled, as though from spending his entire life squinting at poor penmanship. He was carrying a plastic tub, stenciled with U. S. MAIL on its side, as though it were half-filled with bricks instead of thick tan envelopes. He dropped the tub at my feet, sending a loud thud echoing through the marble foyer.

"Perhaps you can get in here more frequently," he groaned, wiping his brow in anticipation of any perspiration that might bead there.

The right thing would have been to remind him that mail piling up would no longer be a problem, since his clerk must have told him I'd showed her Louise's will. Instead, I put on a happy smile and bent down to pick up the box, one-handed. It was heavy, but not like bricks. "I'll keep that in mind," I said.

"I've heard that before," he said.

Already the tub was tugging my hand. "When was she in last?"

"The woman? Not for a while. I meant the fellow before you. He said he'd make sure it didn't pile up." He shook his head. "He hadn't even bothered to bring authorization, just asked for the mail. Like I'd hand it over to a stranger?"

I tried to give him what I hoped was a sympathetic smile—clearly the man's life was a soap opera of unwarranted indignities—but the tub was beginning to tear the ligaments out of my shoulder, and I was afraid my face was showing the pain. I shifted the tub to my other hand, in what I hoped was an unobtrusive manner. "This fellow—when was he in?"

"Two weeks ago. No, maybe the week before that."

"He wanted her mail?"

"Can you believe?"

I could believe, if he'd murdered Louise Thomas and hadn't found what he was looking for in her cottage.

"What did he look like?"

The postmaster gave a dismissive shrug. "Ordinary, very ordinary, like you. Your height, but older. He was slimmer, though."

"Hair color?"

He shook his head. "He wore a knit hat, pulled low, for the cold."

"Eyes?"

"Our conversation was very brief."

"What about Ms. Thomas? What did she look like?"

"Like the star of a trashy Dracula movie." He laughed, trilling against the marble on the floor and the walls. "I mean, every time she came in for her mail, she had on a hooded dark coat and dark glasses. Summer, winter, it didn't matter; she was always shrouded."

"She's dead."

"So my clerk told me."

I shifted the tub back to my right hand. My entire body, from the shoulders on down, was throbbing. "I'll have her mail forwarded to me, so you won't have to bother with it anymore."

He walked me quickly back to the counter and produced a forwarding authorization form. I set down the tub, as grateful as I'd ever been for anything, and reached for the counter pen with a trembling hand.

"Mind you return it," he said.

"What?" Confused, I turned to look at him.

"The container." He gestured at the tub on the floor. I nodded, gave him his form back, and picked up the tub, again one-handed. As soon as I was outside, I put both hands to it so it wouldn't fall from my trembling arms.

There was a white stucco diner across the street with a sign in the window advertising the day's special of chicken-fried steak for $4.99. Chicken for lunch is a requirement of good health. I went in and set the tub beside me on the seat of a red vinyl booth by the window. It was one ten, and like the post office, the diner was empty. I was too hungry to care why nobody was lingering there after lunch.

A matronly waitress in a pink uniform came over. I waved away her offer of a menu, told her I'd have the special. "But only put half the gravy on it," I said. I'd begun the day by skipping Oreos; now I was cutting back on gravy. Soon my ribs would emerge.

She peered over her reading glasses. "We could hold the gravy altogether if you're dieting."

"Half the gravy should do it, thanks," I said, smiling up.

"We could hold the potatoes. You could have fruit."

"Fruit's got a lot of sugar," I said.

"We could hold the fruit."

"Just as I ordered it, please," I said. "Chicken fried steak, mashed potatoes, half the gravy. And coffee, black."

"You know the chicken fried steak isn't really steak?" She wasn't going to yield.

"Is it chicken?"

"Some of it comes from a chicken."

"Will I be able to tell what's under the breading?"

"Probably not," she said, conceding the point, "but to make double sure, we cover the meat and the breading with lots of thick gravy." She tore my order from her little pad and walked to the grill window.

I pulled one of the large envelopes from the tub. It was addressed simply to H. D. and had been mailed two weeks before, from a Smith's Secretarial on Windward Island, in Florida.

It was the same island where the oldest of Louise's newspaper columns had come from.

My waitress came back with the coffee, a basket of rolls, and a dish of little butter tubs the size of sliced doughnut holes. She made a show of turning to walk away, but she was moving slow, hanging back, daring me to butter a bun. I managed a smile for her and went back to the envelope.

By now my fingers were tingling. I ripped open the envelope. Inside was a loose bunch of smaller envelopes along with some photocopies. I turned the big tan envelope to slide everything out onto the table.

Most of the smaller envelopes were white and business-sized, but a few were square, in neon green, yellow, and pink, the kind for greeting cards. I spread them out across the surface of the table. All had been mailed to Honestly Dearest, care of the Bayonne, New Jersey, *Register*. None had been opened.

The photocopies looked to be mock-ups of Honestly Dearest newspaper columns, set in newspaper type.

Reader letters and copies of future advice columns, forwarded up from Florida to an H.D. in Woodton, Michigan.

My mind did loops around the impossibility of it, as I saw again the clutter of newspaper sheets strewn all around inside the tiny, frozen cottage in Rambling, and the old, black typewriter in the bedroom.

I fumbled at opening one of the regular white envelopes. "Dear Honestly Dearest," it began, "I'm a middle-aged housewife, trite I know, who's been having romantic fantasies about the man . . ."

I dropped it back onto the pile and tore open another of the thick tan envelopes forwarded up from Florida. More small envelopes addressed to Honestly Dearest were inside, along with another mock-up of a future column. Something new, too: a white envelope that had been addressed with merely a name, handwritten in large, cursive letters: Carolina.

I slit it with my fingernail. "Carolina!" the same large scrawl had been written on a sheet of white typing paper. "We're about out of backlog! Have you succumbed to the beach in sunny Ef El A?!! RUSH MORE!!!!! Charles."

"Ef. El. A." I mouthed it under my breath. F-L-A. Florida.

"She's sick, you know."

I jerked around, looked up. I hadn't heard the waitress coming. She was balancing a large plate with her fingertips and nodding at the photocopies of the Honestly Dearest columns I'd spread on the table.

She set my plate down a fraction of a second after I got the clippings out of the way. It was mounded with a thick white gravy, the consistency of oatmeal.

"Sick?" I asked, my mind still in the envelopes.

"Honestly Dearest," she said. The gravy started to work its way over the edge of the plate but hung suspended at the lip, too thick to drop.

"How do you know that?"

"More coffee?"

"How do you know she's just sick?"

She left and came back with the glass coffee carafe and a thin newspaper that had been folded twice. She set the newspaper on the table and filled my cup. "Right there at the top," she said.

I looked at the newsprint. HONESTLY DEAREST was printed out in bold letters, followed by "is ill," in italics.

"You read the column a lot?"

"In the *Intelligencer*. Except she's been sick, like I told you, the last couple weeks." She started to turn, to walk away, but then stopped. "You don't look like the type to be reading those columns."

Then she said something else, but her words dissolved into muffled buzzing, crowded out by the flash fire of thoughts raging inside my head. She stood, waiting.

"Nothing else, thanks," I thought to say.

I'd guessed right. She smiled. "I'll leave you to your columns, then," she said.

I looked down at the shape of the chicken fried steak submerged in the puddinglike gravy, a pale porpoise drowning in thick lava. "Thanks for all the gravy," I called out.

"Only way to eat chicken fried steak," she said, not bothering to look around.

I stuffed the loose envelopes and photocopies back into the two tan ones and dropped those back into the mail tub, where, I hoped, I could ignore them for a few minutes.

I cut loose a cube of the chicken fried substance and managed to raise it, quivering as it was beneath its half inch of molten gravy, to my mouth without spilling it, but the traffic in my head was still too busy. My appetite was gone. I needed to get away, find someplace quiet to paw through the mail tub.

I left a ten on the table, hauled the tub out to the Jeep, and gunned down the empty road to West Haven. There were no more answers in the cottage in Rambling, nothing to be learned working out of a room across the street from a Wal-Mart. I needed to get back to the turret.

I left the tub in the Jeep and ran in to grab the Honestly Dearest columns, my duffel, and Louise's old steel typewriter. The desk clerk, a sallow, pimply kid who looked resigned to a life behind a registration counter, stiffened as he told me I'd have to pay for the upcoming night, since it was long past checkout time. I surprised him by not arguing, and he bobbed his head instantly when I asked him to drop Louise's clothes at the local homeless shelter.

H. D. Honestly Dearest. No matter how many times I ran it through my brain, it was unreal. Louise Thomas was Honestly Dearest, the advice columnist. Except she wasn't Louise Thomas; that was a made-up name.

Her name was Carolina.

I had to get back to the turret, to my records, to find a Carolina. To find out why she'd had to lie to me, by using a false name.

Eight

A cell phone rang far away.

"Dek," Amanda's voice said from the sliver of light under my pillow.

"I love you," I said as the phone rang again.

"Your cell phone," her distant voice said, above the ringing.

"I love that, too." I pulled down the pillow to close the little gap.

"Dek Elstrom's phone," she said, much fainter now, outside the darkness.

Several seconds of soothing, dark silence followed. Then, without warning, the pillow was torn away, a thousand daggers of white sunlight stabbed into my eyes, and the rude, cold plastic of a cell phone attacked my cheek.

"Dek Elstrom," I said into the obnoxious intruder, because I had no choice.

"Top of the morning, Mr. Elstrom; Bill Aggert here." I could almost smell the damned mints above his chirping words. "I just called your motel and was shocked to learn you checked out yesterday."

I opened my eyes to squint at Amanda's bedside clock radio. It was seven fifteen. We'd only slept for four hours.

"It's seven fifteen," I said.

"Eight fifteen in West Haven," he said. "You can be back up here before noon."

Amanda stood by the full-length window, looking out at Lake Michigan in the east. The view of the lake from her fortieth-floor condominium was roughly the same as I'd seen in Michigan—waves frozen in midcurl, chunks of ice floating far out—but the view from West Haven didn't include Amanda in a sheer white wrap, made transparent by the sun as it, and part of me, rose.

I propped myself up on one elbow to get a better view. "I found a little key," I said, tossing a morsel to make him go away.

"P.O. box or bank?"

"Louise had her mail held in Woodton. No box."

"Anything in it that affects probate?"

"I haven't gone through it all yet."

"Bring it up today," he boomed, "and I'll go through it while you take that key to the rest of the banks and post offices. Bills and assets have to be included in the inventory."

"You have a deadline to file something concerning her death?"

"The probate court likes timely filings."

Amanda turned from the window to smile. The new view was just as breathtaking.

"I'll call you," I said, not caring much if Aggert heard before I clicked him away and dropped the phone.

I'd called Amanda at nine thirty the previous night, ten seconds after I'd thrown the last of my old business files across my office. There'd been no Carolina.

"I've been in Michigan, in the cold, but I saved myself for you," I said.

"I'm sure I'm not worthy."

"Nonetheless, I'd like to come over."

"What about our one-week rule?"

"I know we must take things slow this time," I said, "but Sunday's horn concert wasn't a date; it was work."

"What about what we did afterward? Was that work?"

"That we must continue to practice. It's why I'm calling."

"No it isn't. There's something else."

"I'm cold."

"I'll call down to the desk."

Now, the next morning, an hour after Aggert called, Amanda and I were sipping coffee in her living room. Like the rest of the apartment, the walls were the palest of whites. She had almost no furniture in the two-bedroom condominium: a simple laminate table and four chairs in the kitchen; nothing in the dining room except boxes of art books; a dresser and an enormous bed, bookended by two nightstands, in the master bedroom; a computer workstation in the spare room.

In the living room, where we were now, there was but one glass coffee table and one soft white sofa, both facing two million dollars of miscellaneous artwork surrounding an eleven-million-dollar Monet. After her house in a gated community had been destroyed the previous year, she'd told me proudly that she'd furnished her new, high-security condo on Lake Shore Drive for less than four thousand dollars.

"Are you teaching today?" I asked.

"Got to pay the bills."

She'd inherited the Monet and the other art from a grandfather, but she needed the teaching money to pay for the taxes, dues, and security system at the condominium. For a woman who owned millions in art, she was just getting by.

She set her coffee cup on the glass table, snuggled closer. "How are you?"

The day was looming fruitless. "I wanted to find Carolina in my files, a previous client from a job. She wasn't there."

"She could have been in the background: a secretary, a clerk."

"That would have been a long time ago. Reynolds told me she bought her car some while ago and never titled it in her own name. She's been running for years, and that's what nags."

She squeezed my arm. "You must have made an indelible impression, for her to remember you from so long ago."

"You should have seen her place, a tiny cottage with missing shingles, set in the middle of nowhere. She was so alone."

"Dek . . ."

"If she'd called, maybe I could have helped."

Amanda straightened up so she could look at my eyes. "She didn't know you well enough for that, Dek. You've got to accept that. People have all sorts of casual relationships. You have to stop making more of this than it is."

"A casual acquaintance, fearing for her life, doesn't worry about an executor, especially not for an estate that has no value. She goes to the cops. A friend, or at least someone who knew me better, would have called me, told me she was in trouble, and asked for help. Unless . . . ." I looked past Amanda, at the frozen lake.

"Unless?" She reached out and touched my arm.

"Unless . . . she didn't think I would help."

"Have you ever refused to help anybody?" Her brown eyes caught the brightness from the windows; a smile, coaxing, played on her lips.

I didn't answer.

Her grip on my arm got stronger. "She was someone you knew briefly a long time ago, someone who went on to write advice columns. Someone who liked to live in seclusion. That's all."

"Or she was someone who knew she was going to die."

Amanda sighed, reaching for her coffee. "What can you do?"

"I'll finish going through all her mail, see if there's some hint in there as to why an advice columnist hides out in Rambling. I'll contact the banks I didn't visit, see if anyone's got a lockbox for a Louise Thomas." Outside her window, everything was white and frozen, easy to see. "But if she rented the box using the Carolina name, I'll strike out. I've only got authorization to act for a Louise Thomas."

"Are you going to call that editor, Charles?"

"If I can rule out that she wasn't running from him. He still thinks she's living in Florida."

She looked out where I was looking. "Such respect for a dead lady," she said.

"I want to know why she chose me."

"What happens when you run through the seven-hundred-dollar fee?"

I shrugged.

"You didn't know her, Dek."

"I want to believe that."

Amanda set down her coffee and turned to touch my shoulder again. "Her house was cold?"

"Her house was dead."

I got back to Rivertown at nine thirty. By then, the jukeboxes that pulsed the tonks had long gone silent. The street drunks with a few bucks had shuffled off to the health center, the ones without to the warm spots beneath the viaducts. The girls who hadn't been girls for decades had made their last slow parade down Thompson Avenue, to ease back to their rooms and drop away their fake furs and peel off the mesh stockings that hid more than they revealed.

Midmorning, when the town is quiet and the sky is clear, helps me make my peace with Rivertown. Midmorning, when the sun hangs behind the dead smokestacks of the abandoned factories and makes them cast long shadows, giving them a sort of new life; midmorning, when the still soft light blurs the accordion fences fronting the pawnshops and the liquor stores just enough to shroud the despair that, come noon, will be sold in those places again. Midmorning, there can be hope in Rivertown.

The little red flag on my rural-style mailbox was up, announcing to the world that I'd received correspondence. Since my business had tanked, it was a rare enough occurrence. I dropped the curved door and found an envelope with a drawing of my turret on its lower left corner. It was from the City of Rivertown. I wanted to wad it up and throw it toward city hall, but reason prevailed. I brought it inside, pinched between my forefinger and thumb, as one would carry an expired rodent.

I went upstairs, nuked cold coffee, and walked across the space that would one day be a hall. My office was warm, fifty-some degrees. In my haste to get away from the files I'd thrown all over the floor the previous night, I'd left without shutting down the space heater. I took off my pea coat, took a sip of coffee, and confronted the envelope.

There was no letter, just a violation notice. The crime, scribbled almost illegibly, as though by a child in a hurry, was "Use of Unhistorical Material in Historical Structure." The fine was one hundred dollars.

It was signed by one E. Derbil, and the bastard had ticketed me for temporarily covering a shattered window with plywood.

Elvis Derbil and I had disliked each other since grammar school. He detested my smart mouth. I detested the way he squealed with laughter every time he did something cruel to a classmate or a small animal. I tried to forget Elvis, like I tried to forget everything about Rivertown, when I fled to Chicago for college and then a career. For years it worked. Then my reputation got ruined, my business collapsed, and Amanda tired of nurturing a whining, self-pitying drunk. I came back to Rivertown and moved into the crumbling turret that had been my grandfather's dream because I'd run out of dreams of my own.

That put me squarely under Elvis Derbil's thumb.

My grandfather had been a small-time bootlegger. According to the mutterings I'd overheard from my mother's three sisters, he'd been broke most of his life. There'd been a time, though, at the beginning of the Great Depression, when his larger competitors had stopped brewing and set instead to killing each other off. In the ensuing shortage, demand for my grandfather's brew soared. Too small to be much noticed before, he now enjoyed great prosperity. But unfortunately, his hinges had not been fully attached. Instead of investing his new wealth in land or equities or even more vats, he bought truckloads of limestone blocks, to build a castle on the Willahock River.

Just after my grandfather began construction, his competitors came to their senses. They stopped shooting and went back to brewing beer, and that disintegrated my grandfather's good fortune. Restored to being broke, he died of a stroke soon after, leaving behind only a lone turret and a small mountain of limestone blocks.

The turret and the limestone sat abandoned until the end of World War II, when the lizards who ran Rivertown sniffed new shakedown opportunities from the coming postwar factory expansions. They'd need a temple from which to dispense building permits and accept gratuities. So they declared the small mountain a public eyesore, seized it and the land on which it sat, and built a magnificent hall of stone terraces and darkened corridors, expansive offices and closet-sized public rooms. They'd had no use for the turret, however, and left that with my grandfather's daughters, accruing unpaid taxes, deserted except for wide-strafing pigeons.

I scoffed when I inherited it from an aunt who'd refused to inflict it upon her own children. It lacked electricity and hot water; its roof leaked, and it was littered with rat carcasses. Then my life unraveled. I got hauled back to Rivertown in a stupor and dropped at the health center like a sack of broken bones, to spend the night in a Lysol-soaked room just vacated by a fellow who'd died in his own vomit. I awoke the next morning looking up, because there was nothing left beneath me. And I quit scoffing. I dragged my clothes to the turret, telling myself that my grandfather's dream could be rehabbed and sold for a grubstake to a new life.

First I needed an occupancy permit.

The person I had to see at city hall, across the lawn, was my old school antagonist Elvis, nephew of the lizard mayor of Rivertown. He looked older now, of course. His hair had receded halfway back on his head and was sprayed straight up, like the comb on a rooster if set perpendicular to its beak. It smelled of coconuts. He still had his squeal, though, amazingly not softened even a fraction of an octave by age.

He'd been waiting. He'd followed the newspaper reports of the corruption trial I'd gotten caught up in, no doubt exhausting his lips as he savored the words reporting my downfall. When I showed up at city hall, he made much of his power, and my lack of it. "Only temporary," he'd said, waving a dirty fingernail over a blank permit application, "and only to fix up the inside. No modifications to the outside." "Why's that?" I'd asked, long removed from the ways of Rivertown. He grinned and turned the form around so I could see. That was the first time I saw the new symbol of the village—my turret—printed right at the top. "It's a historical," he said, the beginnings of a squeal forming in his throat. The turret, though now owned by me, had been zoned a municipal structure in a greasy deal with its former owner, my aunt. The lizards hadn't wanted to own the turret, they just wanted to use it, as the symbol of what they were calling the Rivertown Renaissance, and they'd plastered its image on the town's stationery, the police cars, and the portable outhouses in the town's one park. It was a sleight of hand that could have occurred in no other town on the planet.

I had no choice. I took the occupancy permit, restricted though it was. In the fifteen months since, I'd plodded—renovating the interior as money allowed—and plotted, planning for the day when I could afford a lawyer to sue to get the zoning changed. All the while, Elvis and I fought over each repair. We argued about the color of the new roof, the sheen of the varnish on the timbered door, the hue of the caulk that would stop the winds from coming in around the windows. Everything was a cause for battle. So it was now, concerning the plywood I'd used to temporarily cover a broken window.

I sat at my card table desk, pushed Elvis's citation to the farthest corner, and switched on my computer. Internet directories got me e-mail addresses for the rest of the banks on Aggert's list, and I sent them all letters inquiring whether Louise Thomas had done business with them. It only took a couple of hours, but I was pretty sure it was two hours wasted. Carolina had been a secretive woman, and if she'd used her real name, or any name except Louise Thomas when renting a lockbox, I was stopped.

I sent the last inquiry at two o'clock. My office still seemed hot, but worse, it smelled of futility. I walked into the kitchen, in search of better air.

There was a jar of pickles inside my refrigerator and a third of a bag of Oreos. Between them was a plastic package of ham slices. The ham slices were sweating inside the plastic, in spite of the refrigerated air. I closed the door before the ham started to cry.

Things weren't much better next door. Two generic Lean Cuisine knockoffs rested side by side in the freezer, and otherwise alone. I have a theory that a Lean Cuisine, ingested before Oreos, coats the stomach with a kind of chemical firewall that prevents the absorption of black and white calories. My belt indicates the theory has little promise, but I am still investigating.

I nuked the knockoff that had a picture of a fish dinner on it, but when I removed the plastic cover, I realized I'd been hoaxed. The fish had swum away, and its place had been taken by something that looked and smelled like a puddle of adhesive. I threw the tray in the garbage, poured coffee, and dunked Oreos.

Fifteen minutes later, I called Reynolds, thinking I'd get his voice mail, but he surprised me by answering.

"I've got news," I said. "Louise Thomas's real name was Carolina something. She wrote an advice column syndicated in shopping newspapers."

"A gossip columnist?" He didn't sound excited.

"More like a Dear Abby."

"How'd you find this out?"

"I drove around your neck of the woods, checking to see if a numbered key I found fit a postal or bank box."

"You didn't say you had a key," he said.

"I might never find where it fits. I did learn she was picking up her mail in Woodton."

"Son of a bitch," he said. "All the way over in Woodton."

"There was a lot of mail there."

"Anything interesting?"

"Advice column stuff. Reader letters, copies of her newspaper columns, and a note from her editor."

"Anything else?"

"Like what?"

"Jesus, Elstrom, a clue to her murderer."

"I'm going to read it all this afternoon. Listen, there's something else: The Woodton postmaster told me a guy came in, wanting to get at her mail. The guy didn't have any authorization, so the postmaster blew him off."

"Did he tell the police?"

"I don't think so. You might want to keep a special eye on that cottage."

"You want me to run that key around, check the banks you didn't get to?"

"You don't have the authorization. Besides, I've sent them faxes," I said. "How are you coming at your end?"

"You mean, did I find out if she was wearing a coat when she was killed?"

"With a pack of Salems in the pocket," I added.

He didn't laugh. "We're having some vandalism, petty stuff from the local delinquents. Maybe I should run your key to the sheriff. He can contact every bank in the state."

"You haven't even had the time to find out who's investigating."

This time he laughed. "Get your butt up here with that key. And bring that mail. We can pass that on to the sheriff as well."

I told him I'd be up when I learned something. "If ever," I added.

We both laughed at that.

Nine

The contents of the rest of the large envelopes were the same as of the two I'd opened at the Woodton diner: reader letters, mailed to Honestly Dearest at the *Bayonne Register* in New Jersey, then bundled and sent down to Windward Island, Florida, to be forwarded again, up to Woodton. A third of the large envelopes also contained a photocopy of an Honestly Dearest column, set in type for distribution to the syndicate's newspapers.

By the postmarks, I guessed that Carolina had picked up her last batch of mail at the very end of the year, about the time she'd made out her will.

I read the letters twice through. At the end, I felt like I'd just crammed for a final exam on the continuum of human misery. All the players from the earlier columns had again been present—the cheating husbands, cheating wives, thieving children, unappreciative brides, abusive parents, touchy aunts, and touching uncles—a thousand variations of the species human, reporting up close and personal, in their own woeful words. Such was the pathos of it all that I wanted to raise my coffee with a trembling hand and toast the miracle that the controlling forces of the universe hadn't said the hell with it and dialed up the spinning of the world until it was fast enough to throw us all off.

There were also two more notes from her editor, just as short and whining as the one I'd read in Woodton: "Carolina! YOU MUST STOP DIDDLING! Send more at once. Otherwise will void your contract immediately. Now, Carolina. Charles." And finally: "You are canceled in one week if you don't respond. C."

The editor, Charles, had written truer words than he knew. Around the time he'd scratched out his last note, Carolina's whole life had been canceled.

I stood up and kicked at the listing red vinyl chair. My head was banging from coffee jits and human angst. I'd learned nothing. For days, I'd been chasing a ghost named Louise or Carolina, and I'd discovered only that she wrote columns for throwaway papers and might have smelled of roses and Ivory soap and maybe Salem cigarettes. I put on my pea coat, gloves, and knit hat and went out. A walk in the cold might tamp the failure smoldering in my head.

It was almost dark. Across the vacant strip of land, the merrymakers who played along Thompson Avenue were beginning to gather for another evening of Just Plain Fun. Jumbled juke music drifted over, changing each time a door to a tonk opened and spilled new notes into the discordant mix. Still, there was a certain musicality to it, I supposed, as I walked toward it. Beneath the jangle of competing guitars came the more primal, smoothing rhythms of softly running automobile engines, as the night's first wave of johns slowed to check out the winking inventory of working flesh, to see which looked to offer the least chance of bringing something residual home to mama.

I walked down Thompson, stopping when I got to the video arcade. I hadn't been on that piece of Thompson since the months after high school. I looked up. The girl who'd owned the old Underwood typewriter like Carolina's had lived in the apartment upstairs.

I hadn't been able to figure things out then, either.

I walked on, waiting for the cold and the exercise to calm my head, but the blare from the tonks only made me more edgy. I turned into the quiet of the side streets. Most of the houses in Rivertown had been built in the early 1920s, blocks and blocks of brown brick bungalows, lined up tight on twenty-five-foot lots. Rivertown had factories and jobs, then. And hope. The Slavs and the Poles who worked at the factories had come down the same streets I was now walking, swinging their empty lunch boxes as they headed home to soft lights. If they thought about crime at all, it was probably to smile in anticipation of a pail of prohibition beer snuck back from a corner grocery, or a money game of mah-jongg played in a church basement.

All of that got slapped away by the Great Depression. For with that came the first of the lizards. Elected promising property tax abatements and food subsidies, the lizards instead shrouded the lights along Thompson Avenue and subsidized themselves. They tossed out the groceries and the dry goods stores, replaced them with bars and brothels. They pasted FOR SALE signs on the police station and the city council chamber and spread the word they'd welcome kickbacks from bookmakers and big-time bootleggers, pimps, and prosties.

Three-quarters of a century later, the bootleggers were gone, but the lizards—grandsons and granddaughters now—were still in power, licking quarters from the gambling machines in the backs of the tonks, and bigger money in street taxes from the drug dealers and the pimps. Nobody swung a lunch bucket walking home from the factories anymore; the factories were shuttered. The lights on the bungalow porches were now the biggest in town, bright white hundred-watt bulbs, to keep back the night.

I pounded the blocks east to the city limits, each footfall crunching the snow a loud reminder that I was failing a client. I didn't know what to do next about Carolina. I didn't even know if that was her real name.

I came back up Thompson Avenue. The Hamburgers was open and empty. It had been changing hands and menus every few months, its offerings depending on the ethnicity of its owners. Never, though, had any of the budding restaurateurs bothered to change the big letters on the roof that had spelled, for as long as I could remember, simply HAMBURGERS. So, as the fare had changed from Chinese to Thai, Mexican to Italian, pizza back to Mexican again, hamburgers had always been on the menu. Good entrepreneurs knew it was far cheaper to lay in a few buns and some ground beef than it would be to replace the letters on the roof. That evening's special was a jalapeño burger, a perfect melding of sign and ownership. I took one into the night to eat as I walked.

I couldn't taste it—for the cold, for the noise jingling out of the tonks, for my rage at all the bastards that peopled the world that night: the greasy lizards who were killing Rivertown; the fussy, slow-witted attorney who worshipped a neat desk; the blueberry cop who got too easily derailed by petty crimes; the priss-pot editor of a rat-crap little shopping newspaper. I hated them all, and I hated myself, for being too myopic to see any trace of a woman who'd smelled of roses and Ivory soap.

I crossed the spit of land to the turret.

I stopped.

The slit windows on the first and second floors were casting their usual thin beams of light onto the snow, but that night, there was one too many. A sliver of light showed from the latch edge of the entry. The timbered door was open, just a crack, as though someone had entered and then pushed the door almost closed behind him.

I moved up to the turret, pressed my chest tight against the stone, and reached to push the door slowly open. I saw only the one white plastic chair and my table saw. There was no sign of an intruder. I quickly stepped in and eased the door closed to shut out the noise from the tonks. Coffee nerves, I wanted to think, and maybe a jalapeño or two that stretched the wires even tighter. My front door lock dates from my grandfather's time. The spring bolt could have stopped short when I went out.

Above, light spilled from the open door of my second-floor office. I could have left that open, too, forgetting to shut it to trap the heat. I padded up the circular stairs slowly. They are old wrought iron, and loose; they can ring all the way up to the roof.

At the second-floor landing, I stepped into the kitchen, grabbed the flashlight from the counter, and swept the beam around. The kitchen was empty. I picked up a hammer from the top of an unfinished cabinet and crossed the hall, Mr. Coffee Nerves, with his weapon at the ready.

My office was empty of evil intruders. Starting now to feel foolish,

I padded up to the third floor, found nobody lurking under my bed or beneath the clothes I keep piled on a chair. The circular stairs stop at the fourth floor. Nothing was up there except the ladder I use to get up to the trapdoor to the fifth floor, but it was lying against the wall, right where I'd left it.

I went down to the first floor, worked the lock bolt back and forth. It needed oiling. It must have stuck when I'd gone out, and I'd been too angry to notice.

Back up in my office, shrugging out of my pea coat, my eye caught the small typewriter ribbon box I'd left on the card table. I sat and threaded the ribbon into the old Underwood and typed out "Mary had a horrid little damned, double-damned lamb," because it was a stupid, childish gesture and such things have a place in my life, especially on nights when I'm mad at absolutely everything in the world. The old typewriter clacked and rattled as the carriage chattered to the left, but it laid out a nice, even sentence.

I got up, went into the kitchen, and started a pot of coffee. As it dripped, my anger turned back to Carolina's editor and the harassing tones of the notes he'd sent her. I tried telling myself I shouldn't be angry at the man. He had deadlines to meet and probably wasn't being paid enough to babysit some person to turn in a column. It didn't work. I kept seeing a woman alone and unknown, sitting in a cold cottage, typing out advice to people who had it better than she did. The image ran over my reason, and I did blame him. I did blame that flyspeck of an editor, for not being someone she could have turned to.

The wide, restless anger I'd tried to walk off in the cold was back, but now it was focused on Bayonne, New Jersey. What the hell, Charles; you want input? I'll give you input. I poured coffee, gasoline for an already raging inferno, and went back to my office and fed a clean sheet of paper into the Underwood. "Dear Sir," I began, and stopped. What would be appropriate? "Dear Sir, a woman who wrote for you was brutally murdered a couple of weeks ago. She died alone, in trauma. Her body froze before it was discovered because she had no one, except perhaps you, to ask after her. Yet by the whine in your petulant letters, clearly you were interested only in input for your lousy little news rag. Please submit whatever you owe her in the usual way, you prick, and do it damned quickly."

I stopped and read what I'd typed. It might be a touch aggressive, I allowed. I tore it out, wadded it up, and threw it across the room.

The seconds I should have used to reconsider such a foolish outburst I spent instead rolling in another blank sheet. Then I did stop, for the first faint thoughts of a more appropriate response were beginning to flit around my cranky brain. No, my wise self said, to what I was thinking. Yes, the caffeine countered. The caffeine won, and popped me out of the chair to rootle in the pile of unanswered reader letters. After a few minutes, I found one that made me laugh most inappropriately, wired as I was by the coffee, and the rage.

"Dear Honestly Dearest," it began, "I was a virgin when I married at fifty-six. My husband is a sweet man, four years older, but he was in the navy for forty years, and complains that our sex life is boring because I only like what he calls the mission position. What should a proper girl do? Rigid in Dubuque."

It wasn't funny. It had been written by a woman with a real problem. On the other hand, Charles, the whining editor, wasn't funny either, and neither had anything else been since I started digging through the few remains of Louise Thomas's life.

I took another sip of coffee to keep the jitters dancing and began typing: "Honestly, Dearest, you can be proper and a bit naughty, too. Gourmet chefs will tell you that spice adds flavor to even the oldest meat. Get your sweet self down to the hardware store and buy a couple of eye bolts and one of those child's swings, the kind that has chains and a strap seat to cradle your loving derriere. Hire a handyman to attach it to the bedroom ceiling. And let love be love! P.S.: When sailor hubby asks how you know of such things, look away and smile enigmatically, a Mona Lisa with her memories. Swingingly, Honestly Dearest."

I'd read enough of Carolina's columns to believe I'd captured her tone. My words, though, were sophomoric and stupid, chosen not to advise but to trigger a few palpitations in Charles's chest. I laughed for the first time in days, imagining the horror on his face as he read the faked column. I drank more coffee and rootled again in the unanswered mail.

"Dear Honestly Dearest," the letter from Sioux Falls, South Dakota, started. "My sister-in-law, 'Gladys,' who lives in another state, comes to visit every year, as we go to visit her as well. She's just gotten an older miniature schnauzer from the pound, 'Oofhausen.' Since her husband expired several years ago, we like that she has company when she's not with us. The problem is that Oofhausen thinks he's a cat, and marks his territory everywhere inside our house. During their last visit, Oofy puddled the living room carpet twice, wet the dining room oriental rug in all four corners, and sprayed our fish tank, fireplace screen, and antique map stand. When I mentioned these occurrences to Gladys, she just giggled and said, 'Older boys do lose their arc, you know,' as though it was only his aim that was off. My husband doesn't want to say anything to his sister, but since we are about to visit her, I feel I must use the opportunity to tell her how I feel. Am I right? Snorkling in Sioux Falls."

"Honestly, Dearest," I typed, on fire now. "Of course, honesty is usually the best policy, but it sounds like you've hinted at the problem enough for her to get the point. Short of grabbing her by the back of the head and rubbing her nose in Oofy's aquatic aftermaths, consider an alternative. Before setting off to see Gladys, phone around her town for the name of an agency that will loan or rent you a St. Bernard for an afternoon. Bring the pooch—call him 'Gaseous,' for extra impact—with you when you arrive at her place. As you lead him inside, mention to Gladys that Gaseous is prone to intestinal challenges, and that you hope it won't be a problem. Then, in the kitchen, produce a dog bowl and the quarts of chili you also picked up on the way. As you're filling Gaseous's bowl, ask Gladys if she's got any Lousiana Hot Sauce, explaining that Gaseous is especially fond of spicy things, though it does increase his discomfort. That ought to do it. Assuming Gladys has not fainted, smile sweetly and offer to put Gaseous up in a kennel, if she would prefer. She'll prefer, in a heartbeat, and more importantly, she'll get the point. Dryly Yours, Honestly Dearest."

Cackling as crazily as a loon, I had to open a dozen more envelopes before I found another letter that was bound to offend. “Dear Honestly Dearest, My problem is my college roommate, ‘Marco.’ He says he’s devoutly religious, but he prays to a carrot, ‘Hector the Carrot God,’ that he’s suspended from the ceiling. Sometimes he chants for hours. I want to respect his religious views, but I’m afraid the other guys on our floor are going to think I’m strange, too. Concerned in Champaign.”

I thought for a minute, sipped more coffee, and wrote, “Honestly, Dearest. Eat the carrot. Munchingly Yours, Honestly Dearest.”

At ten o’clock, I made what I swore would be the last pot of coffee and rootled again. The letter was perfection: “Dear Honestly Dearest, I’ll admit I have not lived a perfect life. For the past ten years, I’ve entertained as a clothing-diminished dancer. A gentleman customer, ‘Richard,’ wants to marry me. He is seventy-four and the man of my dreams, and has asked nothing of me (well . . . almost nothing, if you catch my drift, because little works, if you catch my drift) other than, before we get married, he would like me to have removed the names of my former husbands that are tattooed on the inside of one thigh. As he is quite wealthy, he has offered to pay for the procedure. I don’t want to upset him before the wedding—he is not in the best health—but am wondering if he is bargaining for more than he should. The tattoos are small, almost unreadable since I put on weight, and there are only six of them. Nervous Bride in Tulsa.”

“Honestly, Dearest,” I wrote, “the finest business schools in the country teach one thing over and over: Cost-Benefit Analysis. What’s it going to cost you, and what are you going to get? Sounds like you’ve already been to Harvard, honey. Assuming there’s no outlandish prenup, what’s a little lasering when so much more will be gained? Lose the ’toos. Yours for a Clean Slate, Honestly Dearest.”

So it went, me pounding on the old Underwood, overcaffeinated, demented, and giggling. It was catharsis, and it was working.

At one in the morning, the last of the caffeine had vaporized, the giggles were gone. Only a picture of Carolina, alone, frozen, anonymous, and dead, now filled my mind. I’d typed eighteen responses, each crude and ridiculous, each aimed to cause discomfort in Charles, my audience of one.

There was one last letter to write. For that, I had to make up both parts.

"Dear Honestly Dearest, I am the editor of a greasy grocery store tabloid that's best used to blot up hamster droppings. I have an advice columnist, an easily bullied woman whom I've tormented for years. She's suddenly stopped sending in new material. What should I do? Charles."

I leaned back, massaged fingers that were throbbing from punching round metal keys all night, then bent to type the response: "Honestly Dearest, Charles, you kill me. OK, maybe it wasn't you, but it was someone else who gave less than a damn about me. Now I am dead. Terminally, Honestly Dearest."

Black stuff for an ending. No grace, no humor. Later, when I felt kinder, I'd have to send him a proper letter, if only to find out Carolina's last name, but this wasn't the night. I put all the responses in a big envelope, addressed it to New Jersey, stuck it with only one stamp, and took it out to my mailbox. Some would say I'd wasted the night. As I raised the red flag, I told myself I'd come to my senses in the morning and retrieve the envelope. For now, though, it was the best repository for my rage, and best left in the cold.

I went back inside, turned off the space heater, and climbed up to my bed on the third floor. I never sleep well. I'm grateful when I can manage three uninterrupted hours, and those come only after I've spent at least an hour categorizing dilemmas, past, present, and most certainly future.

That night, I had to do no such categorizing. Crawling between the frigid sheets and worn woolen blankets, I felt warmed by my indulgent, childish typings. I had the sense, too, that Carolina would have approved of my pettiness, and I fell asleep almost instantly after my head touched the cold pillow.

Ten

Leo called at eleven in the morning, waking me from the first deep sleep I'd had in weeks. "Apparently banging on your door doesn't intrude into your consciousness."

I mumbled something profane into my phone.

"Let me in," he said. "It's snowing."

I pulled on pants and a sweatshirt from the chair, slipped on Nikes and into my pea coat, which is what one uses for a robe when there's no heat, and hustled down the metal stairs to open the timbered door.

"*Entrez,*" I said, in what might have been flawless French. It's one of three words Amanda has told me I'll need to know if I ever become a doorman in Paris. The other two are "*Merci,*" said with palm up, and "*La patisserie?*" voiced with raised eyebrow, for directions to the nearest bake shop. She assures me they're all I'll need.

"Jeez, it's colder in here than outside." Leo shivered as he stepped in out of the snow.

"Perhaps." I closed the door. "But there's less wind."

Leo wore his usual winter ensemble—the orange traffic parka, the chartreuse knit hat with the purple pom. Today, though, he'd added a lemon-colored wool scarf. "For color," he said, whipping it back with a flourish, like the Red Baron stepping down from his biplane after yet another successful aerial sortie. "Endora bought it for me."

"She alone understands your style," I said.

"Is the heat on in your office?" he asked, already ringing the stairs on his way up.

"Not yet." I clanged up after him and turned left, toward the sink, to make a pot of coffee.

"No time for that now," he said, coming out of my office and shutting the door.

"Where are we going?"

"Do you not own a calendar?"

"It's March first . . . ah," I said, realizing. Then I shook my head. "It's snowing. He might not be open."

"March first is Opening Day. Always. Finish getting dressed, if you own more clothes. I'll wait for you in my car, where there's heat."

He started down, then stopped to launch his eyebrows into a little dance. "Especially this year," he added enigmatically, before going down the rest of the way.

"I don't understand," I said to his back.

"You'll see."

"See what?" I said, but he was already out the door.

I was out to his Porsche in ten minutes. Astrud Gilberto sang softly above a Brazilian guitar as Leo drove us down Thompson Avenue. He turned at the river road and headed down the familiar heaved asphalt toward the concrete piers beneath the overpass. It was snowing harder.

"It's too early—" I started to say.

Leo quieted Astrud and the guitarist a bit as he coasted to a stop. For a minute, neither of us spoke. Then he said, "Behold."

I stared at the horror through the falling snow.

Kutz's Wienie Wagon sat in its usual spot under the railroad overpass, on the same flat tires that had supported it since the Second World War. But its narrow clapboard siding was no longer covered with curling flecks of white paint, as colorless as birch bark.

He'd painted it purple. Not lilac, not lavender, but a ripping, jelly-damned-bean purple.

"What the hell has he done?" I shouted. There were few things in my world that I'd ever trusted to stay constant, but Kutz's flaking hot dog trailer headed that short list. The world might continue to change, and Rivertown might continue to crumble within it, as the lizards went about corrupting it, brick by brick. Never, though, had I doubted that Kutz—eighty-some years old, mean as a snake stuck under a rock—would always, always, be boiling hot dogs under the overpass, and that he'd be doing it, always, always, from that peeling trailer that flicked off bits of leaded paint the way Kutz's always upraised middle finger flicked off the world.

Now he'd gone and painted the thing. Purple.

"Shit, Leo. Double shit."

He switched off the CD, silencing the murmurings of the Brazilian goddess. "Yesterday, at the Discount Den, they told me he'd just bought ten gallons of rubberized paint on closeout, that thick glop you're supposed to trowel on rough walls. I knew what the nutcake was going to do. I swung down here, tried to tell him it would drive away customers. He told me to go screw myself and kept slopping it on, crazy as a jaybird."

"Yesterday?"

Leo turned and grinned. "Yesterday."

"It snowed yesterday."

"Nuts like a jaybird," Leo said again, "out there painting in the falling snow."

"Why?"

"Check out the sign on the roof."

I looked higher. Kutz had amended his old sign to read KUTZ'S WIENIE WAGON AND LATES.

"What are lates?"

"Lattes. Kutz is going in for snoot coffee, lattes and espressos and that stuff." Leo cut the engine, and we got out.

He headed for the order window. I split away and went around to the back of the trailer. Of course, it was purple, too. Worse, it had been smoothed and filled in by the thick, rubberized paint.

Generations of Rivertown's young bucks had carved their initials into the slats on the back of that trailer, guys who were now old men, guys who'd moved away, guys who were dead and never coming back. Since World War II, they'd carved their names, or their initials, or the initials of girls they'd known, or wanted to know, or would never know, with a quick knife cut into the soft, flaking wood. My initials were back there, too, with a girl's, inside a heart carved two months after I graduated high school. Now they were gone like the rest, covered up with rubberized purple paint. Not even the indentations remained.

I walked around to the front. "What the hell, Kutz?" I yelled through the closed Plexiglas.

He bent down and slid open the order window. "Got to change with the times, attract a better crowd than you jerks just buying wienies."

Leo's hand found my shoulder as we waited for our order. He knew what I'd gone looking for on the back of the trailer.

Kutz bagged the six hot dogs, cheese fries, and the two drinks—a Big Swallow for Leo, a small diet for me—and handed them through the window. "Sure you don't want a couple of lates?" he asked Leo.

"Not in this lifetime," I said.

We carried the bags to Leo's Porsche.

"Shit," I said again.

"Trust the weather." Leo started the Porsche up the potholed road.

"What do you mean?"

"Ever see Kutz cleaning anything inside that trailer?"

I shook my head. "Word is, he doesn't even change the hot dog water, lets it sit over the winter because it's too greasy to freeze."

"Exactly." He nosed the Porsche up onto Thompson Avenue and accelerated west toward the turret. "Kutz laid on that glop while it was snowing. No way he scraped or washed that old, flaking wood before he hit it with the paint. Give it a few freeze-and-thaw cycles, throw in some summer rains, and that ground's going to be littered with sheets of rubberized purple, big as the shredded tires you see on the interstate."

"What if the weather doesn't come through?"

Leo flashed me a big-lipped smile that connected his ears with a mouth full of white teeth. "You're crazy. You'll think of something."

At the turret, he went up to the heat in my office, and I went to the kitchen to put on coffee.

"It looks like it's been snowing popcorn balls in here," he called from across the hall. He'd noticed the wadded-up sheets of white paper from my typing frenzy. Then, "Jeez, what the—?" His voice stopped suddenly.

I switched on the coffee and walked across the would-be hall. I knew what had silenced him so abruptly.

He was standing back from the card table desk, the bags of hot dogs and drinks in his hands forgotten. His always pale face was two shades whiter than I'd ever seen it. He was staring at Carolina's typewriter as if he were looking at the dead.

"Just like . . ." He let the sentence die away.

"I know."

He roused his thoughts enough to put the bags on the card table, but his right hand lingered close to the old Underwood.

"There's nothing scratched on the bottom, Leo."

In a kind of exaggerated slow motion, he turned to look at me.

"I checked," I said. "Several times."

He dropped his hand and stepped backward.

"Old times," he said.

"Old times."

His eyes surveyed the mess of wadded-up paper on the floor, hunting, I thought, for a place—any place—to look rather than at the typewriter. "You writing a book?"

"Indulging a fury."

He nodded, without questioning, and pointed at the thick tan envelopes and newspaper sheets stacked beneath the card table. "Louise Thomas's?"

"Carolina's. Her real name."

His eyes had strayed back to the old typewriter. "You knew her?"

"I don't remember a Carolina, either."

He shrugged out of his orange parka. Underneath, he wore a red rag knit sweater, two sizes too long, that on him resembled a sock knitted for a dinosaur. He bent down to peer more closely at the piles of newspaper sheets. "Advice columns?"

"I think she wrote them in Florida and in Rambling. I've read them all. She answered each with compassion, respect, and a good bit of humor. I think she'd known pain herself."

A faint smile touched his lips. "Dek Elstrom, ever the romantic." He straightened up, about to open the bag of hot dogs, when he must have spotted the white envelopes with Carolina's name written on them. He raised an eyebrow. I nodded. He picked one up and slid out the sheet inside. "Her editor wants to know why she's stopped sending in material."

"She quit submitting around the end of last year."

"Because she was killed."

I waved a hand at the litter of wadded-up sheets. "I was up late, trying to find the best way of communicating that to her editor."

He set the small drink and one hot dog on the table for me and took the other five dogs, with the cheese fries and the Big Swallow, to the plastic chair. He would eat all that and still weigh a hundred and forty pounds. It is an injustice. I wear every Oreo I've ever eaten.

I sat in my red swivel chair, unwrapped my hot dog, and took a bite. It tasted as good as ever, though who knew what the absence of lead paint dust would do to the ancient flavors in the boiling water, long term.

"She was nationally syndicated, but she wrote with that old—" He stopped, not wanting to even refer to the old machine. The typewriter had spooked him, the way it had me at first.

"No computer word processor for her."

Leo bit into a hot dog, chewing slower than usual. Always, he ingested Kutz's tube steaks at warp speed. Not today. He'd been slowed by the past.

"It's not hers, Leo," I said.

He looked at me from across the small room. "You're sure?" He was bald, with the shadow of a man's heavy beard on his pale skin, but it was a boy asking the question, the boy he'd been the summer we graduated high school.

I tapped the typewriter next to me. "Nothing under this baby except smooth black paint."

He grinned then, after a fashion, and shook his head as if he were clearing it. "*Saudade,*" he said.

"*Saudade*?"

"Brazilian word, somewhat untranslatable into English, but it can mean a kind of yearning, a grateful nostalgia, for a love past."

I raised my Diet Coke and toasted the typewriter. "*Saudade,*" I said, being bilingual, too.

Leo took a bigger bite of his hot dog. "You said this Rambling, Michigan, place is dirt poor?"

"Everything on its main street is vacant or burned. Half the houses outside of town appear to be abandoned."

He unwrapped another hot dog. "She made a few bucks writing advice columns for shopping rags, lived in a rented shack, drove a clapped-out old car, owned few clothes and almost no other personal possessions?" He was chewing faster, and thinking faster.

"Yes."

"Except for that?" He pointed at the typewriter with the last inch of his second hot dog.

"Except for that."

"If she had nothing, why name any executor? Why name you?"

"I work cheaper than anybody."

It didn't fetch a laugh. "You knew her," he said.

For a moment, neither of us spoke as we pondered the riddle of that.

"I'm guessing Carolina worked at a client's, years ago, before she started writing her columns," I finally offered up. There was nothing else to think.

Leo slid the wrapper of a fourth hot dog away. I hadn't seen him eat the third.

"OK," he said. "Let's get back to the second biggest question. Why was she living in Rambling?"

"Because nobody would know she was there. She had her mail—her readers' mail, notes from her editor—sent down to Florida, then forwarded again, up to the Woodton post office box, which was a half hour's drive from her home. She had no possessions, no personal stuff except a few clothes, a car not even titled in her own name, and a typewriter. She could pack up and be gone in fifteen minutes."

"What about that key you found?"

"That's where she kept what valuables she had. In a bank box."

"Near Rambling?"

"No. The way she cemented the key into that typewriter tells me she wasn't planning on using it for some time. I'm guessing that key works in some bank in Florida, or maybe on the route she took coming north."

I looked at the typewriter, then back to Leo. "But somebody did."

"Did what?" He dropped a limp cheese fry back into the sodden tray.

"Somebody did know she was in Rambling." I told him about the man in the pull-down hat who tried to finesse his way into her mail at the Woodton post office.

"You didn't find any money in her cottage?"

"I don't think she had a bank account. I'm guessing that guy grabbed whatever cash she had in the house."

"It wasn't a random home invasion?" He unwrapped the last of his five hot dogs, bit into it, and waited.

"A home invader doesn't track her mail to Woodton."

"What, then?"

"She'd been hiding from the man who finally found and killed her," I said. "For years."

"That explains why she left Florida, and her secretive life in Rambling. And that brings us back to the number one question: Why name you executor of a valueless estate?"

"She didn't name me. She hired me."

"To do what?" He watched my eyes as he slid the last of the hot dog into his mouth.

There was only one answer.

"She wanted me to find her killer," I said.

Eleven

As Leo walked outside, I saw that the red flag on the mailbox was down. The mailman had come early and had taken the envelope full of nonsense I'd meant to retrieve. I'd have to call Charles now, tell him Carolina was dead, and concoct some story about why that was funny enough to send him an envelope full of sophomoric advice column responses.

The telephone receptionist in Bayonne, New Jersey, didn't even bother to cover her mouthpiece: "Charles, line three," she yelled.

A moment later, a precise voice came on. "Charles Braithwaite," he said, enunciating each of the three syllables carefully.

"I'm calling about Carolina—"

"Carolina!" he said, sucking in enough air to fill a balloon. "You tell her I will not be treated in such a fashion! You tell her that she isn't the only columnist in the world! You tell her—"

I cut him off so he could suck in more air. "You don't understand—"

"No!" he shouted. "She doesn't understand. I need columns; I need them now, and I will not listen to anything that premenopausal—"

I held the phone away from my ear, let the words float away. I'd heard enough to make up my mind. When the noise died down, I brought the phone back to my head. "She hasn't been well. She wanted me to call and tell you that. Also, she didn't receive your last payment."

"Hold on," he said, much more calmly. Papers rustled in the background. "She's wrong. Her last quarterly check was sent out in mid-December. I'm looking at it right now. It got cashed, in Florida, same as always."

"On Windward Island?"

"Of course. As usual, cashed by her service."

"Smith's Secretarial?"

"Of course."

The same outfit that forwarded her mail to Michigan was also cashing her checks. "Could you check the spelling of her last name on the check?"

"Why would you ask that?" Suspicion had crept into his voice.

"Double-checking the details, is all. You know Carolina."

"D-A-R-E, care of Smith's Secretarial. The check was cashed, but maybe they didn't deposit the money into her account, or whatever."

"Probably Carolina just forgot."

"Well, you tell her I haven't forgotten, not about our contract. I've been covering her ass for weeks now, saying she's been sick. I don't care how ill she is, you tell her to send in some columns—"

"When did you last speak with her?"

Too long a silence came from the other end.

"Come on, Charles. How long?"

"You know damned well I've never spoken with her," he said in a small voice.

"Never?"

"Who are you?"

"A friend, helping her. And trying to help you."

"This is what comes from her being a real recluse."

"Not to worry, Chuck," I said. The simpering twit hadn't once asked how sick Carolina was. "She said to tell you she just mailed in a new batch of columns."

"It's Charles," he corrected, "and it's about—"

"Chuck, she specifically wanted me to tell you to pay particular attention to the last letter in the bunch. It's kind of about you and her."

"It's *Charles*," he screamed.

I hung up.

I keep a gym bag in the Jeep for those odd moments when the need to drop the extra pounds I'm carrying overwhelms me. That need doesn't arise often. The gym bag's also there for those moments when I'm angry. That does occur frequently, and since the turret's walls are limestone, tough on the knuckles when punched, I try to hustle my anger over to the Rivertown Health Center, where I can run and talk to myself. The other people there, especially the winos who live upstairs, don't mind; they talk to themselves, some of them, all day long.

I went out, jiggled the lock on the turret door to make sure it had latched tight, and started toward the Jeep and calmer moments. But the day wasn't done with me yet. Across the lawn, Elvis Derbil, in a snap-brim cap worn backward, metal studs glinting off his black leather motorcycle jacket, was scuttling across the lawn toward city hall.

Elvis Derbil, author of the hundred-dollar use-no-plywood citation.

"Elvis!" I yelled across the lawn. Lizards can hear, even if only as vibrations through their membranes. Elvis, though, didn't turn his head. He just hurried through the parking lot door.

I hustled across the frozen snow, over what had once been my grandfather's land, to the city hall built with my grandfather's limestone. Down the stairs, along the dark corridor, through the door marked BUILDING DEPARTMENT, I chased the trail of coconut-scented hair spray. The look on my face sent the department clerk—a dimwitted niece—pattering away; she'd witnessed our confrontations before. Stopped at the counter, I yelled Elvis's name through the doorway to his office. I couldn't see much of him except for one scuffed sole of a pointy-toed red and black cowboy boot, dripping snow slush onto the surface of his desk.

"Get the hell out here, Elvis," I yelled.

"Come to pay your fine?" his voice asked from behind the wall. The dripping boot didn't move.

"Come to protest, Elvis," I said, still yelling.

"I told you: That structure's a historical; no materials not in keeping with the period."

"That plywood is only a temporary cover for a broken window."

His chair creaked, and the boot slid off his desk. A second later, he appeared in his doorway. His forehead, bald halfway back, glistened beneath the overhead fluorescents like Crisco under a stove light. He leaned against his doorjamb and hooked his thumbs in the pockets of his striped cardigan sweater. "You telling me they used plywood in the Middle Ages?"

"You telling me they used window glass in the Middle Ages?"

The tight-lipped smirk on his face opened around yellow teeth. "A 'course they used window glass," he said. "Otherwise, why did they put in windows?"

"High archers," I said, lowering my voice.

The smirk disappeared as if someone had turned off a switch, and worry lines appeared. He was thinking. "What the hell do foot problems have to do with windows?" he ventured, after mulling it over for a minute.

"Not high arches; *archers*: bow and arrow guys, high up."

He nodded vaguely, the most motion he could summon while his brain was frying. "I told you you'd get ticketed for not using authentic material."

"It's temporary, until I can get glass cut."

"Tell you what: I'll cut the fine in half if you get glass in it by two weeks."

"That's still fifty bucks."

"Better than a hunnert."

From habit, I opened my mouth to yell back, but then I shut it. My war with city hall was not winnable through individual battles. I had to wear them down, inch by grinding inch irritate them enough to make them anxious to change my zoning to residential and be rid of me.

And I had reduced the fine by fifty bucks.

I left.

The attendant, a wily fellow who lived upstairs, was pushing shallow eddies of cloudy water toward the floor drain in the basement locker room of the Rivertown Health Center. Normally, the only thing he ever hefted was bolt cutters, and then only when some fool new to the place and thinking a padlock would safeguard a watch and a wallet had just gone up to work out.

"What prompted this?" I asked.

"Toilets," he grunted past the sagging stub of the cigar that had drowned on his lips.

Toilets spit back often enough at the health center. In the past, though, the attendant had left things to air dry rather than lift a mop himself. I could only guess that his new energy was prompted by city hall. The lizards were becoming increasingly desperate to revive the decaying old tank town, to make it worthy of demolition and new construction by upscale developers, for the kickbacks that would bring.

It was slow going. Rivertown was a hard town to make a show of cleaning up. The hookers strutting Thompson Avenue, and their older sisters behind the bowling alley, could outrun police strobes quicker than cockroaches fleeing sudden light. The tonks, too, were untouchable. Most of them were owned by the lizards themselves. As were the vacant factories with their shattered windows, and the boarded-up retail stores dotted along Thompson Avenue like missing teeth.

That left visible eyesores like the Rivertown Health Center. A stained yellow-brick pile, tiger-striped by rust running off its metal roof, it had been defrocked years earlier from being a Y.M.C.A. Its upstairs population of winos and semiretired sex offenders—slowed by age, rather than by any loss of inclination—was a ripe target for a very public cleanup campaign, but even that had limited prospects for success. The grizzled folks who slept, stupored, on the upper floors were rarely seen, staggering down into the daylight only on the first day of the month, and then only to snatch their disability checks from the mail slots at the front desk. The rest of the time, their prowlings were as nocturnal and as furtive as raccoons: fast forays to the liquor store across the street for fresh half-pints, and occasional stumblings down to the Willahock, to admire the stars while urinating in the river. Toppling the health center would send the residents, very publicly and very permanently, into the streets.

Other than the thumpers—small-time greaseballs who lurked in the parking lot, sunning themselves against the abandoned cars like snakes, even on gray days—the only outsiders who came to the health center in the daytime, besides me, were a couple dozen retired tool men and machine operators, veterans of the factories that used to hum in Rivertown. They came to work limber into aching joints and to trade jokes. It was safe enough, so long as everybody got out before dusk, when the dealers nosed their shiny-wheeled cars into the rutted lot, to peddle powders to high schoolers from the affluent, more western suburbs.

I left the locker attendant to his disintegrating cigar and wet floor and went up. As on every afternoon, Dusty and Nick were roosting on the rusted exercise machines. Nick had a new joke that he was brimming to tell, but he forgot it halfway through. I could have finished it for him, since he told it every couple of weeks, but that might have hurt his feelings. So I waited until he remembered enough to finish it with a flourish. In an uncertain world, where any tomorrow can bring tragedy, the opportunity of knowing anything of the future, even if it's only the punch line to an old joke, is always to be cherished.

I began walking laps but kicked up to a run when I started imagining the kind of fear Carolina Dare must have felt, hunkering in that cold, isolated cottage, starting at the sound of every little noise from the fields outside, jerking out of an uneasy sleep every time the wind rattled a loose window sash. I wondered if that kind of living wasn't its own kind of death.

I ran until I couldn't run anymore. Then I headed down to the locker room, grabbed my street clothes—no point in slushing through moisture to shower at the health center that day—and went out, wet from sweat and Carolina's fear, into the gray of the early March afternoon.

"You did what?" Amanda leaned back in the booth at Gino's East, just off Michigan Avenue in Chicago, struggling with the beginnings of a smile. I'd picked her up outside the Art Institute at seven that evening, and now we were drinking sangria, waiting for a cornbread crust pizza.

"I fired off some Honestly Dearest letters to her editor." I shrugged as though it had been acceptable behavior.

"You should have told him, Dek." Her lips twitched, just once. "He was . . . he was . . . her boss. And you . . . you . . ." She lost it then and started laughing. "You as an advice columnist, you . . ." She lost it again.

I took a sip of sangria, felt a little piece of fruit bump my lip. "You don't know how wise I can be." I tried to smile like a sage. It was the first time I'd felt like smiling all day.

She shook her head, still laughing. "I guess not."

We sipped more wine, but the smiles felt wrong.

"He didn't give a damn about her," I said.

"Still, you should have told him."

"I did, actually, in a snotty letter obviously mimicking Carolina's voice."

"Nice."

"I know. I know," I said to the disapproving schoolmarm look she was aiming at me. "I did go to retrieve it, though. I was just too late. And I did call Charles, intending to apologize for what he is going to receive, and to give him the sordid details of Carolina's death."

"Intending?" The marm mouth grew even more dour.

"He's such a priss, Amanda."

She gave it up and asked, "What exactly are the sordid details of Carolina's death?"

"I don't know them yet."

"Yet?" She reached across the table to squeeze my hand.

"It's not just curiosity. It's not even that she set aside what might have been her last seven hundred to hire me. It's that she died without rippling the pond. When her newspapers run a notice, it will sadden her readers, I'm sure. Then they'll forget her, like the cops have forgotten her. Her attorney is only interested in getting the estate closed. The blueberry cop, Reynolds, wants to try, but he doesn't have the time, and her landlady just wants her place back. Nobody cares."

"Except you."

"She was so paranoid she had her checks cashed in Florida and the money forwarded up to Michigan."

"Dek."

"She wanted me to find her killer."

"How?"

"I have no clue."

"You could spend the rest of your life searching for that lockbox."

"Yes, and I don't think I'd get any closer to finding it, if the key even belongs to a lockbox."

"What, then?"

"I'm bothered that there was no coat in the house, which means she must have been wearing it when she was killed. Yet she was inside, supposedly, typing."

"You wear a coat inside the turret."

"She had central heat."

"Maybe the landlady took the coat with the canned peas, or whatever," Amanda said.

"There was an ashtray full of cigarette butts spilled on the floor, yet there were no packs inside the house. Ever know a cigarette smoker who doesn't have a backup pack or two stashed?"

"Not those who don't live in the city, close to an all-night store. Why is that important?"

"Assuming the nimble-fingered landlady didn't take the smokes, the missing cigarettes could have been taken as part of an extremely careful search." I told her about the deep finger gouges in the jar of cold cream in Carolina's bathroom.

"Looking for something small, like that key?"

"Sure. Someone could have come in, bagged all the small stuff, and taken it out to search through later."

"What do you do now?"

"I left a message for Reynolds this afternoon, asking him to get me the name of the person at the county who's been assigned the case. I'll tell the cop about the guy who tried to get at Carolina's mail in Woodton. If Reynolds and I both push, I figure the cops will talk to the postmaster, get a description. Maybe they'll do an artist's sketch."

"Sounds like a plan," she said.

"And they'll send the sketch out to get tacked up on police bulletin boards alongside the other half-accurate sketches, and the death of Carolina, known as Louise, will be forgotten."

"Then you'll drive up to West Haven, hand over the house and car keys to the lawyer, find someplace to donate the car, and be done?" Amanda didn't buy it; she knew where my mind was going. "Because you still won't know exactly what Carolina wanted from you."

"There is that, yes," I said.

Our pizza came. She ate modestly, I ate the rest. Afterward, we braved the cold to stroll up Michigan Avenue and think of better things. We stopped at the gallery where we'd first met, two years before. We didn't go in; we looked through the window, trying to see ourselves through our reflections as we'd been that first night. She squeezed my arm and we walked back to the Jeep. Later, much later, after I left her place and drove south to catch the expressway back to Rivertown, I would have said, if asked, that the world was at last righting itself, that Amanda and I were doing it right this time, carefully, deliberately, spending lots of time on building a solid foundation.

That was before I heard from Carolina herself.

Twelve

The next morning, I drew bigger circles on Fizzy's map of Michigan, then used the Internet to hunt towns even farther out from Rambling, where Carolina might have rented a lockbox. As I'd done before, I sent out e-mails inquiring about a Louise Thomas, but this time I slid in the nugget that Louise might have used the name Carolina Dare. I was hoping that the bankers would check for that name as well. It didn't go well, sliding or otherwise. Nobody got back to me.

Even Aggert sensed the futility of it. "There's too many towns."

I didn't tell him I was only doing it mornings, and then only because I wasn't ready for the guilt of giving up on Louise entirely.

Reynolds didn't answer any of the messages I left on his cell phone. I didn't fault him. He was a watchman, and even watching nothing takes time. Besides, I had asked him to chase down a coat and a pack of cigarettes—the thinnest of threads. Most likely, he figured that Mrs. Sturrow, having emptied Carolina's kitchen of canned goods, would have thought nothing of grabbing a winter coat, and that I was no longer clutching at even whole straws.

It was futile all the way around.

Afternoons, I tried to rest my head and worked on finishing the cabinets in the second-floor kitchen. It felt good to be back touching stains and varnishes, sanding papers and rags. The vapors were dizzying, harsh in my nostrils and at the back of my throat, but there was a rhythmic repetition to it, and the certainty that, at the end of the afternoon, something tangible would result from my efforts.

Amanda and I had dinner downtown several times. Our old once-a-week caution was gone; we were moving faster now, becoming surer that this time we could make it work.

Gradually, as I came up dry phoning banks—by now as far away as Detroit and Lansing, impossible distances from Rambling—I came to accept that the life of Carolina Dare was going to disappear like water spilled on hot sand.

The day was warm enough to caulk in a new piece of glass to replace the one that had so offended the pigeon, and the plywood that had so offended the lizard, Elvis. I was up on the ladder, swaying like long johns on a clothesline, when the postman came.

"Mail again today, Dek," he called up. I suspected he was genuinely pleased that I was beginning to receive mail. For well over a year, I must have been the only person on his route who didn't receive even junk mail. I hadn't blamed that entirely on my reduced circumstances; I doubted Neiman Marcus or Nordstrom launched catalogues at many people with Rivertown zip codes, since neither Neiman nor Nordstrom offered muscatel, switchblades, or auto alarm disablers.

I chanced a look down. He was feeding thick tan envelopes into the curved-top box. "Where are they from?"

He pulled a couple back. "Smith's Secretarial, in Florida, forwarded to here from Woodton, Michigan."

I didn't have the heart to tell him they'd stop soon enough. By now, Charles must have received my made-up columns.

"Oops," he went on. "One of the postmarks is old." He shrugged and pushed the envelopes back into the mailbox. "It happens," he said, looking up. "Stuff gets set aside for one reason or another until someone thinks to send it on."

He started across the lawn to city hall, a happy man with a secure job, and I went back to glazing the window. I was in a hurry to give the putty some setting time in the sunlight before evening dropped the temperature.

Thirty minutes later, as I beaded in the last of the glazing compound, an engine revved down below. I recognized the accent of the exhaust. It was German. Very carefully, so as not to excite the ladder, I turned around just enough to see Leo, bright in orange, lemon, and chartreuse, and topped like a sherbet sundae with a purple pom-pom, behind the wheel of his top-down Porsche Roadster. Gracing the passenger's seat, half a head taller, was the beautiful Endora, Leo's love, model stylish in dark leather and faux fur.

"Go away," I called. "I'm doing honest work."

He revved the engine again, this time louder, more insistent.

I maneuvered to get a better look. Leo was holding up a tabloid newspaper, and grinning so widely that his teeth seemed to split his pale, narrow head in two. The headline was big, but I was too high up to make it out. "Give me a minute," I called down, then turned back to the final bit of glazing. I smoothed out the last few inches of putty against the window and descended as though I were tiptoeing on Twinkies. Safe at last at the bottom, I approached his car, rubbing the glazing compound off my hands.

I could read the bold tabloid headline from fifteen feet away.

"SHE'S BACK!"

Unkind thoughts of an editor with the dimmest bulb in New Jersey flashed through my head.

"No," I said to the world.

"Yes," Leo laughed above the low, tuned rumble of the Porsche.

Endora smiled, but it was with sympathy. She handed me another copy of the paper, something called the *Northway*. "We saw it in an organic food store up in Wisconsin. Leo said we had to turn around, bring it right to you."

"I couldn't wait to see your face," Leo said, all teeth and lips.

I turned to the page listed in the index. Big letters shrieked next to the crossword puzzle: HONESTLY, DEARESTS, I'M BACK.

The uncomprehending Charles had chosen two of my most offensive responses, the ones I'd fired at the middle-aged former virgin, whom I'd advised to get a swing set; and to the college kid with the carrot-worshipping roommate, whom I'd told to eat the offending vegetable deity.

"I'm so clever," I said.

"So we've read," Leo replied, laughing.

Endora reached to touch my forearm.

"Would you like to come in?" I managed.

"Too cold in there," Leo said from the cockpit of his top-down convertible. He made an exaggerated leering face, a wolf in neon clothing, at Endora. "We make our own heat, don't we, darling?"

Endora shook her head, smiling at me apologetically. "Drive away, Leo. Let Dek savor his new fame privately."

I stood by the curb long after they'd pulled away, rereading my juvenile responses, word by unthinking word. Incredibly, it was all there, unedited. In New Jersey, an inmate had taken over the print shop in the asylum and was firing out columns to grocery store tabloids.

It was only after I'd gone inside and reread the inane snippets a dozen times that I remembered the ladder I'd left leaning against the turret, and it was only after I took it down that I remembered to bring in the mail.

There were five of the thick manila envelopes. The most recent had been mailed from Florida just three days before. I slit it open.

This time, the white envelope mixed in with the reader mail was addressed to *Carolina*!; the exclamation point was the tipoff that big news was inside. The note read, "Carolina! Many, many apologies! Wonderful! Your readers are going to just love your more wickedly upbeat tone! Will use the old swinger (clever you, clever me) and the carrot-worshipper right away, and then the others in upcoming weeks. But not the one about me, HA, HA. Send more, ASAP! All Forgiven. Best, Charles."

God, but the man was a fool.

I worked my way backward, by postmark date. The previous three tan envelopes must have been sent from New Jersey before Charles had received my envelope; they contained reader letters only. Apparently,

Charles had given up on Carolina by then and hadn't bothered to dash off any more notes. No wonder he'd sounded so absolutely giddy in his letter about my columns! I didn't open the reader envelopes inside; I'd read enough earlier to know what they contained.

The last large envelope was the one the postman had noticed. It had been postmarked the last day of the previous year, some ten weeks before. It, too, was filled with the usual unopened reader envelopes, but there was another envelope in there, larger and much thicker than the rest. It had been addressed, in what looked like a woman's compact script, to Honestly Dearest at the same New Jersey address as all the other reader mail.

I looked again at the postmark: December 31.

Then I noticed its origin: West Haven, Michigan. And its return address: H. D., care of the Woodton post office.

An envelope mailed from West Haven to New Jersey, forwarded to Florida, to be forwarded, almost full circle, back to Michigan again, to Woodton.

No one would have known to do that, except Carolina herself.

My hands shook as I ripped at the gummed flap. At first, the contents appeared to be the usual batch of reader envelopes. As I pulled them out, though, I saw that they had already been opened.

There were five envelopes, two hand addressed, three typewritten, all mailed to Honestly Dearest in New Jersey. The oldest had been mailed in January of the year before. The most recent had been mailed the past November 22.

There were also about a dozen Honestly Dearest columns in the envelope, cut from newspapers and paper-clipped together. The oldest column, like the oldest envelope, went back to the beginning of the previous year.

There was one additional letter, without an envelope. It had been penned on a wide-ruled sheet of notebook paper, then folded a number of times, until it must have formed a small cube.

I called Aggert. He answered on the second ring.

"This is Elstrom. Did you mail anything to Louise Thomas's New Jersey address a couple of months ago?"

"That newspaper she worked for?" He sounded tired. "I didn't know about New Jersey two months ago. You're the one who told me about that."

"I just got more of her mail. Most of it is recent, the same kinds of reader letters and column copies sent by her editor. But one envelope is different. It was mailed from West Haven the day after she came to see you. I was wondering if she left something behind that you then sent on to her New Jersey address."

"What's in that envelope again?" He spoke quickly, alert now.

"Old letters, all opened, and copies of old newspaper columns. I haven't read through them yet."

"I'd like to see them, too."

"I'll send you copies," I said and hung up.

I looked at the hand-addressed large tan envelope again and realized I was looking at Carolina's own handwriting.

Reader letters and newspaper columns, mailed to get them away from her cottage.

Sent from herself, to herself.

For me to read.

Thirteen

My zip code directory showed the five reader envelopes had been postmarked in Cedar Ridge, Iowa.

The oldest envelope, handwritten with no return address, had been mailed on January 14, almost fourteen months before. Its flap was torn in several places and was finger worn, as though it had been opened a hundred times. The letter inside was written on the kind of three-hole, wide-ruled paper used by grammar school children. "Dear Honestly Dearest," it read, in a big-looped, careful young hand, "My mom married my stepfather a year ago. We moved into his double-wide. Accidently, I was going through a storage tub. Underneath some fishing junk was a newspaper story. It was about a bank robbery. Over a million dollars got took. A bank person was killed. I think my stepfather did it. I don't like him. I'm scared my mom knows. Should I tell. Your reader, Troubles."

The letter hadn't run in any of the Honestly Dearest columns enclosed in the big envelope, but the column clipped from the Windward Island *Gulf Watcher* of February 9 did end with a cryptic note: "Confidentially, Dearest, to Troubles. Just because someone keeps a newspaper story about a crime doesn't mean they're involved. Do you have a grandmother or grandfather, an aunt, or a teacher you can talk to? It would be good for you to discuss this with someone close to you. If not, you can always talk to me. Write Troubles on your envelope, so the people who get my mail will know to hurry it to me. I'll keep everything a secret. Your friend, Honestly Dearest." Carolina had seen something in the letter that made her take the child's fear seriously.

The second envelope was postmarked February 10, the day after the column-ender appeared, and was marked "Troubles" on the outside. The letter read, "Dear Honestly Dearest, I can just talk to you. It is worse. A lot of money is in a golf bag on the underneath of the double-wide. I didn't count it. My stepfather is looking at me strange. I am scared I must run away. I am awful young. Your reader, Troubles."

The column-ender ran on February 26, probably the soonest Carolina could get it into print: "Confidentially, Dearest, to Troubles. Let me find someone in your town for you to talk to. Your friend, Honestly Dearest."

There were no more envelopes from Troubles, but the loose letter that was with them, the one that had been folded several times to form a cube, was written in the same hand, on the same punched, wide-lined paper. "He won't hurt me if I don't tell where this is. You keep it until I say. Your friend, Troubles."

Carolina answered that one at the end of her column of March 11. "I will do as you say, but this is the wrong way. You may be in danger. The police can help you. Let me get them to protect you. Your friend, Honestly Dearest."

Carolina ended each of her next four columns in the *Gulf Watcher*, from late March through the middle of April, with the same note: "Confidentially, Dearest, to Troubles: WRITE TO ME."

There were no more letters from Troubles.

The first of the three business-sized white envelopes, typewriter-addressed to New Jersey with "TROUBLES" typed in capital letters in the lower left corner, was postmarked April 12, also from Cedar Ridge. The letter inside was typed in caps, too, and read like a telegram: "RETURN WHAT DOESN'T BELONG TO YOU TO POST OFFICE AT ORIGINAL ZIP CODE, CARE OF T. ROUBLES GENERAL DELIVERY."

Carolina's column-ender on April 22 responded: "Confidentially to Mr. Roubles: Prove T is in safe hands and will be protected and I will."

The next typed letter came right away: "RETURN OR T WON'T BE SAFE."

She responded with "Prove T is safe" at the close of her next two columns, but Roubles didn't respond until a letter postmarked May 4. As on the others, "TROUBLES" was typed on the outside of the envelope sent to New Jersey.

There were only four words typed on the sheet of paper inside.

"HONESTLY DEAREST, YOU'RE DEAD."

An hour later, I sat in the overstuffed purple chair in the office Leo had built in the basement of the bungalow where he lived with his mother. I'd been there for fifty minutes, watching him examine the letters I'd brought.

He switched off the Luxo magnifying light, pushed its robotlike spring arms away, and slid the envelopes and columns into the envelope Carolina had mailed to herself. Dropping his cotton gloves on the light table, he went to slump into the wood-slatted chair behind the scarred wood desk. He picked up the stub of a yellow wood pencil and started working it between his fingers, end over end.

"Kid finds bank job money, sends it to Honestly Dearest." He shrugged. "Evil stepdad finds out, threatens your Carolina."

"What can you tell me about the handwriting on the first three letters?"

"I go to experts when I need that kind of expertise. For sure I can't tell you if it was written by a boy or a girl."

"Damn," I said.

"At that age, it's hard to tell."

"What age?"

"Hard to tell that, too."

"Damn it, Leo." I pushed myself up from the depths of the sprung seat. His father had died in that chair, years before. Now it felt like it was grabbing for me, too.

The pencil stub paused between his index and middle fingers. "I'm guessing ten to twelve, but the kid could have been older."

"At least now we know why Carolina came to Rambling."

"Running from the stepfather." Leo aimed the pencil at me. "You don't need to be told that this is way over your head."

"No."

"He's killed twice; the kid in Iowa, and then Carolina."

Suddenly I felt like I'd been carrying bricks. I dropped back into the overstuffed chair. "Yes."

Leo started up his pencil, waiting.

"Reynolds said the sheriff probably hasn't done much investigating," I said after a minute. "They'll be interested now. I can show them motive and point them to a zip code in Iowa."

"Slam dunk," Leo said.

"Slam dunk for sure," I said.

I had to call a couple of counties before I got the sheriff's department that oversaw Rambling. A woman named Budzinski answered after I followed the required number of tape-recorded instructions.

"How would I find out who's working on an investigation of a killing in Rambling?"

She paused half a beat. "Rambling, Michigan?"

"That's the place. Happened a month, maybe six weeks ago, on County Road 12."

"Give me the deceased's name and I'll have someone call you back."

"Her name was either Louise Thomas or Carolina Dare."

"Same woman?"

"I think the Louise Thomas name was an alias. Your people thought the killing was the result of a home invasion gone bad. I've got evidence that points to premeditated murder."

"Your interest?"

"I'm the executor of the deceased's estate."

"And you're not sure of her name?"

"I don't even know how she knew mine."

"I'll have whoever's in charge call you," she said and hung up.

A lieutenant named Dillard did, in thirty minutes. "Give me those names again."

"Louise Thomas and Carolina Dare."

"We've got nothing under investigation for either of those names."

"It's probably the state police, then."

"No, it would be us," Dillard said slowly, sounding like he wished he could submit me to a Breathalyzer exam. "Are you sure about the town, and the names?"

"She left a will with a lawyer in West Haven, signed as Louise Thomas. He called me, said she'd named me her executor. The lawyer gave me her keys, which fit a house in Rambling, a house with blood spots in it. Both the lawyer and a local watchman say they got messages from your office, advising them of the death. Now I've received an envelope that might contain significant clues about it."

"Before I called you back, I checked all the state's databases, every municipality, every county. There's been no reported death of a Louise Thomas or a Carolina Dare."

"Any dead Jane Does in the Rambling area?"

"No unknowns in that area for years," he said.

I stared at the turret's limestone walls. A minute passed.

"Mr. Elstrom?"

"Do you want the envelope I've come across?"

"What's in it?"

"Some letters from a frightened child in Cedar Ridge, Iowa, a few newspaper columns, and a very big threat from the killer." Listening to myself, I realized I was coming across loud and stupid.

"The crime is murder?" he said.

"Of course."

Dillard sighed. "And the victim is?"

"Carolina Dare."

"Or Louise Thomas?"

"Of course."

Dillard breathed into the phone.

"There might have been another murder victim," I went on. "That kid in Cedar Ridge who wrote the letters."

"What's the name of the kid?"

"I don't know."

"Boy or girl?"

"I don't know."

"Mr. Elstrom, what do you know?"

"That this information might point to the killer."

"You mean for a murder for which there's no body, or other evidence?"

"I told you, there is evidence: blood spots in a cottage."

"How much blood?"

"A dozen spots, maybe more."

"About the amount you'd get from a cut on a finger?"

"Sure, but . . ." I let the question fade.

He waited.

"Can I file a missing persons report?" I asked.

"Sure." He paused, like he was signaling a drummer in a clown act to pick up his sticks. Then, "Who's missing?"

I could almost hear the drum—and the laughter.

Fourteen

This time Reynolds returned my call. In two minutes.

He sounded out of breath. "What do you mean, no body?"

"Who saw the body?"

"I saw the blood, same as you."

"Did you speak to anybody who saw the body?"

"I told you: I didn't speak to anybody at all. I got a message saying there'd been a death from a home invasion on 12. The place was locked up, but the windows were busted out. I was supposed to keep an eye out when I passed by."

"Who called?"

"The county, I thought. Except now you're telling me they don't know anything? Maybe it was the state. That would explain the runaround I've been getting from the sheriff's office."

"Forget the state. According to a guy named Dillard at the sheriff's office, nobody has a record of any death of a Louise Thomas, a Carolina Dare, or a Jane Doe in Rambling."

"This is bullshit. I'll call you back."

"I've got new information."

"About that key?"

"That's turning out to be a dead end. But Carolina mailed letters to herself that point to her killer."

"How?"

"A kid wrote to the advice column, saying his or her stepfather was involved in a bank robbery in Iowa. Then the kid quit writing, and Carolina started receiving threatening letters, presumably from the stepfather."

"Saying what?"

"Saying, 'Return what's not yours.' "

"The kid had sent something to your columnist?"

"I think so."

Reynolds took a minute to let it all settle into place, then asked, "Like what?"

"Like the money from the robbery, or perhaps just proof that the stepfather pulled the job. I'm leaning toward the money, though."

"You told the county all this?"

"I tried, but Dillard said without a body, or proof of a crime, there's nothing he can do. I'm going to take a run at the cops in Iowa, but I want you to lean on Dillard."

"I'll call you back," he said and hung up.

I called Aggert.

"Elstrom," he said, "I'd given up on you."

"Where'd you get the keys to the house in Rambling?"

"Speaking of keys, how's it going?"

"You'll be the first to hear. Where did you get the house and car keys?"

"The police."

"Which police?"

"I presumed it was the county sheriff. I got a message, telling me about Louise's—excuse me, Carolina's—death and saying they'd found one of my cards at her place. They dropped off the keys in an envelope, after hours. Is there some question about jurisdiction?"

"Was it a man's voice or a woman's on your answering machine?"

"A woman's, I think. What's going on?"

"The county sheriff's office knows nothing about any death in Rambling."

"They must."

"They don't. The security guy out in Rambling is on the phone with them right now, trying to get them interested in what's going on. We've got new information."

"What new information?"

"Carolina mailed herself a few letters, something about a crime."

"What crime?"

I paused as a thought flickered and then raged into full fire inside my head.

"I'll tell you when I know," I said.

Reynolds called back an hour after I hung up with Aggert.

"I talked to the county sheriff's office," he said. "Then I called the state police."

The tone of his voice had already said enough, so I waited.

"Nobody knows anything about a death in Rambling," he finished.

"Was it a man who called you?"

"Is that important?"

"Carolina's lawyer said it was a woman who called him." My mind had spent the last hour skittering over the possibilities.

He chuckled, understanding what I was implying. "It could have been a woman, talking low."

"She faked her own death."

"We've been had." Then he laughed. "She pricked her finger, splattered a few drops of blood, broke some windows, had messages left for me and her lawyer, telling us she was dead. Then she took off. Smart lady."

"Scared lady."

"Maybe, but she was flush with that bank job money from the kid. She could get away, start enjoying the good life." He laughed again, but this time there was a knife edge right in the middle of it. "You can quit wondering about her coat and those cigarettes. She wore the coat when she took off, but my hunch is that where she is now, she doesn't need it. I see her thousands of miles away, on some beach, sipping margaritas and smoking those Salems."

"The charade bought her time," I said. "The stepfather was coming after her. Even if he did eventually track her to Rambling, the trail would disappear at Carolina's cottage. He'd have to give up looking."

"The cops would give up, too, assuming they ever did make the link between the stolen money and your Carolina Dare. The trail would be too cold."

As Aggert might have said, everything looked neat and tidy.

"I'd still like to show those letters from the kid and the stepfather to the sheriff up here," Reynolds said.

"You don't think they're legit?"

"Maybe the kid's are, but Carolina could have forged the death threats from the stepfather. That sends the cops in circles, looking for a body instead of looking for her. Gives her more time to run. Whatever, we need to get those letters to the sheriff."

"I still can't figure why she'd mail the kid's and the stepfather's letters to Woodton."

"I told you: for you to read," Reynolds said. "They point away from her."

"It was a long shot that I'd even discover that she was getting her mail in Woodton."

"Extra insurance? Send you off on the wrong trail, in case you were getting too close?"

"I'm not sure," I said. "You know anybody who does blood work?"

"You mean to analyze the residue in the house?"

"We should preserve the blood evidence," I said, "in case an unidentified body shows up sometime."

"Accept it: We've been had, Mr. Elstrom. Played for chumps."

"We need to preserve the blood."

"Tell you what: I'll cut out one of those small panes of glass on the front porch, one with blood on it, and I'll take it with your letters when I go to see the sheriff."

"I'll do the blood sample," I said. "I want to walk through the cottage again, take some photographs. But first I'm going to call the cops in Cedar Ridge, find out what they know. I'll be up tomorrow or the day after."

"Bring that key for the sheriff to look at, with the letters."

I said that sounded fine.

I tried to call Aggert back but got his machine. I didn't leave much of a message beyond mentioning that Carolina Dare had been crafty about more than her name, and that I'd be running up to Rambling to collect a blood sample that nobody might ever use.

No body, no victim. Everything fit it being a setup.

Except the envelope that Carolina had sent herself. If she'd been planning her own disappearance, it didn't figure that she'd preserve letters linking her to stolen bank money. Better to have burned them.

I got the phone number for the Cedar Ridge, Iowa, police department from the Internet. As I dialed, I imagined a place where Sheriff Andy and little Opie, bamboo rods on their shoulders, were walking down a dirt road to some bucolic fishing hole. I could almost hear them laughing about that apple pie waiting for them back at the house, cooling on the windowsill, as in the background someone whistled theme music from the bushes.

Despite my imaginings, the Cedar Ridge cop who took the call, a sergeant named Patterson, was all pro. "A kid getting killed?" he repeated. "Accident, or deliberate?"

"Deliberate, though it might have been made to look like an accident."

"Boy or girl?"

"Don't know."

"How old?"

"Ten, maybe twelve, guessing from the writing and the notebook paper. It would have happened in the past year."

"Cedar Ridge isn't very big, population-wise, but our jurisdiction covers a lot of miles. What else can you tell me?"

"The child, with his or her mother, had moved recently into a stepfather's double-wide trailer."

"Your interest, Mr. Elstrom?" Patterson's words had suddenly become more clipped.

"I'm following up the disappearance of a newspaper advice columnist. She received three letters from the child. The kid suspected the stepfather was involved in a bank robbery where a million dollars was taken. Then the kid stopped writing. Shortly after, someone, perhaps the stepfather, sent three of his own letters to the columnist, all threatening."

"Your missing columnist thought the stepfather murdered the kid?"

"That's my guess."

"And your columnist feared the stepfather would come after her next?"

"I think so."

"Because the columnist had proof the stepfather was involved in the robbery and in the child's murder?"

"Sure."

"And now the columnist has disappeared?"

"Or was killed. There is blood evidence."

"We'll need those letters, Mr. Elstrom."

"You know of a kid who might have died under questionable circumstances?"

"You want to drive those letters out, or shall I send someone to pick them up? It would be faster if you came to us."

"You know of a robbery that fits with a dead kid?"

"Your choice: come to us, or we come to you," he said.

"I can be on the road first thing tomorrow morning . . ." I let the sentence dangle.

"But?"

"I'd like something to think about on the ride out."

"Lucia Helm," he said. "That's your kid. She died in a trailer fire, along with her mother. Happened last April. A real tragedy."

"Arson?"

"Not even suspected," he said. "Loose fitting on a propane connection. Something sparked it and up it went."

"It could have been arson?"

"The line between deliberate and forgetful is awful fine."

"Who survived?"

"The husband, the stepfather. He was devastated, just devastated."

"Was he questioned?"

"Of course he was questioned."

"And?"

"No reason to suspect him of anything, then," he said.

"What do you mean, 'then'?"

"We need to see those letters, Mr. Elstrom."

"You know about a bank robbery that fits with that child's death?" I asked.

"Have a safe drive," Patterson said and hung up.

Fifteen

I was anticipating music to accompany me west, along I-80, to Iowa. I'd recently bought a new car radio at the Discount Den—the place where Leo got his clothes, and Kutz, the wienie man, his purple paint—and was looking forward to having something to listen to, at last, besides the rattling of my ancient Jeep. It had been over a year since the thumpers had yanked my previous radio at the health center. I hadn't minded the loss so much as the slashes they'd cut in the plastic side curtains. Those had taken a third of a roll of silver duct tape to mend, and that had seriously compromised my peripheral vision. No longer able to be certain of the whereabouts of close-by traffic, I'd had to learn to rely on divine providence each time I changed lanes. I vowed "nevermore" to car radios.

On the other hand, a radio for only $9.95 was too good a deal to pass up. To avoid future slashes, I hung the radio loose on quick release terminals beneath the dash. Though it swung like a pendulum when I drove, at least I could take it inside the health center when I went to work out.

The new radio worked well enough near the bigger towns west of Chicago, and for a time I drove along chirping like a bird, singing rock and roll with oldies stations. In the middle of Illinois, though, the music died, and all I could extract from the static was farm stations, probably being broadcast from the very barns I was passing. It's hard to sing along with crop price reports, so I gave up warbling and concentrated on the snappy agricultural dialogue.

Apparently, the middle of March was none too soon to begin worrying about corn blight and fertilizer and increased yields. At first, I listened casually. The turret didn't have much of a yard, just a circle of dirt, artfully spotted with dandelions that I fertilize because they irritate the groundskeepers at city hall. However, as the miles slipped by, I got caught up in the possibilities of corn, and by the time I hit the Mississippi River, digging up my circle of dirt and growing a dozen stalks was starting to make a lot of sense. I could make corn chowder, corn soufflés, and my all-time favorite, corn bread. I'd need a stove, of course, to process all that corn, but I am at heart an optimist. Someday, I would have central heat, and after that, an oven was bound to follow.

My ten-dollar radio quit grabbing anything thirty miles west of the Mississippi River. Cedar Ridge was ten miles past that, a few fistfuls of frame houses set down on hard snow and surrounded by miles and miles of nothing. There was no Wal-Mart, nor signs that one was soon to be constructed, but I would have bet there was a rutted road leading to a fishing hole, though in March it might still be frozen over.

I drove slowly through the two outskirt blocks of white-sided houses, eyeing the windowsills. I spotted no cooling pies. It was probably too cold for that as well.

The business district was in the third block and consisted of a feed store, a grocery called the NW, and three taverns with neon beer signs already lit to welcome late-morning drinkers. No one had shoveled the sidewalks in front of the taverns, but there appeared to have been no need. The snow had been pounded smooth by the prints of a thousand boots, and perhaps more than a smattering of foreheads.

The police station was at the end of the block. It was a gray cinderblock building that appeared to have been the only thing built in town in the past fifty years. I parked on the street, killing the engine and the static from my radio. I didn't lock the door. No one in Cedar Ridge would have need of such a radio.

Sergeant Patterson sat at a beige metal desk behind the counter.

About forty years old, he had a flat belly and hair that matched his starched khaki uniform. He'd probably done a thousand push-ups before his oatmeal that morning. He led me to a yellow cinder-block meeting room to sit at a brown folding table. Earth tones were alive and rampant in Cedar Ridge. I started pulling photocopies out of the envelope I'd brought.

"You didn't bring the originals?" he asked.

I didn't tell him that the originals were wrapped in plastic underneath the rubber rug in the Jeep, just in case. Nor that I'd mailed another set of photocopies to Leo. That was also just in case.

"Photocopies for now," I said. "Instead of being the executor for a dead woman, I'm hoping I represent a live client, on the run, afraid for her life. She might regard these letters as confidential, because they could tie her to money taken during a bank robbery. Normally, you couldn't look at these letters without a warrant. I'm taking the chance on showing them to you because you might be able to save her life."

"Whew," he said when my wind ran out.

I passed over the first two letters written by the child.

The skin around his eyes tightened as he read. "This is a frightened kid," he said, setting them down. "We can see if Lucia's school has samples of her handwriting to compare. Next?"

I handed him the copy of the letter that had been folded into a cube.

He scanned the few short sentences. "You're thinking the child mailed this with the money?"

"That was folded up more times than necessary for an envelope, and it does refer to something she said she mailed."

Patterson set the photocopy of the folded letter on top of the other two. "You have no idea where your client is now?"

"If I was certain she was alive, I wouldn't want to know."

"Because she took off with a lot of money?"

I tossed it back at him. "How much money?"

Patterson shook his head, parrying as well, and motioned for the rest of the sheets in front of me.

I handed him the copies of the three typed threat letters. There wasn't much to read, but Patterson stared at them for a long time, as though he were looking through the paper at something else.

"No way of telling who wrote these, being that they were typed or computer-printed," he said when he finally looked up.

I nodded, agreeing.

"Of course, the originals might contain fingerprints," he said.

"I'm all ears," I said.

He leaned back in his chair. "A little over two years ago, the Commerce Bank of Ida was held up by two masked men. They made off with one million two hundred and seventy-six thousand dollars. The Commerce Bank normally never kept that much, but that was annual bonus day for a big processor over there."

"Inside information?"

"Common knowledge," he said. "Everybody in town knew it was bonus day. The robbers didn't talk during the robbery; they communicated to the bank president with a written note, which they took back."

"Making investigators wonder whether someone in the bank would recognize their voices?"

"Sure." He nodded. "They were careful, like they were careful to write that they knew about the bait money at the bottom of the cash drawers, the bills that, once pulled, trigger the alarms."

"Inside information?"

Patterson shrugged. "Again, lots of people know banks have bait money."

"How does the girl who died, Lucia Helm, fit in with the heist?"

"Her stepfather, Randall Severs, was a cop."

Reflexively, I looked at the closed door, as though Severs might be lurking on the other side, listening. "You think he was one of the two robbers?"

"No. He was in uniform the day of the robbery, working twenty miles from Ida. But afterward, he was part of the task force working with the Feds to investigate the robbery."

"And then came the fire in his trailer?"

Patterson glanced at the envelopes on the table. "About three weeks after the girl's second letter was mailed."

"You told me he was interrogated?"

Patterson shot me a sharp glance. "Not interrogated, questioned. There was no reason to suspect him of anything."

"It's time to question him again."

"He's dead."

The room went quiet. Then big chunks of facts started moving around in my head. I didn't know what they meant yet, but I could hear them aligning, loud as boxcars being banged together in a train yard.

"We don't really know what happened the night Officer Severs died," Patterson went on. "He was working the evening shift, and we think he pulled somebody over on one of the rural roads a few miles from here. We don't know for what, because he didn't radio it in. About eight o'clock, somebody from out there called the fire department to report a car explosion. It was Severs's unit. By the time the fire department got there, there wasn't much left of Severs."

"When was this?"

Again he glanced at the envelopes spread out before him. "A month after the 'Honestly Dearest, You're Dead' letter was mailed to your columnist."

"No leads?"

"Three bullets, thirty-eights, were presumed to have been the primary cause of Officer Severs's death. We can't match them to anything we have on record. There were two brothers, Lance and Eddie Kovacs, who disappeared at the same time. They were a couple of junior-grade bad guys, with a long list of petty crimes, mostly burglaries they'd pulled off together. There was nothing linking them to the Ida robbery. Our interest in them came only because they disappeared at the same time Severs was killed."

"You think Severs learned something that linked those brothers to the bank job? And that they killed him?"

He tapped the little stack of photocopies on the table. "For now, I'm saying his stepdaughter is the only little girl killed in the time period you're talking about."

"Or are you thinking that Severs could have been involved in planning the robbery, or just stumbled across something that led him to the money afterward?"

"I know, Elstrom; it's tantalizing. Who'd suspect a cop? But as I said, there's no hard evidence suggesting Severs was involved."

"Except the death of a little girl in a double-wide trailer who had proof that her stepfather, a cop, was also a crook? And the disappearance, right after Severs got shot, of two potential suspects?"

"We need more than that." His face tightened. "Like the originals of these letters."

"Why burn the unit if Severs was shot? Why attract that attention?"

He shook his head. "I don't expect we'll ever know."

He caught the smile that was beginning on my face. "You've heard something humorous here, Elstrom?"

"What are you going to do?" I asked, by way of not answering.

He glanced down at the letters in front of him. "I want the originals of these, to see if there are any fingerprints still on them."

"And if there are no known comparison fingerprints of Lucia, and the typed letters are clean?"

"We'll get Carolina Dare's photograph from her Florida driver's license, perhaps put out a bulletin." He frowned at the grin I thought I had under control. "What's so damned funny, Elstrom?"

"You know all of this is futile?"

"That's funny?"

"That's perfect." This time I let the laugh out, at the relief of it. "Carolina Dare is so far gone no one will ever find her."

"We'll—"

"Sure you will," I cut in, before he could make something up. "How hot is the money?"

"Meaning, was it marked with secret ink, or the serial numbers recorded, so when it starts getting passed at the Seven-Eleven, we'll be able to race to the scene and apprehend the villain?" For the first time, part of a smile was beginning to play on his starched pale face as well.

"You funnin' with me, Sergeant?"

"Just trying to wipe that shit-eating grin off your face. I don't like being handled."

"Me either, but you've got to admit, this wasn't handling, this was finesse, born of necessity. Because of that bank job, and then the murder of that little girl and her stepfather, Carolina Dare had lived in fear that someone was coming for her next. Until she figured out how to make that bank money work for her."

He scowled, but it faded away. "The money was not marked. We'll never know if it is being spent."

For a minute, we concentrated on not looking at each other. Then I asked, "If I gave you a dried blood sample, would you have it analyzed, store the results?"

He looked at my eyes, trying to figure if I'd said it for show. "To see if it belongs to your client?"

"Yes."

"I thought you'd convinced yourself she was gone, with the money."

"That's what I want to believe, because she deserves it. And because it ends things for me. I don't have to keep going around screaming that something bad has happened to her."

"So why the blood sample?"

"Just in case."

"I'd need a known comparison sample, one that definitely belongs to your client or a close relation."

"It might take time to hunt down a relative."

"Years, maybe decades?"

I stood up, felt in my pocket for my keys. Carolina's flat key rested thin next to the one for the Jeep. I was beginning to think of it as a key to nothing, a false clue. That made it all the more comfortable in my pocket.

I went out to the Jeep to get the originals of the letters.

Sixteen

Driving back east across Iowa, as the sun eased into the horizon behind me, I let my mind play over the good certainty that Carolina Dare was alive.

She'd known the town from the zip code. After the box of money had arrived on Windward Island, the letters from the girl had stopped, and the threatening letters had begun, Carolina would have called out to a local paper or the police department in Cedar Ridge. She would have found out about the death of a girl in a trailer fire. More chillingly, she would have learned the girl's stepfather was a cop, someone with resources good enough to find anybody.

Scared, she fled Florida. She found her way north, to Rambling, Michigan, a place cheap enough to get by on her column income, a place desolate enough to hide from a cop. She arranged to have her checks cashed and sent with her mail to a post office half an hour away. She locked the girl's money in a bank box, because it was her only insurance, should the cop somehow find his way to her.

As safe as she could make herself, she stayed vigilant. She kept track of Severs, because by now she knew his name. She must have called the Cedar Ridge Police Department every day or two, from a pay phone, asking if the officer was in. "No, ma'am," she would have been told, "can we have him call you?" "No need." She'd laugh, relieved that he was still in Iowa, as she fired up another Salem.

Then one day she called and learned Randall Severs would no longer be in. He'd died in a car fire.

I could almost feel the way her lungs must have filled, deep, perhaps for the first time in over a year. She wouldn't have let herself feel safe, not at first. Too many months of running and hiding couldn't be erased like chalk off slate, and she must have suspected that somebody involved in the bank job had killed Severs. Still, Severs's death must have muddied the trail to her.

She stayed put, kept writing her columns, trailing out to Woodton for her mail. She stayed edgy, too, running to the window every time a car drove by or a branch snapped at the side of the house. After a time, she must have seen her life unraveling like that, living scared in a sagging, drafty cottage on a desolate piece of dirt. It was then that she must have seen—really seen—that lockbox with one million, two hundred and seventy-six thousand dollars in it.

Money that nobody knew she had.

She considered all the angles, chose something simple: Leave the white cotton panties, the sensible JCPenney bras, the twenty-year-old Dodge, and the damned generic cans of food that, by then, all tasted the same. Hunt up someone to name as executor, someone she'd met at a job long ago, someone who wouldn't remember her and make it personal, trying to find out what happened to her. Find a lawyer, some lethargic fellow working above a junk store, drop off a will. Then visit the lockbox, fill the bag or the backpack, spend a little of it on a used car, privately advertised in the *Intelligencer*. Then, after dark, daub a little blood, smash a few windows, slip on the coat, tuck the smokes into the pocket. Stop in West Haven, slip the keys though the lawyer's mail slot. Then, after a few hundred miles make a couple of last calls from a pay phone someplace, talking low through a wad of Kleenex, to tell the answering devices of the lawyer and the blueberry cop that Louise Thomas was dead. Be gone.

I'd been had, by a terrified, hunted woman. It felt good. I was done.

I thumbed Reynolds's number on my cell phone, got him on the second ring. "You should be a real cop, Reynolds. You've got a good nose."

"I called you twice."

"I've been to Iowa." I told him about Carolina's connection to Lucia Helm, the bank robbery, the two brothers who took off, and the late incinerated stepfather cop, Randall Severs. "All that gives the Iowa cops a fresh angle. That might get the Feds interested in the Kovacs brothers."

"Think they'll find her?"

"I hope not. She's running with enough money to become invisible."

"You're that sure she's running?"

"It's been weeks, and no body has surfaced. She might be free as a bird, forever."

"That stepfather . . ."

"Severs."

"Yeah, Severs. How does he fit with the bank?"

"For now, only through his stepdaughter's letters to Carolina about the money. He might have been involved in the robbery planning, or maybe he just stumbled onto the money during the investigation. We'll never know. The only thing that's for sure is he was torched in his police car."

"By those brothers?"

"That's the supposition."

"You'd better be careful," he said.

"The Kovacs brothers don't know I exist," I said, "and I gave the letters to Patterson. I've got nothing they need."

"You've got that lockbox key."

"The money's gone. That box, wherever it is, has already been emptied."

"You're probably right." His voice was barely audible.

"I'll still come to Michigan tomorrow, to give the house and car keys to Aggert. Afterward, I'll swing out to Rambling, take a last look around the cottage, and grab that blood sample to send to Patterson, but it won't do him any good without a known relative."

"We're done?"

"She's on a beach, watching sunsets."

I let myself fantasize for a few miles, then, about corn, and it wasn't until I was almost to the Illinois line that I thought to check my cell phone for messages. There were five: the two from Reynolds he'd said he left; two from Aggert, both asking if I'd returned to Michigan; and one from Amanda.

I called Amanda.

"I was thinking we ought to have dinner tonight," she began.

"That is good thinking, though this incessant violating of our one-week rule might lead to us becoming overcome with passion and trigger chaos."

"How soon can you get downtown?"

"Where downtown? A restaurant, or that huge bed you have overlooking Lake Michigan? I can get to your bed hours quicker."

"Restaurant." She laughed. "We need nourishment for what I've got in mind."

"Your sense of urgency is encouraging."

"Where are you now?"

"Suspended above the middle of the Mississippi River, on a bridge."

"You sound like that's making you chipper."

"My burden has been lifted. I believe Carolina is alive, with enough money to hide well and long. We will celebrate tonight."

"Our trattoria, at eight?"

"I'll fly."

"I'm sure," she said.

The last of the orange had gone out of the sky, and it was now appropriately dark enough to call Aggert. He'd left a phone number different from his office.

"Are you back up here?" he asked, right off.

"I've found another reason why I'm done being an executor," I said.

"You found the lockbox?" There was traffic noise behind him; he was on a cell phone.

"Even better. I'm pretty sure your Louise is very much alive. I've just been to Iowa, talking to the police in Cedar Ridge. Your client received some money stolen from a bank near there. She was afraid the robbers would track her to Rambling, so she took off, but I think she's safe."

"You didn't find the lockbox?"

"It was a ruse. She would have taken the money with her. Wherever the lockbox is, it's empty now."

"For the purpose of the court—"

"Tell the court there's no corpse." Traffic was slowing now that I was getting closer to Chicago. I'd need both hands for the steering wheel and the gear shift. "I'll be up in Rambling tomorrow, for one last look around. I'll drop off the keys."

"All the keys?"

"The Iowa police might want that numbered one." I said it to be a jerk—and maybe to give Carolina just a little more cover.

"What time will you be here?"

"Probably after lunch," I said, recognizing the reality that a foot of onions served on a stick just across the street would inhibit any attempt I might make to go directly to Aggert's office.

Traffic congealed almost solid just west of Chicago, so I drove straight downtown. Amanda was already at the restaurant. She'd ordered a bottle of wine.

"Truly, we are celebrating," I said, sliding into the booth across from her.

"I think so, yes." She poured me wine. "To survival." She raised her glass.

I took a sip and set down the glass. "Anybody's survival in particular?"

"Ours."

"You're referring to the fact that, in a scant two years, we've gone from being whirlwind lovers to newlyweds to divorcés to recoverers to occasional daters to lovers again?"

"Still a whirlwind." A smile played on her lips.

"I don't understand, but I've been in Iowa."

"I'm wondering if we should turn up the centrifuge, start spinning things a bit faster."

"You mean start seeing each other even more frequently than we have been?" I reached to pour us more wine. I would certainly drink to that.

"More than that."

I looked at her across the table. What I thought had been a smile was actually a suppressed tremble. Her eyes were shiny. She was about to cry.

"Hey," I said. "We're celebrating. We're survivors."

"Are we healing?"

"Stronger every day, especially since I took my vow of poverty."

She didn't laugh, and I knew why.

"You're worried," I said, "because since we met, I've gotten poorer, and you're still . . . ?" I stopped, because it was a topic she liked to ignore.

The unfinished question hung in the air for a minute, until she said, "Rich?"

"Art rich," I corrected, "which is quite unimpressive, except to snoots. Rubes like me don't recognize the stuff on your walls as being worth millions. To us, it looks like the paintings they sell at warehouse events."

"You rubes."

"Ah, but in our eyes, you are redeemed by your beater Toyota and your cheesy starting-out furniture."

"I don't have cash. What I make at the Art Institute goes for condo dues, taxes, and the security system."

I pounced. "So you see, it wasn't the money that did us in. As the counselors might say, we had a different, unresolved issue: me. I got duped in a high-profile court case, and the newspapers trashed me. My clients flew away like birds. I sulked, like a child. Also like a child, I took it out on you. You were handy, you came from rich—the daughter of a major executive and political player—and I came from Rivertown. The money difference was never the problem, it was the weapon I used against you. That's what made us go away."

"We came back together," she said, managing a small smile.

"You conveniently forget that I had to help blow up your house to get you to pay attention to me."

She laughed, and for a moment, it touched her eyes. Then her face turned serious. "Will we ever know if we're surviving surviving?"

"I don't understand," I said. Though, of course, I did.

"We can't just survive; we have to move on."

She'd just said the words I'd been living to hear for over a year. But I was wiser now.

"I need to get my livelihood back in order," I said, "establish thick links to bedrock. Rivertown isn't coming around like the lizards had planned, which makes selling the turret a ways away. And most of my former clients remember the stories in the *Tribune*; they're still reluctant to use me to trace documents or photograph accident scenes. Still, things are picking up—at glacial speed, perhaps, but they're picking up. I'm wobbling, but I'm upright, and I'm aimed down the right road."

She smiled and took a sip of wine. She was still unsure.

"It's you that I want," I said. "It's only you that I want."

She smiled bigger and reached for my hand under the table.

There wasn't time, then, to tell her about my plan to ring the turret with cornstalks and make soufflés.

Seventeen

The door to the turret swung open as soon as I touched the lock with the big old-fashioned key. Returning home to an unlatched door at eight thirty in the morning, when the sun is up far enough to chase away most of the bogeymen that might be hiding in the shadows, is not as creepy as coming home to a picked lock in the middle of the night. It's close, though. Especially considering that I'd been double-checking the lock on my way out ever since the evening, a few days earlier, when I'd come home to find the door ajar.

I bent down; the bolt was stuck. I had to thumb the latch several times before it popped out. I'd oiled it, but it needed more.

But the bolt had caught when I left. I was sure of that. I nudged the door open. Inside, in the narrow beams of sunlight streaming in from the slit windows, the table saw and the plastic chair were exactly as I'd left them.

I went up the stairs, letting them ring loudly. At the second-floor landing, I stopped, holding my breath. The turret was like a crypt, dead to outside noise. I gave it a long count, strained to listen. Nothing moved.

I stepped into the kitchen. Every unfinished cabinet stood right where it had been. My tools lay scattered in the same places that I'd left them. I crossed the hall, opened the office door.

Carolina's old Underwood typewriter was gone from the card table.

Her old newspaper columns lay in jumbled piles on the floor, next to the haphazard stacks of boxes of my old business files. I could have left them that way, or they could have been pawed through. I couldn't tell.

For sure, though, the typewriter had been there.

I ran up the stairs. The third-floor bedroom was a mess, clothes heaped on the one chair, the bed unmade, but it was the mess I'd left. Running up more stairs revealed the undisturbed dust on the fourth floor. The ladder I used to climb up to the fifth floor still lay tilted on its side against the wall. No one had set it under the trapdoor to the top floor. I was alone in the turret.

I went back down to my office, and this time, I saw what I'd overlooked. A small note lay on the card table, where the typewriter had been.

"D," he'd written. "I hope you don't mind, but I used my key to grab the old typewriter. I want to give it a solid going over. Call it indulging a ghost. Leo."

I didn't mind, not even the thrill he'd just given me by being too preoccupied to remember to lock the door. For years, that same ghost had visited me, too, more days and nights than not. That was long ago, and hardly ever since I met Amanda.

An hour later, I was in Indiana. It was going to be a good day, I told the radio, swinging beneath the dash in perfect concordance with the music and the jolts from the potholes along the interstate. With luck, I'd get the blood samples from Carolina's cottage, ingest a foot of onion rings, drop off the keys at Aggert's, and be back in Rivertown before the evening rush hour. I supposed the trip was unnecessary—I could have overnighted the keys to Aggert, and the blood sample would likely never be used—but it was a fine March day, alive with sun and the promise of onion rings.

I got to the West Haven Wal-Mart at eleven thirty, took a right, and blew through the husk of downtown Rambling twenty-five minutes later. At County Road 12, I turned left.

On the passenger seat beside me, two small pieces of plywood rested beneath a hand saw. They would replace the two panes of blood-splattered glass I was going to remove from Carolina's front porch. It was sure to excite Mrs. Sturrow, but I planned to leave money to replace the glass with Aggert when I dropped off the keys.

I slowed for the driveway that was about to appear past the copse of trees on my left. As the trees passed and I began to turn, my feet reacted quicker than my mind could absorb, and I hit the brakes too hard. The Jeep skidded off the ruts of the drive and slid twenty feet into the snow-covered yard before shuddering to a stop.

I stared through the gap between the tape strips on the side window, disoriented. I looked to the right and to the left, for anything that was familiar. The thin, spindly trees at the sides and back of the property were the same, as were the wind-glazed fields beyond, bright now in the glare of the late-morning sun. It was the same clearing, my brain told my gut.

But Carolina's cottage was gone.

It lay in a blackened heap, burned down to its cinder-block foundation. At the end of the rutted drive, the garage was gone, too, its boards charred and collapsed, mounded onto the shape of the old Dodge Aries.

I got out. The rancid stench of fire hung in the air like fresh death. Here and there, wispy tendrils of smoke curled up from the pile.

I walked up to where the porch had been, bent down to feel the rubble. Even in the cold, the cracked fragments of siding and twisted pieces of studs and boards were still faintly warm—and drenched. My hand came away wet and blackened. The fire had just been put out.

I walked around the smoldering debris. None of the glass was intact. It lay shattered here and there in the pile on the ground, a million bits of blackened crystal, trying to sparkle in the sun. I wondered if the windows had been blown out by the force of tremendous heat. There was no blood evidence anymore. There was no evidence of any kind anymore.

I went back to what had been the garage. Parts of the old Aries showed through the charred boards, soot-streaked, gray-primered in the spots where the pale blue paint had blistered away.

I looked back at the house. I'd been around enough insurance fires to recognize arson. Almost all accidental fires are irregular, totally destroying some parts of a structure while leaving others eerily pristine. This destruction had been complete. The fire had consumed everything, boards and glass and plaster—and fingerprints and blood traces. It had been carefully set to destroy everything.

I walked back to the Jeep, sat behind the wheel, and called Reynolds. His cell phone asked for a message. "I assume you already know that Carolina's cottage was torched." Then I said what I was struggling to understand. "Question number one: Why didn't you call me? Question number two: Who set the fire, Reynolds?"

I still had the number of the sheriff's department. Dillard was out. I asked for the phone number for the firehouse closest to Rambling. It was in Bangor, ten miles away. A lieutenant said he could see me as soon as I got there.

"Happened last night, around midnight," he said fifteen minutes later. He'd been waiting for me on the wide drive out front. "By the time we got there, the structure was down."

"And the garage?" I asked.

"Simultaneous."

"Arson," I said.

"Absolutely," he said, "but we'll never find out who set it. We get fires like that one. Kids mostly, bored, looking for something to do."

"Could it have been landlord lightning?"

"Set to collect insurance? We don't have the resources to investigate for that."

"It was very destructive, for an amateur job. Nothing remains."

He whistled under his breath. "Professional? Why would anybody torch a claptrap cottage in Rambling?"

"The woman who lived there, Louise Thomas, went missing a month ago."

"I hadn't heard that. Is the sheriff working on it?"

He raised his eyebrows when I said Dillard could fill him in on what wasn't being done. "There wasn't much evidence in the cottage," I went on, "just a few smudges of blood, some broken windows, and overturned furniture. Nothing that pointed conclusively to an abduction."

"And now even that's gone."

I nodded.

"I'll call Dillard," the fire lieutenant said, "make sure he knows about this fire."

I drove back to West Haven and climbed the stairs to Aggert's office. His door was locked. It didn't matter. There was no point anymore in dropping off keys to a house that had burned down and a car that had just been destroyed. There was no point, either, in hanging around. I got on the expressway and headed south.

Just after 196 turned onto 94 West, I called Sergeant Patterson in Iowa. "I'm up in Michigan, just done staring at a burned pile that used to be Carolina Dare's house. It's gone, all of it, gone."

"Not accidental?" He'd caught the tone in my voice.

"As accidental as that trailer fire that killed Lucia Helm."

"You think your client may not be running?"

"She didn't set the fire. Someone else did, someone who wanted to destroy whatever was still in that cottage."

I listened to him breathe for a minute, and then he said, "We do what we're doing. We find something with Lucia's fingerprints still on it, make sure she was the letter writer. We kick up the suspected charges on the Kovacs brothers, include suspicion of Severs's murder, get federal help to find them. But I don't know if any of that gets you the guy who set your fire, or the whereabouts of your columnist."

"Did you get a driver's license photo of Carolina Dare?"

"I submitted a request this morning."

"You need that right away, to send around to every police department."

"More curious now about who hired you?"

Something queasy played at my gut. "I'm not so sure anymore that she's running."

Eighteen

Leo's silver Porsche was parked in front of the turret. Light came out in thin beams from the slit windows on the first and second floors. I parked behind him and walked up to the door. It was locked tight.

"Hi, honey, I'm home," I called up, inside. There was no responding laugh. After the dark ride home I could have used a chuckle, even a friendly insult, and Leo was always good for those, but nothing came back at me from the second floor. I went up the stairs.

The kitchen was dark. Across the hall, what passes for a blast of heat in my stone cylinder blew at me when I opened my office door. Leo sat huddled next to the space heater, shrunken inside his traffic engineer's parka. He was staring into an inch of brown whiskey he was swirling inside a clear plastic cup as if he were seeing his future—and not liking what he saw.

"Problems?" I asked, shedding my pea coat before I got used to being warm.

"You could say," he said. He turned to look at the card table.

He'd brought back the old Underwood.

I followed his eyes as he looked back at me. He tried for a smile, but his lips had begun to tremble.

"No, Leo."

His eyes were glassy in the light from the sculpted plaster lamp.

I looked again at the typewriter on the table.

"No," I said louder, as if I could null what he'd done.

The air in the office clawed at my chest. Suddenly, it was too hot to breathe. I went to the space heater, knelt to turn down the dial. Beside me, Leo sat motionless, slumped inside his jacket. I had to focus now, on the doable, on what I trusted. That meant starting with setting the dial just right.

"Want some coffee?" I said when I stood up.

"Not now, Dek." His voice was soft, indistinct almost. Slurred only by the whiskey, I wanted to think.

"I'm going to make coffee."

"Dek . . ."

"I need coffee." I didn't need coffee; I needed time, time to quiet the drummers that were beating on the inside of my chest, time to calm the pumpers who were sending too much blood to my ears.

I walked into the would-be kitchen. It was different now, different than it had been that morning. Then, the five new cabinets hanging on the stone walls, and the six still stacked on the floor, waiting, had been the future. Now, they looked like failure, the artifacts of a fool's life.

I peeled the plastic lid off the coffee can, measured out four scoops, holding each one up to the light to make sure the dipper was filled exactly level. Precision was necessary now, that and focus and concentration. It would take time, but I had the time; Leo could wait. I smoothed the grounds in the paper filter, ran water into the reservoir, and switched the maker on. I wanted to scream at the pounding in my ears, drowning out the coffee dripping into the carafe. I could have watched it all night, except for the pounding.

After a time, Leo came in, still swirling that damned inch of brown whiskey. Raising it to his lips, he finished it, then set the cup on the makeshift plywood counter. He leaned against the refrigerator, small in his big coat, and watched me watch the coffee. He waited. He didn't say anything; he didn't have to. We both knew the conversation we were about to have. We'd already had it, in the fraction of a second when I'd turned from the typewriter to see the confirmation in his eyes. We just hadn't said it with words.

It had been his loss, too.

The coffeemaker burbled and stopped dripping. He pulled a quart bottle of Jack Daniel's out of one of his enormous orange pockets and raised his sad, black eyebrows. I nodded. I half-filled two coffee cups and held them out to him. He added an inch of the Jack to each.

"Whatever we don't drink, I am taking away," he said, capping the bottle and setting it on the plywood. I do not have a good history of being left alone with whiskey.

"Sounds prudent," I heard myself answer.

He took one of the cups, and we walked across to my office. The room was still too hot, but that was all right. The room was cold, too. Leo eased down into the white plastic chair; I sat on the red swivel, took a sip, felt the fire of the Jack Daniel's burn its way down my throat.

For a minute, we stared into our coffees. Then I said, "OK, Leo."

He set his cup on the floor, pushed himself out of his chair, and moved, like an old man with arthritic legs, to the card table. He grasped the typewriter and turned it upside down so that it rested on its platen. Then he unscrewed the little finial bolt on the top of my ridiculous swirled plaster lamp, removed the pleated shade, and aimed the bulb at the bottom of the old Underwood. I stood up. The black paint had been chemically removed from the underside of the front rail.

"I didn't remove any more paint than was necessary, because I knew where to look," he said quietly, angling the bulb further so I could see the old metal.

I wanted to turn away.

"As you can see, nothing was left visible to the naked eye." The metal had been scraped with a bastard file, leaving rough, cross-hatched grooves along the rail. "But she didn't obliterate it all." He set down the desk lamp and reached inside his pocket for a photocopy folded lengthwise. He handed it to me.

It was the same cross-hatched pattern of file marks, enlarged enough now so that they looked like slashes from a knife. Mixed in with the cuts was a series of specks, grouped in clusters.

I handed back the sheet. "Do you think I don't know what you're showing me, damn it?" I took another pull at the coffee and Jack.

"You'll see it the way I did," he snapped. He pulled another photocopy out of his jacket and started to hand it to me.

"No."

He started to say something, then shrugged and set the sheet on the table next to the Underwood. "I don't have the equipment or the training for picking trace images off metal. I do know a guy who gets called in on thorny gun registration questions, the ones where someone has filed off a serial number." He was back to sounding calm, speaking in the almost trancelike voice he used in his lectures to art examiners, but I knew he was struggling for control as hard as I was. "Often, there's nothing he can do. Occasionally, though, the attempted obliteration was too rushed to totally eliminate what was there, and traces remain, invisible to the naked eye, but not to great magnification." He looked at me. "I didn't tell my guy what I was looking for," he added.

I took another sip of the spiked coffee. It tasted bitter, like death.

"Go on," I said.

He took the second photocopy from the table. "I asked him to reconstruct what he thought remained," Leo said, "kind of like connect the dots." He held it out.

This time I took it.

M F RE NE was scratched in uneven letters on the underside rail in the photocopy.

"You remember when she—?"

I crumpled the photocopy and threw it across the room.

"Dek—"

I reached to touch the bottom rail of the old Underwood. The metal was cold. I kept my hand on it until the metal warmed to my touch.

Of course I remembered.

She asked us, after school, to come with her. "For moral support," she'd said, smiling mysteriously. We'd go, certainly; Leo and I were weeks past needing any kind of justification to follow her anywhere. So it was, on a gray afternoon in early February, that the three of us marched from Rivertown High to one of the dingy side streets off Thompson Avenue.

She laughed when she stopped us in front of a junk shop. "Behold," she said, and with a grand wave of her hand, as though she were presenting the crown jewels, she pointed to the old black typewriter in the window, set alongside a weed whacker with a frayed rubber cord, a girl's faded pink tricycle with a cracked front tire, and a set of chipped floral teacups. "I'm going to write my way out of this town," she announced as we went in.

The junk shop smelled of mildew and used-up lives. The crafty old character inside told her the old Underwood had been reconditioned, but when he pulled it out of the window and set it on the counter, we could see that all he'd done was turn a hose on it and leave it to dry in the sun. He wanted fifty bucks for it; she offered twenty. Leo and I lounged by a rack of women's clothes that smelled of sweat and mothballs, high school senior males, clueless but striving for cool, as she and the old man dickered in the gloom. She was golden and blond and blue-eyed, tenacious as a ferret. He was grizzled, big-bellied in a stained undershirt, and had a greasy bald head that looked hardened, like a crustacean's shell, around a brain that must have been haggling for fifty years. Still, we were betting on her, and we almost applauded when she ended up giving him twenty-six for that old Underwood; her crumpled twenty, four of mine, two of Leo's. I suspected it was less her willpower that ended it than the old crafty's recognition that twenty-six was all we were packing, and that there was little chance that anyone else would want that old typewriter. Folks in Rivertown communicated more with whiskey drinks and longnecks than with small words typed on a page.

With our princess between us, Leo and I traded off lugging the old iron back to her father's apartment above the pinball place. Because we were boys, bent on impressing a girl and supposed to know of things mechanical, we turned it upside down on the kitchen table and slathered it with too much oil from a can some tenant had left under the sink.

She went to a drawer, came back with a fork. M.M.'S FUTURE MACHINE, *she scratched on its underside, in scraggly letters. Then she hid it in the back of her closet so her father wouldn't see it when he came stumbling home, late that night, stinking of whatever was on the skin of the women who worked the men behind the bowling alley.*

I crossed the room, picked up and smoothed the photocopy I'd crumpled and thrown, and looked again at the connections Leo's expert had drawn between the specks. M F RE NE. It wasn't hard to fill in the rest of the letters: M. M.'S FUTURE MACHINE.

Leo took my cup off the card table, went into the kitchen, and returned with more coffee and Jack. He'd made the mix stronger this time, at least fifty-fifty. He sat by the space heater, I sat back down in my desk chair, and for a little while we said nothing.

Sometime later, his voice came through the whiskey. Except it wasn't his voice, his adult-Leo voice. It was the voice he'd had when he was in high school, creaking and starting, prone to change pitch without warning. "Can we hope Maris is still alive?" that voice asked.

I drank more and told that voice I didn't know.

Nineteen

Leo met her first. In high school, Leo met everybody first. It was hard not to notice him, afire in his mismatched madras plaids, fluorescent stripes, and outrageous red tennis shoes. At five foot six, he was the shortest boy in the senior class, weighed not much more than a hundred pounds, and was already balding. However, with a ready grin and an intellect as bright as his plumage, Leo sparkled in a thousand colors, bright as the Hope Diamond. Sooner or later, everyone got drawn to Leo.

"You wouldn't believe this girl in my American lit class, just transferred in," he said as we walked home at the start of the second semester. "She's a junior, at first glance as bland as an egg white scrambled with skim milk." Leo was contemplating a career as a novelist then and spoke of everything in terms of metaphors, similes, and other things I didn't understand. "Until she smiles, and then, man, her face lights up like"—he paused, because only a brand-new simile would serve such a goddess—"like the Encyclopedia Britannica in a silk dress."

I laughed, picturing blue-bound books dressed for a prom.

He stopped, his pale, narrow face intent. "I mean it, Dek, she is the most beautiful, the most wondrous, most amazing, smartest—"

I held up my hand to silence the spew. "All right, she's perfect. And you're in love . . . again."

"She wants to be a writer, too; a George Eliot, a—"

"What's this new girl's name?"

"Don't laugh; it's sort of a boy's name," he said.

"I got branded with 'Vlodek' at birth; I never laugh at names."

"Maris."

"Like Roger Maris, the Yankee slugger?"

"Indeed," he said. That was a word he was using a lot, our senior year. Indeed.

"What's her first name?"

"That's it." He smiled. "Maris. Her last name is Mays, like Willie Mays. Her mother told her she named her Maris Mays so boys would never forget her."

We started walking again.

"It's a perfect name for a great woman writer," he said after we'd gone another block. "Like George Eliot, like—"

"Indeed," I shouted at the corner where I turned off to go to work at the laundry. I didn't think he heard me; I didn't think he even noticed I'd peeled away. For all I knew, he kept talking about Maris Mays all the way to his house.

I spotted her the next day, a blond shadow of medium height, in an almost colorless gold-tinted corduroy jumper, keeping to the walls as she moved between classes. Rivertown High allowed that, allowed anonymity, perhaps more than most high schools. Like all schools, Rivertown had cliques: the jocks, the activists, the physically superior—the noticed. They were small groups, though, for those were days of marauding Japanese steel and murderous Taiwanese efficiencies, when Rivertown students came home to announcements of layoffs and factory shutdowns, predictions of financial freefalls, and fits of uncomprehending rage. A pall hung over Rivertown, as noxious as any of the clouds of smoke that used to blanket the town, only this time it extended past the factories to darken the halls of the high school as well. Most of the students at

Rivertown lived under that cloud, stunned, just trying to get by. There was no time for cliques.

A week later, Leo grabbed my arm outside the door after school. "You've got to meet Maris."

"Indeed," I said, trying not to grin at my perfect one-word sarcasm.

She came out a couple of minutes later. She wore an open green coat, a starched white blouse—a novelty at RHS—and pale gray jeans. Her blond hair hung straight down to her shoulders, framing a face that at first glance might have been unremarkable.

She smiled. Leo was right. It transformed everything.

Leo stood up and shrugged out of his traffic-stopper orange parka, warm at last. He held his hand out for my cup. "We're under control," he said. "We can have another."

When he came back, he handed me my mug, then snapped off the plaster lamp. The outlines of Maris's old typewriter blurred just enough to give us some distance. I squeezed the coffee mug with both hands for warmth.

Leo sat down. "So now you know who your client is," he said again, for perhaps the fifteenth time. All fifteen times, it hadn't been a question, it had been a prompt.

My head was a muddle of too many images, old and new, mixed together, of a blond girl and a burned cottage, of the smell of spring and the stench of fire, of blue eyes and red blood spots. Each of them flew by, too quickly to seize. I didn't know what to say. I didn't know what to think. So I offered up what I'd said the previous fourteen times. "It changes everything."

I stared for a while at the space heater, because there was no place else left to look. I didn't want to look anymore at Maris's typewriter, and I didn't want to look at Leo, because it would just prompt him again.

"What will you do?" he said anyway.

"What will you do?" Maris asked. We were two blocks from school by then, marching three abreast on the sidewalk. Or

rather, they were marching on the sidewalk. I was trying to keep up beside them, hobbling over the small mounds of snow on the fringe between the sidewalk and the street like a man new to wooden legs.

"Go to college, I suppose," I stammered. It wasn't her beauty that was making me stutter, though she had that, in aces. It was her directness, the unblinking way she asked me the question, and then waited, as though what I was going to say might change her life.

"Where?" she asked.

"I don't know."

"Surely you must know. You're going to graduate in five months. Surely you must know what you're doing after high school."

On the other side of her, Leo arched his eyebrows in a pantomime of Groucho Marx. He knew that in the places I lived, college was never discussed. The only future I had was to be shoveled out, like ash from a fireplace, as soon as I graduated. Nonetheless, he was enjoying the discomfort that was knotting my tongue. He was my best friend.

"I don't know," I stammered again.

"Maris." Leo laughed, rescuing me. "Don't get bogged down in what Dek doesn't know. It will stop your life."

She laughed then, too, and they marched, and I hobbled, on.

"All this time, I believed . . ." I stopped, sipped coffee and Jack, and tried again. "All this time, I believed she was . . ."

"Dead," Leo finished for me.

"Disappeared forever." I couldn't say "dead," not for Maris. Even during the worst months, in the dark times between two and four in the morning, I'd never said that. "I just figured if she were OK, she would have found a way to let me know."

"Everybody thought she'd been abducted."

I looked at the low, partially shadowed thing on the card table. "I know."

"It's good; she had a life."

I turned to stare at him.

He looked away. "Sorry," he said, "I just meant at least she wasn't abducted and killed back then, like the cops thought."

"I don't know what to make of it."

"Her disappearing?"

"Sure, that. And the rest." I was angry at her now. I wanted to throw her old Underwood onto the snow. "But that charade, that Louise Thomas business about a will." I set the cup down on the floor, hard, spilling. "That was cheap."

"I'm sure—"

I cut him off. "Crap. She could have called."

"Back then?"

"Damned right; but now, too. If she needed help, why the hell didn't she call, ever? I wasn't just some fucking jamoke."

Leo got up, went to the kitchen, and came back with the bottle and a paper towel. He blotted up the coffee and Jack. "Mr. Daniels and I are going home," he said, reaching for his parka.

We walked down the stairs.

"I would have gone to her," I said.

"Of course."

I opened the door. "Then, or now."

He stepped out, then turned around. "I couldn't help it. I had to have that old typewriter examined."

Ludicrously, a fragment of an old, better moment came to me. I smiled, remembering the word.

"Indeed," I said.

Twenty

"You're rousting me at home because you just realized you know your lady columnist?" Patterson said quietly into the phone.

I'd started calling the Cedar Ridge Police Department at five thirty that morning. At seven, when I'd called for the fourth time, they finally told me Patterson wouldn't be in for another hour. I said it was an emergency. Patterson called five minutes later, from his home.

"And because her home got torched. I think she's being tortured for what she knows about that bank money," I said.

"Not after a month. She's running or she's dead."

"You've got to find her."

"Why the sudden panic, Elstrom?"

After Leo left, I stayed up the rest of the night, pushing back at the arms of the past so I could think of something to do in the present. I came up with nothing except to jump-start Patterson. Too many of the wrong words, though, would make Maris the target of a police manhunt, if she were running. Too few wouldn't get Patterson started.

"She's an old client," I said, because that's what I'd decided upon somewhere around five in the morning.

"An old client you just remembered?" He exhaled disbelief into the phone. "Look, there's no way of telling whether those letters sent to Honestly Dearest were written by Lucia Helm. Her school has nothing of hers anymore, her family is dead, and none of her old friends have anything they can be sure she touched. We're at a dead end on that."

"Assume Lucia wrote the handwritten letters. What about the typed ones?"

"Common stationery, common computer printer, and not a fingerprint on them. You want to guess Severs sent them?"

"Yes."

"Be my guest. Dead man, dead end."

"That leaves us with the Kovacs brothers. Did you send out bulletins saying they might have been involved in Severs's murder?"

"Because a guy named Elstrom thinks he may have known a woman who wrote an advice column, who may have received stolen money from a girl who's now dead, who found it hidden, perhaps, by a cop who's now dead, who may have gotten the money from two brothers who may have stolen it, but whose only provable deed is that they left town around the time the cop died?"

"What have you got that's better?"

"Circulate Carolina Dare's driver's license photo. It's coming in this morning."

"And then what?"

"We wait for a response."

"Can't you take the lead on anything?"

"You mean like calling her editor in New Jersey?"

"I already did that. He doesn't know anything. He's never even spoken to her."

"Then tell me who to call, Elstrom. And after you've done that, give me the link between Carolina Dare and any crime. I can't rustle too deeply into her background without reason. For now, all we can assume is that the lady just left—picked up and headed for a new life."

"You'll e-mail me her driver's license photo?"

"What aren't you telling me, Elstrom?"

I looked at the old black Underwood on the card table and hung up.

"I'll come along," Leo said simply, when I called to tell him I was driving back to Rambling. He didn't ask why I was going, didn't remind me that

I'd already said there was nothing left up there. He didn't waste words expressing outrage when I told him that Patterson had effectively back-burnered the case, nor did he suggest we wait a day, because snow was coming down heavy, and the roads were slick enough to make even Hummers do pirouettes. He didn't tell me that he had a right to be involved, either. I knew he wouldn't say any of that, but that's not why I'd phoned him. I called because I didn't want to go to Rambling alone.

Now, I was parked at his curb, and he was talking at me through my unzipped side window. "I don't know why I shouldn't drive," he was saying. "I've got shock absorbers, an adequate heater, treads on my tires, and"—he paused to gesture at the Discount Den radio dangling underneath the dash—"a CD player for when you bore me."

He was trying for light. We both knew the drive up to Rambling would be grim business, like two men going to the funeral of the woman who'd deserted them both.

"A hundred-thousand-dollar Porsche will make people too distrustful of us rich city folks to answer questions."

"Whereas a clapped-out Jeep will get us invited in for generic beer and pork rinds?" Leo grinned, but not much.

"You'll see lots of cars like mine—"

"Up on blocks, rusting."

"Get in and zip the window."

He got in, closed the zipper around the scratched plastic, and smoothed back a flap of duct tape that was dissolving in the moisture. "You ever hear from that security guy in Rambling?"

"No."

Leo turned to look at me. "He doesn't know about the fire?"

"You mean the fire that occurred right after I told him I'd be coming up for the blood evidence?"

"Ah," he said.

"Reynolds knows about lots of things. That's why he won't call back. And that's why we're going to Rambling."

I concentrated on moving us through the thickening snow, out of the side streets, onto Thompson Avenue, and up the ramp to the tollway. It had been plowed, but not recently. Cars and trucks were crawling, strung out like a convoy carrying nuclear waste. I supposed Leo was as grateful as I was for the snow; having to squint into the white ahead for the sudden flash of brake lights gave us an excuse not to look at each other. Or to talk.

It wasn't until an hour later, after I pulled away from the second tollbooth, that he said to the windshield, "I dreamed about her last night, how she was in high school."

"Not me," I said.

I felt him turn to look at me.

"I didn't sleep at all," I said.

He nodded a bit and went back to looking out the windshield. And we moved on, the three of us, with Maris Mays right in the middle. Just like old times.

January gave way to the beginning of February, and Maris and Leo, brought together by words, became Maris, Leo, and Dek, brought together by Leo. Leo knew everything that went on at school, because he talked to everybody, and walking home—Leo hugging the inside of the sidewalk, outrageous in mismatched neon garb; Maris quiet and beautiful in the middle; and me wobbling on the rough terrain by the curb—we laughed as Leo pantomimed a self-important jock's lips struggling with the words on a science exam, or mimicked the soft wonder in the homecoming queen's voice as she bragged that so many of her male teachers offered to tutor her on weekends. The details, though, were only half of it. It was Leo's sense of the absurd, the way his thick eyebrows danced in disbelief, the way his lips stretched into the most wicked of grins, that made us laugh so hard we couldn't breathe.

Leo had been cracking me up like that for years, but I had the sense, sneaking looks at Maris, that laughing hard was new to her, that she'd never had much occasion to see anything that was funny in her life. I think Leo saw that, too. His walking-home monologues seemed to acquire a bit of polish as February moved along, and I had the thought that he might have been practicing his delivery at night, at his house.

I would have, if I could have been that funny. I would have, if I could have made Maris laugh like that.

"She lived here?" Leo poked the toe of his boot at the black end of a charred board poking through the snow.

"It's where I found the typewriter."

It had stopped snowing, but the sky was dark with another approaching storm. It wasn't yet noon.

"Nobody should live here." He looked down the rutted road at spindly, stunted trees, black against the charcoal sky. "Too desolate."

I kicked at a charred board. "That was the attraction."

He shook his head as we walked back to the pile that was the garage, covered now in clumps of fresh snow. "Her car?" He pointed at a corner of the blistered trunk, exposed under the pile of boards where the snow had slid off.

"Just like the inside of the house, she was careful to leave no clues of her identity in the car," I said.

He turned to look at me. "She bought that car years ago and managed to never title it in her own name?"

"That's what Reynolds said."

"Which name might that have been?"

"You mean, was Maris using the name Carolina Dare before she'd ever heard from the girl in Iowa?" I knew where he was going. "I think yes. She changed from Carolina to Louise when she got up here. And I think she had other names before that."

"She wasn't just running from bank robbers."

"No."

His eyes searched my face. "So she could have spilled a few drops of blood, then run, like—"

"Like last time, Leo?"

"Like when we were kids." He turned to look at the ruined remains of the cottage, covered now by a blanket of clumped snow. "There was no fire then."

"She didn't set this. No way she risked coming back to torch the place."

"She's got to be running," he said.

I tried to find the words for Leo, a grown man in an orange parka and a purple-pommed hat, very much the boy he used to be. A boy looking for hope.

"I can't tell you she's still alive," I said.

He turned to walk back down the drive, not wanting to hear any more.

Twenty-one

We traversed the roads within a two-mile radius of the burned cottage, looking to find someone who had ever noticed anything happening at the cottage, or who had seen the fire. There were fourteen homes in that two-mile square. Nine of them had enough broken windows to indicate their owners were long gone. Five appeared to be occupied, but at two, no one answered my knock. At the three houses where somebody came to the door, no one had ever seen a commotion at the cottage, until the night of the fire.

"Roaring inferno," the unshaven man in the flannel shirt at the second house said, making a careful whoosh with a can of Bud Light. "Even from this far, I could see the flames had burned way down by the time the fire department got there. No saving that place."

"I don't suppose you knew the woman who lived in that house?"

"No time for chitchat, then or now," he said, closing the door.

It went the same way at the other two cottages.

"What now?" Leo asked at four o'clock.

"Local phone book."

We drove to West Haven and parked in front of Fizzy's discount store. Aggert's windows above were dark. We walked across the street to the restaurant.

"Beer?" he asked.

"No sleep, no beer. Just coffee and a cheeseburger." I pointed him toward the hostess smoking by the door and started for the directory hanging by the pay phone in back.

There was a listing for a Southwest Michigan Growers Association in Rambling. I called and got a machine message saying they were closed, but it included an after-hours emergency number. That number had an answering device, too. I said I was looking for a John Reynolds and was in the area only for the evening. I left my cell number.

I got back to the table at the same time as a waitress with a tray. Leo had spotted the specialty of the house, because she was setting down two poles of onion rings, two double-thick cheeseburgers, and an extra plate.

"I figured you should cut down on fat." He cut one of the burgers and put the small half on the extra plate for me.

I nodded at the wisdom of that but quickly slid one of the poles of onion rings out of his reach, before he developed wisdom about those as well. The truth was, though, that I wasn't so much hungry as starved for banter.

"I came up here one last time, expecting nothing, and nothing is what I'm getting," I said.

"Is this a dead end?" Leo asked.

"Maybe it's supposed to be," I said. "Maybe it's nothing more than Maris, if it is Maris, sending me a signal that I'm misinterpreting."

He brightened. "Like what?"

"Like this." I pulled out my key ring and held up the flat numbered key. "She knew I'd recognize that typewriter, knew, too, that I'd find the key she'd glued up inside. She named me her executor because that would give me access to her mail at the post office box, and from that I'd learn about the bank job in Iowa. Maybe all she wanted was for me to tip the cops about the real cause of Lucia Helm's death and let them take it from there."

"Kind of a roundabout way of doing things, isn't it: faking an abduction, leaving a will? What's wrong with a simple telephone call to the cops in Iowa?"

"She couldn't be sure they'd catch all the people involved in the bank job before the robbers caught up with her."

"And it spared her from having to get in front of the cops and explain why she's been changing her name, and why, a long time ago—"

My cell phone rang.

"Wilbur Watson over at the Fruit Growers," a man's voice said. "You're looking for John Reynolds?"

"I've been working with him on the disappearance of the woman who lived in that cottage that just burned on County Road 12."

"You want to swing by my office in an hour?"

I started to ask him why we couldn't talk on the phone, but he cut me off, gave me directions, and hung up.

"Man of few words?" Leo asked.

"Must come from talking mostly to blueberry bushes."

Leo nodded, but his mind was wandering someplace else. "She could have left you a note, with instructions, instead of running you all over the place."

"It's been a long time, Leo. People change."

A grin grew on his lips. "Not me," he said, tapping the orange parka draped on the chair next to him.

I laughed then, a real laugh, and as we ate, we talked about the old pictures on the wall, of sailing ships, and men cutting huge logs, and my theory about beckoning women plying the shores of Indiana in the good old days. I made him laugh, and that made me laugh some more.

On the drive back to Rambling, he asked, "You really think she took all that money and ran?"

"Why not? She'd been running for years, since she was a kid. Why couldn't she get fed up with it all and grab something for herself?"

"But do you really believe it?"

"I need to hope it, Leo."

The fruit warehouse was a big corrugated-metal structure, two stories tall. A shiny blue pickup truck was parked on the gravel in front, in a circle of light cast by a fixture above a large overhead door. We got out and tried the small door at the side of the building. It was unlocked. We went in.

A single string of fluorescent fixtures, high up, barely lit the rows of empty gray metal storage racks. A yellow forklift truck with its forks dropped was parked at the edge of the light, next to three stacks of wood pallets. The warehouse smelled of fruit and diesel fuel.

"Elstrom?" A man's voice came from an open door to a small, metal prefab office.

We walked over to stop in the doorway. "And Leo Brumsky," I said.

Watson looked up at us from his chair. He was about sixty and looked to be tall and beefy enough to eat Leo for lunch. There were no other chairs in the cramped office.

He didn't get up to extend his hand. "What's this about John Reynolds and some woman that lived in that cottage that just burned down?"

"I ran into him at that cottage. He told me he works security for some of the growers around here."

"Which growers?"

"I didn't think it mattered."

"And you?"

"The missing woman's lawyer called me, said she'd died and I'd been named executor of her will. What do you know about Reynolds?"

"Your John Reynolds showed up here just before Christmas. Said he was looking for security work. I told him we weren't hiring."

"Do you know where he works?"

"That's why I asked you to stop by. I wanted to see your face. After we talked on the phone, I called some of the smaller growers, to make sure. Nobody hired your John Reynolds to work security." Watson's lips worked at a small smile. "Nobody hires security in the winter." His smile grew larger. "If you look around, Elstrom, you'll see there's nothing worth taking, unless you fancy chipping a frozen blueberry bush out of the ground."

Watson stood up.

"You're not interested in the woman who might have disappeared from that cottage out on 12?" I asked.

Watson paused before reaching to snap off the light to his office. "Don't much care about anything, other than somebody passing himself off as working for us," he said.

Outside, not even the cold winter air could cut through the sudden heavy weight of fatigue. I handed Leo the car keys and went to the passenger's door. "You drive," I said.

"Reynolds?"

"I'd like to think he was an insurance investigator, looking for a line on the robbery money, but insurance investigators don't torch crime scenes on their way out of town."

"Someone involved in the bank job?"

I shut my eyes. "It's exhausting, being played for a chump."

Twenty-two

I called Leo from Midway Airport at seven o'clock the next morning. It had only been a few hours since we'd pulled up in front of his bungalow. In a calmer world, he would have been still sleeping. As would I.

But the world had changed, again.

He answered on the first ring. "You couldn't sleep either?"

"Are you in your office?"

"Yes, trying to get my mind off—"

"Switch on your e-mail."

I pressed the cell phone tighter to my ear and listened to him tapping keys. "E-mail forwarded from you to me," he said, reading off the screen. Then, "E-mail to you from your cop Patterson in Cedar Ridge: 'Carolina Dare's driver's license photo received from Florida secretary of state. Who is she, Elstrom?' " Leo paused, and I could easily imagine the relief growing on his face as he studied the photo on the screen. "Hell, Dek," he said after a minute, "I'm with the cop: Who is the woman in the photograph? That can't be Maris." He sounded almost giddy.

I looked at the copy I'd printed for myself. "Look at the photo again, Leo."

"I can see," he said, not ruffled. "She's got dark bangs down to her eyebrows, hair framing the sides of her face. Lots of makeup, sloppily applied. Especially the lipstick; too much lipstick, blurring the contours of her lips. Thick, black-rimmed glasses; puffed-up, fat cheeks, like she'd stuffed them with cotton balls . . . jeez, it's like . . ."

"Like she deliberately tried to conceal her facial features?"

"It can't be Maris," he said.

"That license was issued three years ago."

"You're surprised she was hiding out three years ago, long before she'd ever heard of Lucia Helm? You always figured she ran from Rivertown."

A boarding announcement for another flight came over the loudspeaker above my head.

"Where are you, Dek?"

"I'm going to Florida."

"You're at the airport already?"

"I've got to be sure it was Maris down in Florida, and up in Rambling. That driver's license photo gives me nothing."

"What about your blueberry cop?"

"When I get back, I'll pass on what I know to Dillard in Michigan and Patterson in Iowa. First, I've got to be sure about Maris."

"I'll come along," he said.

"You want to help? Keep an eye on the turret. If you've got time, get somebody to put another lock on the door."

"What?" Surprise, mixed with anger, came through the phone.

I told him about the two times I'd come home to an unlocked door. "I'd feel better with another lock."

"You're dusting me off."

"I'd put the lock on myself if I had the time."

"Dek."

"And I want you to call Aggert, get his e-mail address, and forward that photo to him. See if that's the woman who came to see him."

"Crap, Dek. You're giving me crap to do."

"I have to go to Florida alone," I said.

"Because?"

"I have to be sure it was Maris down there."

Leo let it go because we'd been friends since seventh grade, but the anger was still in his voice when I hung up.

I bought coffee and a *Chicago Tribune*, and for a half hour I tried to be like everybody else waiting at the gate, staring at a paper, lulling time into a stupor, but I couldn't focus the blur of the letters in the headline. I kept seeing Maris's face, on a rare bright afternoon, early in February.

Leo raised his palms to the sky, a rural preacher begging divine guidance.

"Help me understand!" he shouted, done telling us about Elvis Derbil, delinquent senior, who'd taken to sneaking up on students passing in the halls and twisting the backs of their shirts and blouses into crumpled knots. "The principal having to tell you he was going to make your mother come to school to iron clothes for the kids you'd been grabbing?"

I started to laugh, but stopped as Leo's face suddenly froze in pain. He was looking at Maris.

"Oops," Leo said.

Maris touched Leo's shoulder. Then she turned to me, smiling. "Leo is oversensitive about my situation."

On the other side of her, Leo kept his eyes far ahead on the sidewalk, his face a red mask.

"After my mother died," Maris went on, "my father started complaining about all the things he'd lost with her death: He had to make his own coffee, push his own vacuum cleaner, and press his own shirts. Exactly the sort of grief an eight-year-old girl who's just lost her mother needs to hear." She sighed. "My father still whines about his loss, every night when he's on his way out to the bars, but what he doesn't say is that, by the time I was nine, I was making the coffee, running the vacuum, and pressing his shirts."

"His slave," Leo muttered.

"It's not so bad," Maris said.

She stopped, and we stopped. "Do you really work in a laundry?" she asked, feigning horror as she looked at my own rumpled shirt. Then her face lit up the world with a huge smile. "Do you even know what ironing is?"

Leo laughed in relief.

"I'm affecting a weary intellectual look," I said, my face warming from her attention. "This young man is too busy tending a huge brain to be bothered by trivia like appearance."

Maris laughed, and we started up again, she and Leo and I, and I was sure I would remember that laugh for the rest of my life.

I called Amanda when my flight to St. Petersburg was five minutes from boarding.

"Why is it when I finally agree that we should start seeing each other more frequently, you quit calling?" She asked it laughingly, but the tone behind it was worried.

"I'm off to sunny Florida," I said, trying for sun-shined Vitamin C in my voice.

"What's in Florida?"

"Oranges, alligators, and a lead on this case I'm working."

"Your seven-hundred-dollar-fee case?"

"I tend to get involved" was all I said, to my shame.

She started to ask something, but I was saved, as I'd planned, by the boarding announcement, and I clicked off in too much of a hurry to tell her I loved her.

Leo and Amanda. I'd just shut them both out. It's not every morning a man gets the chance to trash the emotions of the only two people on the planet who care about him.

The St. Petersburg airport still used roll-up staircases to deplane passengers, and for a second, as I stepped out into the blinding white heat at the top of the platform, I felt like I was in one of those old Hawaii travel ads, where disembarking tourists were greeted by hula girls with leis, waiting at the bottom of the stairs. I scanned the tarmac below, adjusting my expectations now for girls with baskets of Florida oranges, holding alligators on leashes. Such was travel to a vacation destination in the new millennium: Only one person waited below, an overweight ramper with a three-day beard, sweating in blue coveralls.

I rented the cheapest car they had at the Alamo counter—a micro-compact with a name I'd never heard of, put together in an Asian country I'd never heard of, and then, I supposed, just affixed with postage and mailed over—and headed south on 275 to 75 to Bradenton. The car was right for my wallet but wrong for my six feet four inches. I drove with the windows down and my knees up, gripping the steering wheel as if I were aiming a go-kart.

Never having been to Florida, I had some expectation of roadsides lined with grass-topped huts selling seashells and coconuts. Apparently I'd arrived decades too late. There were no such huts, but there was a huge Wal-Mart, the biggest Wal-Building I'd ever seen. Its sign said it contained a food store and an auto repair center. It was big enough to also house a hospital, though the sign didn't mention any such thing. That was just as well, because the idea of continuous price rollbacks on bypass surgery was not comforting. I swung in, depleted their supply of Doomsday Oreos by one bag, and was out of there in five minutes, prepared now for anything.

Windward Island was south and west of Bradenton, across two bridges, one of wood, one of steel. It was not so much an island as it was a sandbar, bisected by a two-lane road. The Gulf of Mexico was a shell's throw to the west, and an inlet waterway was a shell's throw to the east.

Smith's Secretarial, the service that forwarded Carolina's Honestly Dearest mail north to Michigan, was in an aluminum-sided building on the northernmost part of the island. It was on the second floor, above a beauty supply shop. The woman inside, smoking a cigarette at a desk behind a computer, looked not to have bought anything from the store below.

I introduced myself, said I was there representing Carolina Dare.

"We don't give out the names of our clients," she said.

"I'm a court-nominated executor," I added, trying the same bluff I'd used on the landlady in Rambling.

This woman was sharper. "What the hell is that supposed to mean?" She crushed out the stub of her cigarette and pulled another Marlboro from the pack on the desk.

"Nothing," I said.

"She dead?"

"I hope not."

She lit the Marlboro. "If you'd like to leave her a note," she said from behind the smoke, "I'll be happy to pass it on if she ever comes in."

"I know you're cashing her checks and forwarding her mail to Woodton, Michigan."

"Then you can mail your note up there," she said.

"I've been reading her mail."

"Then you can read your own note when it arrives up there."

"I don't know how to get in touch with her."

"I can't help you."

The dim bulb that occasionally lights my attic flickered. "Maybe I can help you."

"How's that?"

"Are her bills with you paid?"

"We bill quarterly, in advance, fifty bucks a month." The woman wasn't going to give anything away.

"I imagine she sent in her payment in December. That would cover her through the end of this month?"

She said nothing, and I realized my mistake. Maris hadn't needed to send in any payments. Smith's would just take their fee from the New Jersey checks and forward the balance up to Woodton.

"I would imagine there are laws preventing you from making any deduction if Carolina wasn't around to authorize it," I said.

That got her attention. She crushed out the new Marlboro, half-smoked. "Go on."

"How about I make you a deal?" I pulled out my checkbook. "I'll pay her account six months in advance, for April through September. If she contacts you, authorizes you to make further deductions from the checks that you cash, you return my three hundred."

"Fair enough." She set a pen down at the edge of the desk.

I didn't pick it up. Instead, I pulled out the copy of the driver's license photo Patterson had sent to my computer. "Is this her?"

She studied the photo through the smoke, then looked up. "Mister, that isn't anybody."

I wrote the check for three hundred and handed it to her. "One more thing, which shouldn't violate your confidentiality restrictions: Ever hear of a woman named Carolina Dare?"

"Sure." She grinned, sliding open her desk drawer and dropping in my check. "She used to waitress at the Copper Scupper, north point of the island."

"Used to?"

"Worked there for years, then took off sudden, a year ago. Nobody's heard from her since."

"Nobody?"

"I would have heard. This is a small island."

I started for the door but stopped and asked the question I'd wanted to blurt at the beginning.

"What did she look like?"

"I thought you said you were her executor," the woman said, reaching for another Marlboro.

"Court-appointed."

"Of course." She laughed up a bit of phlegm. "Court-appointed people come down here all the time, looking to settle the estates of women who made the big bucks waitressing at beach bars."

I reached for the doorknob. "What did she look like?" I asked again.

"About your age, slim, medium height, blond, blue eyes. Ordinary looking," she said.

I started to turn the knob.

"Ordinary looking," the woman said behind me, "but damn, when she smiled, it changed her into the most beautiful woman in the world."

I walked down the stairs.

Twenty-three

It was only three thirty, but already both lanes of the imaginatively named main road, Shell Drive, were packed with crawling vehicles. Half of them were putty-colored sedans filled with gray-headed, putty-colored people. They were the used-to-be working class, retired to planned activities and dinner at four on Windward Island. The other half were dinged trucks, faded SUVs, and beater Jeeps like mine. They were driven by sun-darkened people, the still-struggling service class. Both lanes were choked, so I couldn't tell who was coming or going, but maybe that's the way it always was on an island that had only one main road: Everyone was always coming and going simultaneously.

I supposed that was what I was doing, too. I was coming and going simultaneously; chasing a woman who might be alive, or who might be dead; hunting a girl who'd changed my life, or a woman I'd never known. Or both.

I followed the throng inching south toward the middle of the island, scanning both sides of the road for a place to stay. Windward was going upscale. Interspersed along one stretch of classy-looking restaurants was a barbecue joint with a skull-and-bones sign, a garage that did oil changes and repaired marine engines, and a shack trying to pass itself as selling authentic Chicago-style hot dogs. It was a fraud, that shack; its outdoor counter was lined with ketchup bottles. Chicagoans know that ketchup has as much place on a hot dog as motor oil.

Every motel had a NO VACANCY sign dangling out front. That was no surprise. It was March, the time when the hordes from the north descend on the Florida beaches to blister themselves, incubating little carcinomas. A digital sign outside a bank said the temperature was ninety-two degrees.

Ten minutes later, but only a mile down, I spotted a turquoise two-story motel with pink shutters and an almost empty parking lot, right on the beach. Its sign said simply ROOMS and appeared to be too solidly rusted to its metal pole to creak if there'd been a breeze. The place looked just seedy enough to offer cheap rates. I swung in, parked next to the pickup truck that was the only vehicle in the crushed shell lot, and extracted myself from the micro-rental.

I pushed open the screen door. The lobby was dark, and so dank it made me wonder why the old guy behind the counter wasn't wearing a snorkel.

"Nine hundred for the week," he said.

I turned to go.

"What were you looking to spend?" he asked from behind me.

"Fifty a night," I said to the screen.

He laughed. "In tourist season?"

I put my hand on the door handle. A screen on a windless, blistering day explained the empty parking lot.

"One ten a night," he said.

"You got air-conditioning?"

"Make it ninety."

"Fifty-five a night," I said.

"How long you going to stay?"

"Maybe a week." I turned and walked back to the counter. It wouldn't take that long to check out the details of Carolina Dare's life. If I became certain that she was Maris, though, it might take that long to walk the beaches she'd walked, smell the salt air she'd breathed, see her dawns, feel her sunsets.

It might very well take a whole week to kiss a ghost.

I gave the guy a check for two nights.

"You told me a week," he said.

"Depends on whether I can catch a breeze in the room."

I carried my duffel and my Oreos up the outside staircase. My room had windows facing both the beach and Shell Drive. Depending on the breeze, if one arose, I'd either be savoring salt air or sucking auto exhaust. Of such is life.

The hot and cold water worked, and the toilet flushed. The bed's headboard and the top of the dresser were sticky, as though the salt air were dissolving the laminate. I took that to be a good sign. If I was sharing the room with cockroaches, they'd stick to the Formica and might drown in the humidity, standing up. I unzipped the duffel, changed into a red knit shirt and blue plaid shorts, colors made all the more vivid by my northern skin, and went out.

Traffic was easing as I started back up Shell Drive toward the northeastern part of Windward Island. The bank thermometer said the temperature was now ninety-four degrees. It was getting hotter as the sun was setting. I wondered if that was a sign of Doomsday and regretted not buying more Oreos.

The Copper Scupper was at the very tip of the island, a bleached-board place with white metal furniture, green umbrellas, and a planked deck on the sand. The waiters and waitresses wore khaki shorts, and Hawaiian shirts like Leo's, except that theirs fit. A sign said to wait to be seated, so I did, watching a guy in an orange parrot shirt and pink baseball cap plug in an electric keyboard—readying himself, no doubt, for Margaritaville music.

A hostess, deeply tanned, fiftyish, and with the courage to let her hair go gray, came out from the inside dining room. She led me to a table at the end of the deck, mercifully the one farthest from the would-be Buffett. She handed me a menu and told me a waitress would be right with me. The waitress was, in less than a minute, and I ordered a gin and tonic.

While I waited, I pulled my cell phone out of my shorts and checked for messages. Nobody had called, not Leo, not Amanda. That was no surprise. I owed them both apologies, but I wouldn't know what to say, or how to say it, until I finished up on Windward Island. My drink came. For a time, I let the sun and the gin and the tonic wash at the knots in my head as I watched the sun make curving silver lines on the crests of the waves in the Gulf of Mexico.

My waitress came by and asked if I wanted another gin and tonic. It seemed that kind of night, so I said sure. Before she could leave, I asked my question.

"Did Carolina Dare used to work here?"

Her eyes narrowed, but she could have been squinting from the sun sinking toward the water.

"You a friend?"

"I don't know," I said.

She smiled because she was a good waitress, used to clever lines from solitary male drinkers. "There's no Carolina Dare working here," she said.

"What I meant was, I didn't know her by that name. It was a long time ago. I could be asking about the wrong woman."

She kept the smile fixed on her face. "Why would you be asking at all?"

"I'm getting her mail, and it's being forwarded from here."

"From the Copper Scupper?" She grinned, still parrying.

"From Windward Island."

"Have the crab cake sandwich and float another one of those," she said, pointing to the lime resting at the bottom of my empty glass. She walked away.

Twenty minutes later a server, a girl, twenty, taut and tanned, brought me my food and the second drink. She left too quickly for me to ask her about Carolina, perhaps afraid that the whiteness of my skin might leach the bronze out of her like a sponge in a glass of water. The crab cake sandwich was delicious, flaky, and free of mayo. It was the best I'd ever had, though in truth, it was the only crab cake sandwich I'd ever had. Restaurateurs in Rivertown, like Kutz, don't go netting in the Willahock for delicacies, rightly fearing that something bigger might come back at them, angry, from the tires in the murky water.

By the time I'd finished, the Copper Scupper had filled with music lovers, sitting with their backs turned to the now-crooning Buffett and his rhythm machine. I searched the crowd for my original waitress. She'd known something, and I wanted another chance to use my clever investigative techniques on her. I didn't see her. When my server passed by, I asked for my waitress.

She smiled big, white teeth at me from a safe distance. "Mary? She got off a half hour ago."

A change in clever investigative technique was in order. "I'm an old friend of Carolina Dare's," I said. "She used to work here?"

The sweet young thing smiled again and shook her head. "I'm just taking a break from college," she said. "I've only been here a month."

I asked her to bring me coffee. The sun was low over the water, changing the silver-tipped eddies to red. A couple walked on the beach, close, one slow silhouette against the setting sun. It was a good night for lovers.

"I have to stay after, get some help with physics," Maris said in the hall before the last period of the day. It was the third week of February.

"I'll wait," I blurted, and then suddenly froze at what my mouth, with no provocation from my brain, had just said.

She smiled. "I'm glad."

Two hours later, we went out the back doors of Rivertown High. The sun was beginning to set.

"Leo tells me you have no parents," she said as we got to the bottom of the concrete steps.

"My mother took off a week after I was born. She was a sophomore right here at Rivertown High."

"And your father?"

"Some guy named Elstrom but otherwise unknown, at least to me."

"You live with her sisters?"

"The three of them pass me around, from living room couch to living room couch, a month at a time. I'm like the pea that carnival

guys hide in those three-walnut shell games." I was trying to sound metaphorical, like the literary heroes she and Leo shared.

She was too kind to laugh. "They don't like you?"

"One sister, Lillian, does. When I stay with her, it's like a vacation; good food, television, sometimes a movie at the theater. The other two say I look like my mother. I keep my stuff in a suitcase that I never unpack."

Walking home, it was easy to tell her things that, until that afternoon, I hadn't known to tell myself. We talked about everything and nothing and lingered outside the pinball parlor below her apartment, oblivious to the cars passing by and the other people jostling us on the sidewalk. It wasn't until five forty-five that I realized I was an hour late for work. It didn't matter. I ran to the laundry sucking air ten thousand times purer than I'd ever tasted before.

"Will there be anything else, sir?" Another young, Hawaiian-shirted waitress was back with the pot of coffee. She'd brought the check a half hour before, about the time the sun disappeared into the water. She hadn't known Carolina Dare, either.

"Thanks, no. I've taken up this table long enough." I signed the credit card slip and made my way across the deck to the exit, bringing with me just enough residue from the gins to make me feel old.

"Carolina Dare," a voice said from the shadow of the entrance to the bar.

I stopped and turned. It was the hostess, the gray-haired woman with the deep tan.

"You've been asking about Carolina Dare."

"Yes," I said.

A group of three couples came up then, smelling of whiskey. She motioned for me to wait, walked them to a table by the sand, and came back.

By that time, another couple had come up to stand next to me.

"Coffee at nine tomorrow," she said to me and named a restaurant.

"On Shell Drive?" I asked.

She smiled. "If it's not on Shell Drive, it's in the water."

I drove back to my motel and climbed the stairs to the second floor. My room was hot. I opened the windows to catch a breeze, should one come along, took off my clothes, and lay on the bed. Outside, somewhere in the dark along the beach, intermingled with the soft sounds of the surf lapping at the shore, young voices were laughing. I heard Maris's among them, lilting and light.

"Vlodek," she teased, "you're so serious."

Twenty-four

I managed five hours of sleep, more or less, but it came in ragged twenty- and thirty-minute chunks, each one ending when a dream of Maris jerked me awake. I'd long ago buried most of my memories of Maris deep enough for me to move on, but that night they all came back, as bright and hot as fires in dry brush. I sat up, finally, at eight, drenched by the humidity and the past.

I spent some minutes staring at my cell phone, then set it down and took a shower. It wasn't that I didn't want to talk to Amanda, it was that I didn't want to lie. After I got dressed, I put the phone in my pocket, still turned off, and went out.

Traffic was almost devoid of putty-colored people. I guessed they were still inside, reading their newspapers, and bracing for another evening's dinner that afternoon. The still-struggling folks were out, though, buzzing north and south on Shell Drive, on their ways to tend to pools and sewers and stores. The temperature at the bank was already past ninety. Motoring along with the car windows open, the heat felt good after the dampness of my motel room. I wondered if Maris had come to Florida for the heat. Or because it was about as far away from Rivertown as she could get without dropping into the ocean.

I got to the diner a half hour early and took a booth that looked out over the water. Already the sand was littered with beach umbrellas, blow-up balls, and vinyl alligators. Nine thirty was family time for mothers and fathers and toddling kids. The sun was not yet high enough to burn. It was safe, then, on Windward Island.

Maris and I never called it love, that thing growing by glances and smiles between us. We didn't come from places where that word was used. But neither was it one of the vague, restless, ever-shifting fixations I'd felt for other girls at school. Those had been the stuff of fantasies, of heroic athleticism, or courageous rescues played against historical backdrops: Dek rescues teen queen, bound to the tracks, from onrushing railroad train; Dek fights duel, saves honor of teen queen; and teen queen rewards Dek with . . . well, I didn't know exactly what the reward might be, but I knew enough to hope it would involve getting at least partially naked.

What joined Maris and me was something else, something born of our histories, of being out of place, like red pawns in a black and white chess set. We sought distance from what we didn't have, and shelter in each other. We found reasons to stay after school, she and I, just long enough for Leo to have to walk home alone. And what had begun as grand camaraderie, of Maris and me, both pale and unformed, orbiting around the flash and sizzle that was Leo, changed. Our orbit began to wobble, and then it broke free, and then everything began to orbit around us.

"Name's Dina," the gray-haired hostess from the Copper Scupper said, sliding into the booth. "And you are?"

"Dek Elstrom."

Our waitress appeared almost instantly, perhaps because people in Florida hear the clock ticking louder than in other places.

"From where?" Dina asked, after we'd both ordered scrambled eggs.

"From Rivertown, just west of Chicago. I'm trying to trace down Carolina Dare."

"You a friend?"

"I'm not sure." I pulled out the copy of the driver's license photo and gave it to her.

She pulled reading glasses out of her purse. "Who's this?"

"Carolina Dare?"

She stared at the photo for a minute, then shook her head. "That's a frightened woman, Dek Elstrom, some woman who didn't want to be photographed." She handed it back. "Tell me," she said.

She was direct, like Maris, and it was easy to like her. So I told her most of it, beginning with Attorney Aggert's phone call, the Louise Thomas will, my poking around the Rambling cottage. I told her, too, of discovering the name Carolina Dare in the mail forwarded from Windward Island, but I offered up nothing about Honestly Dearest, the Iowa bank robbery, the letters from Lucia Helm, and the threatening letters that followed.

"Are you withholding a lot?" Dina asked when I finished.

"Enough."

Dina looked out the window. The sun was higher now. Most of the families had left the beach.

"A girl that pretty . . ." She stirred her coffee, then looked up. "You think she's dead?"

"I'm hoping she's running." I told her about the blood spatters in the cottage and the subsequent fire.

"Like somebody's destroying evidence of something?"

"It's better for Carolina if I don't get into that," I said.

Our eggs came. She stabbed at hers for a minute, then set down her fork. "You told one of my girls you didn't know her as Carolina Dare."

"As I said, I got hired by a Louise Thomas."

"There's a third name, isn't there?"

"Perhaps, a long time ago."

"I can respect that," she said when I didn't say any more. She pushed away her uneaten food. "I've been afraid for her since I first met her, going back over a dozen years. She answered an ad I had in the paper for an attic apartment, said she was hoping to find work. Poor kid, she looked like it was time for her to catch a break. I rented her the apartment, got her a job waitressing at the Scupper, and became as much of a friend to her as she would allow."

"What do you mean?"

"Carolina was always looking over her shoulder. You see that a lot down here. Mixed in with the tourists is a different bunch, people leaving something behind. They come here thinking it's warm enough to live cheap, sleeping in their cars even. Carolina was like them. She was guarded and kept to herself. I noticed it right off, with the pictures."

"Pictures?"

"We have staff parties at the Scupper, rum punch and beach volleyball things, two or three times a year. Her first one, she faded into the shadows whenever somebody started snapping pictures. She didn't want to be photographed. And there were times when tourists, men, wanted her to pose with them—you know, pretty young local thing. She always found a way not to. I figured she had her reasons and never asked her about it."

"Do you remember her car?"

Dina nodded. "I took her over to buy it. A blue something."

"A Dodge Aries?"

Her eyes narrowed. "You know that car?"

That was it, then. "It was in the garage that burned down."

Dina looked out the window, the glare bright in the watering in her eyes.

"She have any boyfriends, anybody else she knew on the island?"

She shook her head. "When she wasn't working, she was upstairs in her apartment. Pretty girl like that, she got talked to a lot at the Scupper, but I don't think she ever once went out. I think she read a lot."

"She wrote, though, didn't she? On a typewriter?"

Dina smiled at the memory. "I'd hear that, yes."

"What was she writing?"

"Never knew. She didn't leave any of it behind."

"She ever get any mail?"

"Thick envelopes sometimes, from a newspaper in New Jersey. I figured she was sending stuff in, articles maybe, for publication. And getting rejected."

"When did she leave?"

Dina leaned back in the booth, sipped coffee for a minute. "A little over a year ago. Left me a note with her key." She opened her purse, pulled out a folded piece of typing paper, and handed it to me.

"Dina," she'd typed. "Thanks. C."

"Just this?"

"Like I said, I think she was running from something."

"But no boyfriends?" I had to ask it again.

"Other than you?"

I started to deny it, then stopped.

"You got that look." She smiled.

"It was a long time ago."

Dina looked back out the window. "No boyfriends, but there was one guy. He came into the Scupper a few times right before Carolina took off. Sat at the bar inside, making two or three drinks last the whole evening. You get that, slow drinkers. Owner doesn't mind, so long as they're not taking up a table all night."

"This guy was different?"

"He was real watchful. Guys sitting by themselves at the bar, they mostly look down, like they're self-conscious, or else they stare at every passing girl, hoping to catch a look back. Not this one. He was interested only in Carolina, kept his eyes on her all night. He stayed until closing, those nights, so I made sure one of the busboys walked Carolina to her car. She laughed it off, but there was something in her eyes that told me she was taking it serious. She never said anything, but after a few days, she was gone."

"Because of him?"

"That's what I thought."

"Did the man ever come in after she took off?"

"Just once, the next night. But he left early. I'm thinking he asked around, found out Carolina had quit."

"What did he look like?"

"Six three or four, your height. Brown hair, about the color of yours. And blue eyes—" She stopped, looking at my face.

Something oily was working its way up my throat. She could have been describing John Reynolds.

"Have you rented her apartment?" I asked.

"Didn't seem right, after she went away," she said slowly. "She'd cleaned it real thorough, and there's no trace of her left, but I've just never gotten around to putting another ad in the paper. I guess I was keeping it for her, in case she ever wanted to come back. Everybody needs a place to come back to."

"Can I see it?"

Dina dug in her purse, took out a ring of keys, and detached one. She handed it to me. "I've got to get to the Scupper, but you can look around." She told me where she lived and said to bring the key to the Scupper when I was done.

I walked her to her car in the parking lot. She got in and started the engine with the door open, to let the air-conditioning blow out the superheated air. She looked up at me as she reached to pull the door closed.

"She ever say anything about a family?" I asked.

Dina looked at my eyes until I thought to take sunglasses out of my shirt pocket and put them on.

"A family?" she repeated.

"She ever mention anybody at all?"

"You mean like parents?"

"Anybody at all."

"I don't know about any family," she said and drove away.

Twenty-five

It was the first warm day of spring. We were a half block, and three minutes, from where she would turn for her apartment and I toward the laundry.

Suddenly, she took a couple of giant strides to get in front of me, turned, and stopped. "So what about it, Vlodek?" She grinned. One of her eyeteeth was slightly crooked. It was enchanting.

"What about what?"

"Taking me to the Spring Dance."

"I don't go to proms," I said, hoping that the blush warming my face didn't betray me. I wanted, more than anything I'd ever wanted, anytime, anywhere, to hold Maris Mays, to make contact, flesh-to-cloth-to-cloth-to-flesh.

But I didn't dance. I had never danced. I believed fervently that were I to try, my legs would knot themselves twice or three times over, and I would collapse into a lumpy, gnarled skein of limbs and elbows and knees and pointy head, a pathetic pretzel.

"I don't have a suit," the stuttering idiot who managed my mouth said.

"I'll find you a suit."

"Leo," I stammered. Leo and I barely spoke anymore. I told myself it was because there was no time. We passed in the halls,

smiled, flashed a thumbs-up like always, but it was a charade. He knew that Maris and I had been hanging back, every afternoon, just enough to be alone. He knew about me and the girl who had caught his heart.

"Leo?" she asked.

"He loved you first." Baboons were loose in my mouth now, throwing pots and pans out with the words.

Her eyes, always as blue as the best of skies, widened in surprise. She leaned closer, and I could smell Ivory soap and roses and spring and a moment that might never come again.

"Take me to the dance, Vlodek," she breathed.

Dina's house was like most I'd seen along Shell Drive. It was a two-story white-sided box with shallow balconies and dark windows, set up high on cinder-block piers. Noah wouldn't have gotten any ark-building assignments from the folks who lived in such places, for they knew that when the floods did come, they'd be safe enough, high up in their stilt houses, to sip mai tais and eat Oreos and watch, with impunity, as streams of donkeys and geese, coconut palms and yachts and Wal-Mart trucks, got washed away to oblivion right beneath their very own verandas.

I parked on the crushed shell driveway and walked around to the back.

A week before the dance, Maris found me a four-dollar suit. It was an itchy brown wool thing with big lapels, and it stank so badly of mothballs that the tea-sipping lady at the resale shop threw in a wrinkled floral necktie and a yellowed shirt with a long, pointy collar.

"Twenty-three skiddoo," I said, copping a line from an old gangster movie, as we walked out. Maris laughed. I'd gotten far wittier in the weeks since I'd been walking with Maris.

I climbed the outside staircase that led up the two flights to her apartment. A clutch of yellow flowers bloomed in a red clay pot on the second-floor landing. I bent to sniff them, but they didn't smell of anything.

The key turned easily in the lock, and I stepped inside.

The night of the dance was warm, scented with the lilacs that blossomed, mostly untended, in old bushes in many of the backyards in Rivertown. Maris was waiting for me on the sidewalk, which meant her father was still upstairs, splashing on cheap cologne, before he set off for another night of groping for love in the tonks on Thompson Avenue. I'd only met Herman Mays twice, and then only at the base of their stairs. We'd disliked each other instantly; he, I thought, because he saw me as unmarked, yet to live the disappointments he cried about, Maris said, even in his sleep. My dislike was simpler. I despised him for the rage he directed at Maris.

Maris wore a blue and green leaf-patterned dress of thick brocade—like my suit, too heavy for the warm evening—and tiny sparkling earrings.

We walked to the high school, both of us dressed for winter, because it would have been unthinkable to ask my aunt Rosemary—one of the bad aunts—for the use of her Ford. She'd barely looked up as I cut through her apartment in my big-lapel brown suit and razzmatazz necktie, trailing my musk of mothballs, as though it were usual for me to go out dressed as a junior-grade gangster.

As Maris and I stepped into the gymnasium, I saw, to my horror, that most of the girls were wearing corsages. Embarrassment heated my face; I had not thought to buy one for Maris. "It doesn't matter, Vlodek," she said, squeezing my hand.

The dance passed in a blur. There was a punch bowl, filled with some fruity red mix that I joked would never be noticed if spilled on the riot of flowers that was my necktie. There were bright overhead lights, excellent for spotting basketball fouls, just as good for spotting hands rising for social fouls. The music was fast, dialed up on the treble to shut out the bass, lest something primal be aroused. And everywhere there was a teacher, eyes darting like a falcon's, making sure minimum intervals, flesh-to-cloth-to-air-to-cloth-to-flesh, were being maintained by all the couples on the gymnasium floor. There was nothing for them to worry about with Maris and me. We danced awkwardly, as stiff as back patients recovering from surgery.

There was an after-dance party, a rec room affair in the basement of a two-flat, five blocks off of Thompson Avenue. A friend of Maris's, another junior, invited a dozen couples. There were fluorescents in the ceiling there, too—strong and white, like in the gym, and quite overpowering a low lamp with a straw shade—switched on by the girl's mother, switched off as soon as she climbed the stairs.

The music was vinyl and old, slow love songs of the fifties and sixties, played on a portable record player. It wasn't listening music, it was rubbing music. And it was there, in that two-flat basement, lit softly by pale light from a straw-shaded lamp, that itchy brown wool at last met heavy blue and green brocade. At the end of the first dance, a blessedly interminable Johnny Mathis swoon, I looked down, Maris looked up, and the orbiting at last was complete. We kissed, nervous lips on soft lips, her smelling of Ivory soap and roses, me of mothballs and wonder.

And from somewhere behind the straw-shaded lamp, the vinyl band played on.

The second-floor rooms were hot, at least a hundred and ten degrees. I stood by the opened door for a minute, to let the scorching air rush to the lesser heat outside. Hoping, I suppose, to inhale some scent, some trace of Maris. There was only old air, trapped in the heat.

The tiny apartment combined a living room with a kitchen setup. An open door offered a glimpse of a bedroom and, beyond that, a bathroom.

All the walls were a pale yellow, and completely blank. The vinyl tile floor was a bright, clean white, free of heel scuffs or scratches. They were rooms that had been decorated and then never marked, rooms occupied by someone who'd been careful to leave nothing of herself behind.

Everywhere, there was sun, lots of sun.

I walked through the living room to open one of the windows that faced Shell Drive. The soft white curtains stirred for an instant, then collapsed back against the screen.

It was good that everywhere, in those rooms, there was the sun, the bright yellow-white sun.

Maris liked the sun. She liked that it was the color of her hair.

For the first days following the Spring Dance, we were tentative, fellow adventurers who shared a secret but were afraid to put a name to it, for fear its magic would disappear if we spoke of it aloud. Passing each other in the halls at school, we smiled but then quickly averted our eyes. Walking after school, it took us two or three blocks to say anything at all, and then our words were careful, of assignments and tests and term papers, things that neither of us heard. It was prelude.

On Monday and Tuesday, we kissed on the sidewalk in front of the door that led up to her apartment, a quick, furtive brushing of lips. On Wednesday, we stepped just inside the street door, into the dark at the foot of the stairs.

The weekend was interminable. Her father was home, not about to allow his daughter to slip out to see some boy. He had need of her. There was cleaning to do, and ironing. Things a wife would have done.

On Wednesday of the following week, we went upstairs to the landing outside the door that opened to her father's apartment. Not that many days later, we moved inside that door, to the nubby orange couch in her father's front room.

No longer did we find reasons to stay after class. There was no time. From the last bell until I had to be at the laundry, we had a narrow window, seventy-five minutes, and we learned to manage them with the cunning of museum robbers. We met outside the southwest door of the high school at three eighteen. By three twenty-one we had passed the parking lot, walking purposefully, not saying much for fear it would slow us down. We crossed to Thompson Avenue at three thirty-one if the truck traffic was light; three thirty-two if it was heavy. By three thirty-seven we were up the stairs to her landing, and she was fumbling with her key. A second or two later, she'd have the door open, our books would drop, and we would be on the nubby orange couch, daring only to touch each other's face.

I moved through the tiny apartment, trying not to place the girl I'd known on the beige upholstered chair, hear her lifting a Coke or a lemonade from the kitchen counter, or see her picking up a book of poetry from the lamp table.

In the far back corner, by the stove, refrigerator, and sink, there was a yellow kitchen table and a white ladder-back chair. She'd sat on that chair, eaten at that table, alone, for over a decade. The boy I'd been the summer of high school graduation wanted to rejoice; she'd shared her meals with no one. The man that boy had become wanted to cry at the loss of it.

From the doorway to the bedroom, I looked at the twin bed, made up with a white bedspread pulled tight. Next to it was a night table with a frilly-shaded lamp, and across the room, a painted four-drawer dresser. It was the bedroom of a woman alone. Or that of a young girl.

People called Lillian, my mother's youngest sister, flighty and scatterbrained. Perhaps that was true. She was easily overwhelmed and took care to lead a spinster's ordered life, taking the train downtown to Chicago to work in the ladies' coats department of Marshall Field's.

She was the kindest of my mother's three sisters. She was the one who fussed over my clothes, made sure the sheets for the sofa were clean, and kept meals warm for me for when I came home at midnight from the laundry. I looked forward to every third month, when I could stay at her apartment.

Her funeral was five days before my graduation. It was a fine day late in May, heavy with the scents of flowers and beginnings, a day too bright and alive for burying a woman who'd lived quietly and demanded nothing of anyone. I rode with her two remaining sisters and their husbands and children from the funeral home west on Thompson Avenue to the cemetery but stood apart from them, at the back of the small cluster of people, as the minister mouthed words that made no sense on such a beautiful day. When he was done, Lillian's sisters dropped roses onto the coffin that rested on low metal poles, and everyone began walking away from the opening that had been ripped into the ground.

My skin was tingling. Crazily, every breath I took went deeper into my lungs than ever before. The sky was bluer than I'd ever seen it, the smells of spring stronger. Time raced. No matter where I looked—the dash clock on the funeral home Cadillac, the Timex Lillian had given me for Christmas—minutes were disappearing, fast and forever, like petals thrown to a gusting spring windstorm.

Still in my Spring Dance wool suit, I ran to the high school, waited for Maris outside our door. When she stepped into the bright sunshine, agonizing minutes later, I grabbed her books, then her hand, and half-pulled her across the grass, toward the parking lot.

"Vlodek! Where's the fire?"

I had no words and no time to tell her that the flames were all around me. The whole world was ablaze with life and death and vanishing minutes.

Inside her apartment, I tugged her past the nubby couch. She put her hand to my chest at the door to her bedroom, bright from the sun at the window. Never before had I touched anything except her face, her arms, her hands. She paused, trying to see what was raging behind my eyes, but it was only for an instant. Then we were inside, and I was pulling at her clothes, ripping at my own, and we were naked on her narrow twin bed.

I was somewhere else, then, looking down at her, at me. I saw her face change from acceptance to need and then to something that I didn't understand. She started to cry. I saw myself stop. She shook her head. "No," I heard her whisper. And I saw myself start again. I was not that boy slowly moving on the bed; I was watching, detached, entirely accepting the inevitability that I was seeing down below. When the boy who was me at last stopped, she continued to hold me against her, her hands clenched around my back, her face wet against my shoulder, until we started again, and later, again. I left at six o'clock, late for the laundry. In all that time at Maris's, I had not uttered one word. I didn't know what I could possibly say.

I walked around the bed, to the door to the bath, and stood for a moment, holding on to the jamb. There was nothing of her left in that heat, of course. Nothing at all.

My cell phone rang, echoing loudly off the tiled walls of the empty, hard room. I almost dropped it, fumbling it out of my pocket.

"Where are you, Dek?" Amanda's voice, light and trusting.

My hand shook as I pressed the phone tight against my ear, guilty of being caught in another woman's place, in another woman's time. I walked quickly out of the bath and through the bedroom to sit on the white chair at the yellow kitchen table in the sun. "Still in Florida," I said.

"Are you all right?"

"Of course."

"You sound a little . . . unsure."

I made a laugh that sounded like a cough. "Maybe a little preoccupied."

"I was hoping you'd call me last night, when you got settled." It was a soft rebuke, and though mild, it was unusual for her.

"Sorry. I checked into a motel—a dump, but affordable—then went out for something to eat. I had a crab cake sandwich, a couple of gin and tonics, and watched the sun set."

"And thought of me?" There was doubt in her playful question, realization that something was wrong.

"That, too," I said after a beat.

She inhaled sharply, as if she'd been struck. I'd taken too long, and spoken too flatly.

"Of course I thought of you," I added, but that sounded even clumsier. I am not inexperienced at lying. Mostly, however, I lie to myself. With Amanda, I'd always blundered ahead with the truth. That day, though, in that kitchen, I was spewing deceit—and Amanda had heard it.

She said something. I missed the words. My eyes had quit searching the room, stopped by some discolorations on the kitchen table in front of me. There were four little circular rub smudges, spaced evenly in a square pattern.

"Dek?" Amanda's voice cut through.

"Sorry. What?"

"I asked when you're coming back."

"I don't know." I knew what those little smudges on the table were from.

"You're making progress?" Her voice was far away, from another place.

"I'm trying," I heard myself say.

She said something that I didn't catch. I said that sounded fine, and I'd call her soon. It was only after I clicked off that I realized she'd told me she loved me.

The little circles on the kitchen table had come from old rubber typewriter feet.

I went down to the car, came back up with the tissue-thin car rental agreement, and used it to trace the markings on the table. I knew the pattern on the laminate would match the footprint of the typewriter, right down to the little wedge-shaped piece missing from one pad that had caused the one irregular smudge on the table. I didn't need the tracing to be absolutely certain that this had been Maris's apartment; I needed it to preserve the one mark she'd left in those rooms.

Perhaps an hour later, I stood up from the yellow table. My shirt was soaked from the heat. My eyes burned from the sweat coming off my forehead. I closed the window, locked the door, and walked down the long stairs.

Twenty-six

The *Gulf Watcher* office was in the middle of an L-shaped strip mall, between a hardware store and an Irish restaurant with a Budweiser sign in its window. Inside were three desks and a red-haired woman talking on the phone. I sat on a vinyl chair next to the door and took a copy of the paper from a wire rack. On page eight, next to an article about ridding the Florida house of palmetto bugs, the Honestly Dearest column offered advice to a love-starved teenaged service station cashier, an elderly gentleman afraid that his lady-friend bridge partner had given him herpes, and a bowler who worried that his shirt made him look fat. I barely remembered writing the smart-assed answers and wondered who was the bigger fool: Charles, the editor, or myself.

When the woman hung up, I said, "I'm looking for information on one of your columnists."

"We only have the one, writing on senior citizen issues. You look a little young to be offended." She smiled.

"Honestly Dearest," I said.

"Ah, you mean a syndicated columnist." Her smile grew broader. "She's getting a little more feisty, don't you think?"

"Most assuredly. I heard she lives around here."

"I wouldn't know about that," she said, but the corners of her eyes had tightened.

"This is a small island."

"We buy her columns from a syndicator in New Jersey."

"I'm not asking you to betray any confidences. All I want to know is whether a guy came here, asking about Honestly Dearest."

"Like you're asking?"

"He was up at the Copper Scupper, too. You could ask Dina, the hostess."

The wariness stayed in her eyes.

"Dina told me it was about a year ago."

She shrugged. "I really don't understand what you're talking about."

"About a year ago?"

She looked past me, out the window. "I told him nothing, because there's nothing to know."

The temperature at the bank was ninety-four degrees. On impulse, I swung in.

"Not one of ours," the lady at the lockbox desk said, handing me back the numbered key. "Matter of fact, that key looks too old to belong in any bank built in the last fifty years."

"Are there any other banks on Windward Island?"

She said no, and I left.

Dina was in the bar, talking to a waitress who was holding a tray of silverware wrapped in napkins. The Buffett was nowhere to be seen. He was probably warming up at home, strumming his electric thing, on his front porch swing. I sat at a high table at the back.

A few minutes later, Dina brought over two cups of coffee. "You don't look like an afternoon drinker," she said as she sat on the other stool.

"Not anymore." I set her keys on the table.

"Any luck?"

"Immaculate rooms."

"That's the way they always were. The few times I went up, I never saw any clutter. She lived like she never unpacked."

"Except for the typewriter."

"There was that. Clacking away, sometimes, until all hours of the morning. I never minded it, though."

"Her typewriter left little marks on the kitchen table."

"I hadn't noticed."

I set down the copy of the *Gulf Watcher* I'd gotten earlier. I'd folded it open to the Honestly Dearest column. "Ever read that?"

"Honestly Dearest?" She shook her head. "I've gotten enough bad advice in my life."

"Carolina Dare."

Surprise widened her eyes. She looked down at the page. "I'll be damned," she said, after looking at the paper for a long minute. "I never asked what she was typing. She was so private . . . I'll be damned."

"You know of nobody else she might have had a relationship with?"

"She didn't even have a phone, cell or otherwise. She was either in her apartment or here at the Scupper."

We sipped coffee in silence. Outside, a waitress on the deck was setting out silverware on the tables. She was a brunette, and at least ten years younger, but when she moved in the shadows next to the building, she could have been Maris.

Dina set down her coffee. "Earlier today, you asked about a family?"

I turned away from the window. "Yes."

"Do you know of a family?"

"Just her father. He died long ago."

"What were you asking, then?"

I wanted to go out on the deck and tell the waitress to make wise choices in her life. "I don't know, exactly."

Dina's eyes were steady on my face. "You were asking if she had a child."

The waitress came in from outside. Even in the dim light of the bar, she had no resemblance to Maris, none whatsoever.

"There was no child," Dina said.

I laid one of my business cards on the table next to her keys and stood up. As I went through the door, into the sunshine, the Buffett man, dressed in a ridiculous shirt with frolicking lobsters on it, passed in front of me, carrying his keyboard. I looked back at Dina. She was staring out the window at the water.

I caught the day's last plane out of St. Pete.

Florida was dead.

Twenty-seven

The sky looked like it was about to throw down serious snow when I drove over to Leo's at ten thirty the next morning. The radio weatherman, undoubtedly medicated, was chirping that it was going to be a fine day nonetheless when the quick release terminals gave way and the radio clattered to the floor of the Jeep, silencing the fool. I took that as a good omen and whistled the rest of the way.

Now, below the hem of the red terrycloth robe, behind the storm door, I could see pajama legs that had World War I biplanes on them.

"I'm here to complain that you didn't put a lock on my door." I smiled, striving for the same cheer as the medicated weatherman.

"I worked until four in the morning." Leo rubbed his eyes. "You're supposed to be in Florida."

The glass on the door was starting to cloud up from the heat inside, and the biplanes were disappearing into the mist.

"I need coffee and remembrances," I said.

He pushed the door open. "Jeez," he said, yawning.

I followed him through the living room. Several folding chairs and little tray tables holding almost empty bowls of pretzels, nuts, and bridge mix were grouped to face the big-screen television.

He turned to put his finger to his lips. "Ma's still sleeping."

"Porn again?" I mouthed, gesturing at the semicircle of chairs.

He nodded. "All the ladies have premium cable," he whispered as we passed his mother's bedroom door. "Each is supposed to take a turn hosting, but Ma's got the biggest screen, and with their eyes, at their ages . . ."

"They're all widows, right?" I asked in the kitchen.

"All except Mrs. Roshiska. Her husband's still kicking, but he's almost ninety. God help that poor bastard when she comes home after watching television here. I have nightmares of her charging him in her walker." He reached into a cabinet for a can of generic coffee and set it on the counter. "Make java," he said, heading for the hall.

I measured out four scoops of coffee, added ten cups of water, and switched on the machine.

Ten minutes later, as the coffeemaker belched a last puff, Leo reappeared, this time in jeans and a purple Sesame Street sweatshirt. Both Bert and Ernie, embroidered on the sweatshirt, were wearing tuxedos. There was a message there, but I was too tired to figure it out.

I poured coffee into two of Ma's scratched porcelain mugs, and we sat at the kitchen table, its top dulled almost opaque from Ma's relentless scrubbings with wire pads and kitchen cleanser. It had been colorless even back in the day when Leo and I had built model airplanes at that table.

"What did you find out in Florida?" Leo took a sip of the coffee and grimaced. I make weak coffee, especially for the morning, but compensate by drinking too much of it.

"Maris was a shadow down there. She lived in an attic apartment, acquired nothing but a car and a passing friendship with her boss at the restaurant where she waitressed. She moved from her apartment to the restaurant and back to her apartment."

"Completely safe. Completely anonymous."

"Somebody followed her down there, somebody who looked like Reynolds. He traced her to the restaurant where she worked. The hostess there thinks it's why she took off."

Leo pushed his one hundred and forty pounds out of his chair as if he weighed ten times that and went to the counter. He dumped the pot of coffee I'd just made into the sink.

"You're sure it was her?" he asked without turning around.

"There were marks on the kitchen table. I made a tracing, checked them against the little rubber feet on the Underwood. They match."

"Shit."

"Yes. Did you call Aggert?"

He shook out the grounds basket, put in a new filter, added many scoops, and filled the water reservoir. "He gave me his e-mail address, asked me whether I knew if you found her lockbox. I told him you'd call, and I forwarded the driver's license photo up to him."

Leo turned to look out the window, the coffee forgotten.

"OK."

"Did you call Iowa?" he asked, still looking out the window. There was nothing out there except a wall of bricks. And maybe Maris.

"Today. I'll tell Patterson I think Reynolds is one of the Kovacs brothers and that he followed Maris down to Florida. He'll send me photos of the Kovacs brothers. I'll I.D. the one posing as Reynolds."

"Progress."

"Absolutely."

He flicked on the coffeemaker and came back to sit at the table. For a few minutes he told me about the ancient urns he was authenticating for Sotheby's. Neither of us was listening, but it passed the time until the new pot of coffee was done.

"What do you remember about . . . about that August after we graduated?" I asked, after he reached for the pot and filled our cups. Even after all the years, I couldn't use the right words.

Leo took a sip, studying me over the rim of the mug. "You mean about Maris's disappearance?"

I nodded.

"Her first disappearance?" he amended.

"Her first disappearance." I didn't want to ever say she was dead, either.

"Jeez, Dek, you were there, closer to everything than me."

"Nobody talked to me. They asked questions, made accusations. Nobody talked to me."

Leo set down his mug. "There was fear, mostly: 'Killer Stalks

Rivertown.' I remember my parents talking low, hush-hush, when they thought I couldn't hear. Rivertown was rough then, sure—hookers, gambling, like now—but there were no murders. Obviously that changed when Maris's father was killed and she was thought abducted and presumed killed. Ma made me quit McDonald's the moment she heard, no notice, no nothing. She hustled me downstate to a motel near the college two whole weeks before freshman orientation."

"And forbade you to talk to me," I said.

"There was a lot of whispering, Dek. You were seen arguing with Maris the day before she vanished."

Remembering that still wanted to suck the air out of my lungs. People I didn't even know suddenly gave me a wide berth on the sidewalks. Even my two aunts wouldn't look at me directly.

"Besides," Leo went on, a sly smile lighting his face, "I called you plenty from that motel pay phone. Used up my *Playboy* money, as I remember."

"I can't believe it."

"That I used up my *Playboy* money to talk to you? Me neither." He put on a frown, still trying for light.

I looked at him across the scuffed old table. "That she never called to tell me she was all right."

"You're pissed now, along with being worried." Since we were kids, there'd been no fooling Leo about much of anything.

I shrugged, the best I could offer up.

"Maybe she really was abducted, Dek, like everybody thought. She could have been kept as a slave or something, and only broke away later. That kind of fear would make anybody want to hide for the rest of their lives."

I shook my head. "She ran scared from Rivertown, too."

"I'm not a virgin, Vlodek," Maris said.

We were sitting on the bank of the Willahock River, in front of my grandfather's turret. We went there a lot, because it was choked with weeds and thorny bushes and nobody else went there.

Although almost three months had passed, that was the first time she'd spoken of the afternoon in May. Certainly, I'd never brought it up. In the days immediately afterward, I'd come to dread the last bell of the school day. Walking home, I couldn't even reach for her hand and had begun inventing lies about having to be at the laundry an hour early. I'd been a beast.

Until after the last day of school. We were walking down Thompson Avenue when she stopped suddenly, grabbed my arm, and told me to stop being a damned fool. Most of the weights came off my chest then, and we did resume our explorations, although never again did I let myself get close to what I'd done the day of Lillian's funeral. Even now, in August, I was still ashamed of my lust that afternoon, ashamed of that boy I watched on her bed. She wasn't a virgin, and it was my fault.

"I know," I said.

She looked at me, and I saw that she was trying to smile, but it touched only her mouth. Her eyes and her forehead were frozen with something—shame, too, I thought, though it had not been her fault.

"No." She shifted closer so that her body rested against mine. "I didn't mean it that way."

I turned to look at her, surprise and relief muddling in my mind. "What, then?"

She was looking past me, through the bramble, at the Willahock. The river was running strong that afternoon, and for a minute we watched a small Styrofoam ice chest work its way west. Then she stood up and tugged at my arms. "Buy me a Coke," she said.

We followed the path along the river, past the limestone enormity of the city hall, and when the path disappeared into brush, we cut through the junkyard, the used auto lot, and behind the convenience store where the chief convenience was that it sold pocket-sized bottles of wine. We ran under the railroad overpass and down to Kutz's.

It was lunchtime, and there was a line of businessmen in suits, construction workers in dusty dungarees, and rig drivers in white

T-shirts and ball caps. I started toward the end of the line, but Maris held out her hand and led me around to the back. All of the wood-planked tables were filled by people eating, and dozens more stood around the clearing, balancing paper soft drink cups, and hamburgers and hot dogs wrapped in thin paper.

She squeezed my hand, keeping me tight beside her, until she stopped up close to the back of the clapboard-slatted trailer. For a minute, we looked at the carvings of initials inside hearts, some deep, some tentative. It was an old tradition, going back to World War II, when Kutz's old man ran the stand. My father's initials, whoever he might have been, could have been cut into that wood, maybe with my mother's, maybe with someone else's. All I knew of him was he was a Norwegian named Elstrom. When I was small, I used to sneak down to the back of Kutz's and hunt for my mother's initials, but I never found any that matched. She'd left no trace. Still, it was an old habit, and even that day, with Maris, I looked.

Maris gave my hand a hard last squeeze and let it go. She reached into her jeans and came out with a bone-handled penknife. Stepping back, with a grin as wide as Montana on her face, she studied the wall like a sculptor planning a first cut. Then, still smiling, she began to trace our initials with the point of the knife, MM+VE, in a small blank space and surrounded them with a tight heart. She worked silently, concentrating, the tip of her tongue protruding slightly past her lips, oblivious to the people at the tables and, I thought, only faintly aware of me. Over and over, she cut into the lines of our initials and their protecting heart, until it was the deepest carving on the side of the trailer. Finally, she stood back. Satisfied, she wiped the blade of her little knife clean of old white paint and specks of wood, folded it, and slipped it back into her jeans.

"There," she said. "Forever."

Neither of us came from a place that believed in forever, but that day I came as close as I thought I ever would. "It must be forever, Maris," I managed, "if it's on Kutz's trailer."

She reached up to kiss me. Somewhere behind us, at one of the tables, somebody clapped, and in a second, everybody in the clearing was applauding. We turned, and Maris, ever Maris, curtsied to the crowd.

She vanished a week later.

"The way she disappeared back then matters now because . . . ?" Leo stood and walked to the kitchen window. It had begun to snow, a light, halfhearted snow that wouldn't amount to anything.

"I don't know," I said.

"But you do know. You think what's happened now has to do with that August?"

"I don't know."

Leo turned from the window. "Tell me again that she's alive."

"She had money enough to fake her disappearance from Rambling. She could have found somebody to torch the cottage, if she didn't come back to do it, to eliminate the last traces of herself."

"You're thinking of telling the cops in Iowa her real name?"

"I can't risk that."

"She was never a suspect in her father's murder, Dek."

"Because they never found motive." I got up and put my cup in the sink.

"Then why does any of that old stuff matter now?"

I looked at his eyes, maybe the only pair of eyes that had trusted me in that long-ago August, when I said I'd had nothing to do with Maris's disappearance.

"I don't know" was all I could say.

We walked out of the kitchen, through the living room, to the front door.

"She had no motive, that August." He opened the door for me.

I drove to the Burlington station and caught the twelve twenty into Chicago.

Twenty-eight

I called Patterson when I got off the train at Union Station. "I've got a lead for you to do nothing with," I said.

"Lovely to hear from you, Mr. Elstrom."

"That blueberry cop I was working with up in Rambling?"

"Security guard for a growers' association."

"He's not."

"Not what?"

"Not a security guard."

"Who is he?"

"I think he's a Kovacs, and that he followed Carolina down to Florida. From there he, or they, tracked her to Rambling. You need to send out photos of those two brothers."

"To whom?"

"To the cops on Windward Island. Ask them to show the photos to Dina at the Copper Scupper and the woman who runs the *Gulf Watcher* newspaper." I thought for another minute, then added, "And have them send a set of photos to a Lieutenant Dillard at the sheriff's office in West Haven, Michigan. He doesn't see a crime yet, but he will if you do your job."

"And a set for you?"

"Of course. I can identify which one of them is passing as Reynolds, at least."

He said he would.

At least.

The Harold Washington Library in Chicago is modern and huge. Outside, it is home to enormous green owls at its roofline. Inside, it is home to microfilms of most Chicago newspapers, some going back to the 1850s. My shoes made loud clacking sounds as I went up the empty broad staircase to the second floor.

I started with the *Chicago Tribune*. Once I threaded the correct microfilm spool into a reader, it took only a few seconds to fast-forward to the right page. I knew the date better than my own birthday.

The headline for August 12 was in big type: MACHINIST MYSTERIOUSLY MURDERED. The one-column story underneath, slugged at the top with "Daughter, 16, Feared Abducted," began with a vivid summary of the gore: At noon on August 11, Herman Mays had been found slumped onto his kitchen table, facedown in a puddle of blood. The back of his skull was caved in. His daughter, Maris, was missing. Police feared she'd been kidnapped by the murderer or murderers.

Herman Mays had been discovered by a coworker sent around after Herman had failed to punch in. A factory representative said Mays had been a top-form die and mold maker, and his work was considered vital to fulfilling a government contract the company was under great pressure to complete. After ringing the outside bell, the coworker noticed that the sidewalk door, though closed, was unlocked. He went in and found that the upstairs apartment door was also unlocked. After knocking several times, he went in and discovered Herman facedown on the kitchen table, dead.

Because nothing in the rest of the apartment appeared to have been disturbed, Rivertown police theorized Herman Mays had not been killed as the result of a robbery and were focusing their efforts to find the missing daughter through contacts the father and daughter might have had with other people. Though newly arrived in Rivertown, Herman Mays was well known to patrons of some of the bars along Thompson Avenue. All described him as a solid, sociable working man, though still grieving the death of his wife some years earlier.

More promising, the *Tribune* reported, were witnesses who had observed Maris Mays engaged in an argument with a young man on the sidewalk outside the family's apartment, the day before the murder and her own disappearance. Police were actively seeking the young man.

At eight in the evening on August 11, I was in the alley behind the laundry, loading plastic-bagged clothes into a truck for the next morning's delivery, when two police officers drove up in an unmarked black Ford sedan.

The driver, a beefy guy in a long-sleeved white shirt and maroon tie, called to me from his open window. "Vlodek Elstrom?"

"Yes, sir?"

"Come on over here, son."

I walked over, still holding several bags by their hangers.

"Do you know Maris Mays?"

Those were the last clear words I heard. My head went into a sort of sensory delay. My breaths came loud and hollow, as if I were a deep sea diver, breathing through a regulator. My heart pulsed in my ears, in rhythm with my slow, gasping lungs.

"When did you see her last, son?" the beefy man's voice asked from far away. His face was close, less than a foot from mine. He had thin, spidery veins in his cheeks, and gray mixed in with the black of his hair. But his words were distant.

"Is she all right?" I could feel my mouth moving, but it wasn't my voice. It was slower, like a robot making mechanical words in between the loud, hollow breaths.

"When, son?" the beefy man's lips asked.

"Yesterday. She didn't answer the phone today. It was yesterday, before work."

"Got along with her all right?"

"Got?" The blood was pulsing so loud now I could barely hear myself. "You mean get. She's my girlfriend. We get along fine. Please, is Maris all right?"

"What about her father?"

"A son of a bitch. Is Maris all right?"

The cop was looking at me like he was inspecting meat. For a moment, the only sound came from my lungs, working in and out. The rest of the world had gone away.

"How much of a son of a bitch?" he asked.

"He treats Maris like crap."

"She's missing," he said.

"I just talked to her."

"When?"

"I told you: Yesterday, about four thirty. Before I came here."

I stepped back. The beefy cop's partner had gotten out of the car. He was thin and had white skin. The pulsing in my ears slowed; the hollow machine-breathing quieted.

"Please," I asked the thin cop, "what's going on?"

They told me, after they put me in that black Ford sedan and drove me to the police station and questioned me at a metal table in a back room for over twelve hours.

"What were you arguing about?" they asked, over and over.

"Nothing," I said, over and over.

"C'mon, kid." The beefy cop hitched at his pants, standing over me. "She wouldn't put out?"

I glared at him.

The beefy cop put a fake smile on his fat lips. "You got to have urges, right, Vlodek?" He drew my name out, derisively: Vah-low-dek. "Lots of girls need a little nudge."

I lied then, lied to wipe that fat smile off his fat mouth. "I told her she was crazy to want to be a writer," I said. "That's what we were arguing about yesterday. I said she ought to do something sensible with her life, like other girls: be a teacher or a nurse, normal stuff that women do." I made myself shrug, acting it out. "She got mad," I said.

Perhaps he bought it because he was a Rivertown cop and I was a Rivertown kid, and nobody in Rivertown aspired to much of anything at all. Still it was only after the medical examiner fixed Herman Mays's time of death at around ten o'clock the previous evening—a time, the laundry owner said, that was in the middle of my shift—that I was allowed to go home.

The story dropped off the front page the next day, but the *Tribune* had a paragraph on page two. "Kid's Alibi Solid," the little story was titled. "Police have cleared the young man seen talking with Maris Mays, the missing daughter of Herman Mays, who was found bludgeoned two days ago. The young man, a June graduate of Rivertown High School, was at work during the time the attack occurred, according to his employer."

The *Tribune* hadn't printed my name, or the name of the laundry where I worked. It didn't matter. By the time I'd been allowed to go home, most of the people in Rivertown knew who I was.

I walked the town every morning, searching the sidewalks and the alleys; the gangways between the houses and the roads between the factories; the way from her apartment to the flower shop where she was working; and the path along the Willahock we'd taken on the way to Kutz's, the day she'd carved our initials on his trailer. I didn't know what I was expecting; I knew she wouldn't be there.

Afternoons, I haunted the police station on my way to the laundry.

"What are you doing to find Maris?"

"The usual," the desk sergeant said.

"Which is what, exactly?" I asked, louder and louder. The days were trickling by. Nothing was happening.

"We've notified all the surrounding police departments, as well as the state police."

"What about getting off your asses and combing the town? What if she's trapped in one of the abandoned factories?"

"What if you got too smart a mouth, kid?"

"She's being held someplace."

"You know something about that?"

"She wouldn't have taken off without telling me."

"What else do you know, kid?"

Then I'd leave. Cops in Rivertown had wide latitude and narrow tolerances for teen-aged kids who weren't connected to the lizards that ran the city.

I wasn't connected to anybody anymore.

I left on Labor Day.

Four months earlier, I'd enrolled at City College. I was thinking I would go on as before, except now I'd be taking the train into Chicago for classes. I'd still live with my mother's sisters and, not coincidentally, hang around Rivertown for Maris's last year of high school.

Except now Maris was gone, and I'd become the stink in the family. My aunt Rosemary suggested, if that was the word, that my days of rotating between my mother's sisters' couches should come to an end. She blamed it on Lillian, saying that since she was no longer around to do her share, it would be unfair to expect the two surviving sisters to continue shouldering the load. I wanted to be hurt, even get angry; I wanted to believe that the issue was about my continuing to take food and space. I knew, though, there was something else: I was a suspect, no matter how tangential, in a murder and a disappearance.

I moved to the city, into a partitioned square in the basement of a student rooming house that was mine if I shoveled the snow and fed the coal-fired furnace in the winter, put up the screens and cut the grass with a rusted push mower in the summer. I grabbed at it as if it were the last life preserver tossed off the Titanic.

I went to the school library every day, to comb the newspapers for any mention of Maris. Mondays, Wednesdays, and Fridays, I called the Rivertown police. By the first of October, the desk sergeant started hanging up as soon as he recognized my voice.

Weekends, between jobs, I took the train out to Rivertown and prowled our old paths. Sometimes, if I could stand it, I'd walk to

Kutz's and go to the back of the trailer to look at the initials she'd carved there.

As November blew away the last of the leaves that had curled on the ground, I had the thought that Maris could be dead.

I never said it aloud.

And most nights, I dreamed of Maris Mays.

Twenty-nine

My cell phone began to vibrate, again, as I rewound the last of the microfilm spools. The display said it was Amanda, calling for the third time. That I'd let her calls go straight to message, unanswered, was because I was in a quiet room of the library. That I hadn't walked outside to return any of them was because I didn't know the answers to the questions she was going to ask.

I put back the spools and walked down the stairs, anxious now to get out of the library. I'd learned nothing new. The story had disappeared from the *Tribune* and the *Sun-Times* two days after Maris disappeared, dead from a lack of leads.

Outside, I walked underneath the elevated tracks, then north along Dearborn. I passed a store-wide patch that had been grassed over after a demolition the year before. Plans must have changed; nothing had been built on it. Now it was covered with filthy snow, dark from the splatters of the truck traffic and the trains that rumbled overhead.

I sat on a bench by the bus stop. The air smelled of oil and diesel exhaust, and it was cold, too cold to sit on a bench. I wanted that; I wanted to feel the cold, instead of the paralyzing, futile heat of an old August.

My cell phone rang again. This time, it was Patterson, calling from Iowa. I got up and moved away from the noise of the traffic on the street.

"I e-mailed you photos of the Kovacs brothers," he said.

"I'm not at home."

"Let me know if one of them is your security guard." He started to say good-bye.

"Wait," I said before he could hang up. I'd just spent a few hours searching for an investigation that had never taken place. Now I was seeing another one not happen, all over again. "Did you send them to Michigan and Florida as well?"

"Yes."

"Is that all you're going to do?"

"What more are you suggesting?"

"Ace police tracking," I said. "Stay on top of Michigan and Florida, make sure those photos get shown around. Find those brothers. Force them to tell you where Carolina is."

"You think she disappeared in Iowa?" he asked.

"Of course not." I took a breath. "You know what I want."

"Recognize what I can do, Mr. Elstrom: I can ask around about a couple of brothers who have absolutely no links to the bank robbery, and maybe I'll stumble across something to interest the F.B.I. But I can't commit major resources, because I have no justification. I can't pursue a disappearance in Michigan, either. If you think your Carolina was taken across state lines, give me something I can take to the F.B.I."

"Find those Kovacs brothers, you'll find her."

"Then get your ass to your computer and check out the photos. Tell me which Kovacs you saw in Michigan."

I phoned Amanda. She'd called from her office. It was only a few blocks away.

She started bright. "How's the sunshine? It's miserable here, dark and gray and very Chicago."

"I know. I'm back."

"When?"

"Last night."

"Late?"

"Too late to call." It sounded dismissive, a greasy, quick excuse. "Listen, I just got done with some stuff at the Washington Library. I thought I'd swing by your office, use your computer to check my e-mail, then take you to lunch."

"It's way too late for lunch."

"Dinner, then. I'm starved."

"It's too soon for dinner."

I looked at my watch. "It is not."

"It is, for us."

"I'll come over to the Art Institute, we'll have coffee from a machine."

"Go back to the library; use their computers to check your e-mail."

"What the hell do you want, Amanda?"

"I'll see you in the lobby of the Palmer House in a half hour," she said and hung up before either of us could do more damage.

There was a Starbucks on the way, but there's a Starbucks on the way to everyplace, except perhaps the moon. Someday, they'll move all the Starbucks inside the Wal-Marts, next to the Oreo displays, and that will mark the last time mankind will see the sun. I don't like Starbucks coffee; it's too bitter, too strong, for a dishwater man like myself. I bought a small cup anyway, because I needed a prop, something to do with my mouth when it wasn't ruining a relationship. I sipped it while I walked to the hotel.

The lobby of the Palmer House is an enormous room of cathedral ceilings, painted with scenes of bare-breasted ladies being comforted by muscular men and children playing flutes. It is a place of arched entrances, marble staircases, and second-story balconies worthy of any weeping Juliet. Its widely distanced sofas make it the kind of grand setting where a Cary Grant, impeccable in a soft gray suit and solid, unencumbered tie, would choose to meet a regal blonde in understated silk—an Eva Marie Saint or a Grace Kelly. The surrounding bustle of people going up, coming down, and traversing the ornate rugs gives almost-lovers good last cover, as they decide whether to order a drink and ponder safe, small next steps or say the hell with it, rent a room, and go up to screw their brains out.

The Palmer House lobby is also a place for soon-to-be ex-lovers to meet, because that same surrounding bustle demands civility and restrained, last good-byes.

Amanda sat at the end of one of the large sofas in the middle of the great room. I sat at the other end, turned to rest one arm along the back of the sofa, and tried to grin like a man not haunted.

"You look awful," she said. "And you hate Starbucks."

I set the vile brew on the low table in front of us and told her of Leo's examination of the typewriter, told her the woman who'd named me her executor had been a girl we'd once known.

"You *and* Leo?" she interrupted.

"More me."

" 'Known?' "

"We dated my last semester of high school and into the summer." I reached for the Starbucks, saw that my hand was trembling slightly. I left the prop where it was. "Until she disappeared," I finished.

"You never mentioned any of this when we were married."

"I always thought I would."

"Someday?"

"Someday."

"Why do you have to be the one carrying this now?" It was a reasonable question, but not what she was really asking.

"No one else will."

Her eyes narrowed, seeing half-truths.

"No one else must," I said, finally.

"You really think she's still alive?"

"If so, she's safe someplace with a pot full of money."

"If not?"

"If not, she died several weeks ago, tortured by someone who wanted that money."

"She's an old love," Amanda said.

"We were kids; we went out for a few months. Her father was murdered and she disappeared." I paused. "I have felt responsible."

"How?"

"It took me a long time, years, to accept the possibility that she was dead, though that was what everyone was saying. She never called, and gradually . . . I always figured, if she was all right, she would have found a way to contact me, to let me know . . ."

"Maybe she's a bitch."

The urge to get up, walk away, came burning. Just as quickly, it passed. Amanda was right. And she loved me.

"I have to see this through," I said.

"Because that's what you do: see things through?"

"Not always, Amanda, but this time."

She stood and reached down to touch the side of my face lightly. Then she was gone.

I joined the throng of purposeful people, sure of their next steps, hurrying to Union Station. The five fifty-three, west to Rivertown and better places, was a slow train that stopped at every crossing. That was fine. It was late enough to get a window seat, and for a time I let myself shut down a little, watching the passing stores and flashing lights, listening to the other riders talking on their cell phones about meetings and class schedules and things that were sure to make them rich.

At Rivertown, instead of crossing Thompson Avenue to head to the turret, I turned the other way. The sun was long gone, but the sidewalk was bright with neon and smiling ladies. Rivertown was shrugging itself to life.

I stopped on a very particular square of cement, three blocks down. Just ahead, multicolored lights pulsed from the street-level windows, in time with high-tech pong, ding, and zoom sounds from digitized machines. The pinball parlor had evolved with the times. It was now a video arcade and, according to rumor, a drug depot for high schoolers.

I'd come to that building every day, right after Maris vanished. I'd stood at the exact square on the sidewalk, in front of her door, where we'd argued that last time. Crazily, I'd tried to believe that I could change time, summon her back if I just stood there long enough, willed her back hard enough. Then that horrible August ended. I went to school in Chicago, and sometime after that, I gave up coming back to Rivertown altogether. When I did return, years later, I looked the other way each time I passed by her old door.

I stepped to the curb, looked up at the apartment on the second floor. A light burned in the bedroom that had been Maris's. The window was covered by soft white curtains, as when Maris slept there. I stared up for a minute or two, half expecting to see a female shadow cross behind the curtain.

I walked on and turned off Thompson Avenue. Leo's mother's bungalow was in the middle of a block of identical bungalows. Ma Brumsky's windows flickered the most brightly, from the biggest television screen on the block. Even from several houses away, so many primary colors were bombarding the pulled-down shades, and with such ferocity, that a stranger to the block could easily have assumed that fireworks were being set off in the parlor. Which, in a sense, was true enough.

I went into the narrow gangway next to his house. A light shone up from Leo's office. I tapped on the window. He pulled open the curtain, grinned, and pointed to the back. I walked around and waited until he opened the porch door.

"I've got to come around back, like the service class?" I asked as I stepped in. His screened back porch was piled high with two-liter bottles of Diet Pepsi, for the effervescence; bags of potato chips, for the salt; and cans of fruit juice, for the regularity. Wintertime, those babushkas still left in Rivertown used their back porches as walk-through refrigerators.

"Ma's lady friends are due here any minute. They'd get embarrassed if we were upstairs, to see them come in."

"Always a risk when you're running a porn theater for septuagenarians."

I followed him down the basement stairs, then sat in his desk chair and switched his computer on to the Internet.

"Iowa?" Leo asked.

I nodded as I opened the e-mail Sergeant Patterson had sent.

"Nice to know people are recycling motor oil," Leo said, looking over my shoulder.

It was true. The police photos of the Kovacs brothers showed shiny, slicked-back hair, acne scars, and the sullen, face-on expressions of the newly arrested.

"No bingo," I typed in a reply to Patterson's e-mail: "Neither one is John Reynolds."

"Shit," said Leo.

"Exactly. It means we've got a third man in the equation, somebody else who wanted to hunt Maris."

I stood up and moved to the overstuffed chair as Leo extracted a bottle of Jack Daniel's and a tube of plastic cups from a desk drawer. "Snort?"

"I told Amanda about Maris," I said.

"Definitely calls for a snort." He poured two inches of Jack into each of the cups, set one down at the edge of the desk for me, and dropped into his desk chair.

He took a sip and asked, "How much did you tell?"

"Most of what I understand."

He raised his glass in a kind of toast. "Which isn't very much, then or now. Besides, you were kids."

"I'm not a kid now," I said.

He leaned forward, to speak carefully. "If she's alive, she's running with plenty of money, and she's safe. If not, it doesn't matter anymore."

"It matters, Leo; either way, it matters."

He looked away, realizing he'd stumbled with the words.

Upstairs, the front doorbell rang, and for a time we sipped Mr. Jack's golden elixir and tried to grin, listening as Ma's lady friends shuffled in, chattering excitedly in Polish. I finished the Jack and got up, and he walked me up the basement stairs.

He paused at the back door. "You told Amanda all of it?"

I knew what he was asking. He was the only person in the world, save Maris, who suspected how much there could be, but in all the years since that August, he'd never asked.

"I've never told anybody all of it," I said. "Not even myself."

Thirty

The answering machine light was blinking when I walked into my office late the next morning. For a second, I let myself hope it was Amanda, but then realized she would have dialed my cell phone. Aggert, I guessed then, calling to chastise me for not reporting in. I was wrong again. It had been Lieutenant Dillard, calling from Michigan. I called him back.

"There was a fire at the house of that woman you were looking for," he said. "The fire department in Bangor forwarded me a report."

"Days ago," I said. "You people move fast."

"Faster now, Elstrom. How soon can you get up here?"

"You have new information?"

"We found a body underneath the car in the garage."

It took a few seconds to get the word out: "Female?"

"We don't know yet."

"Don't play with me."

"Come on up and find out, Elstrom."

The county sheriff's department was just north of West Haven, in a tan brick building with windows that needed paint. It looked like a place where people went to hear bad news.

Dillard was a big cop, my age, but a couple of inches taller and packing fifty more pounds. With his brush-cut hair and clear eyes, he could have been a drill sergeant in a recruiting poster, except for what he was holding in his big, meaty hand. It was a porcelain teacup, dainty and painted with little dark grapes, and it was steaming up something fruity. He led me down a cinder-block hall to a windowless office in back. More of the sickly sweet smell wafted from an electric teapot set on the low filing cabinet behind the metal desk. We sat, and when I said no to coffee, he asked if I'd like a soft drink. I said no to that, too.

"Well, then, how about some blueberry tea?" he asked, raising his cup. I'd been wrong; the dark circles painted on the cup weren't grapes, they were blueberries.

Sweet Jesus O'Keefe.

"Was it a woman's body?" I asked.

He sipped from the dainty cup. "Still don't know."

"How much damned time do you need?" I asked, this time loud enough to be heard in the hall.

"The coroner is backed up; two kids in a motorcycle crash. Tell me everything you know about that woman on 12."

I hurried through the Louise and Carolina version of the story, beginning with Aggert, ending with my trip to Windward Island.

"You're thinking Carolina Dare might not be her real name, either?" he asked when I was done.

"I don't know. The body was under the car?" I still couldn't believe I hadn't seen it.

He studied me for a long, maddening minute, then nodded. "Jammed right under."

I wanted to grab his teacup, smash it on the tile floor. "When will you know if it was a woman's?"

"Got some photos from a Sergeant Patterson in Cedar Ridge, Iowa. A couple of brothers named Kovacs."

"I already e-mailed Patterson that neither was passing himself off as the John Reynolds I met up here."

"We'll tack them up on the board anyway. Maybe somebody will remember seeing them."

"How about calling the coroner, find out if it was a woman under that house?"

He paused at the door before going out. "You should try the blueberry tea. It soothes the nerves."

Measured by the number of times the ants crawling in my gut multiplied, Dillard was gone a long time. According to my watch, though, he was gone only twenty minutes before he came back, carrying a green file folder and a cup of coffee, black, for me.

"The coroner said it was a man's body."

Some of the air came back into the room. It was too warm and stale with my sweat, and it disappeared too quickly into the sticky smell of the tea, but it was easier breathing. I drank the coffee while he opened the folder. He took out computer-printed photographs of two men and slid them across the table.

"The Kovacs brothers," I said. "I told you, neither was the one posing as John Reynolds."

"Your Cedar Ridge friend, Sergeant Patterson, said these ne'er-do-wells, Eddie and Lance, never went beyond petty crime. The only thing that ties them to the bank is timing; they disappeared at the same time an Officer Severs—your suspect for killing his daughter—was found dead in his police unit."

"Severs is not just a guess. The letters to Carolina Dare point to him."

"Patterson faxed me the letters, too," Dillard said, nodding agreement. "We best be sure before we start pointing fingers at a cop."

"A dead cop," I said, "and likely a dead, dirty cop." I pushed the photos on the table back toward him. "You could show these to the Woodton postmaster. Perhaps it was one of the Kovacs brothers who tried to get at Carolina's mail."

"And who was then found as toast underneath a car on County Road 12?"

"It could have been a Kovacs," I agreed.

"So who killed him?"

"Same person who then torched the place: John Reynolds."

"Close." Dillard smiled. "My first guess is that Reynolds is a private investigator who got wind of the money trail. That doesn't make him a killer. My second guess is he was one of the bank robbers. That does. Either way, I don't see Reynolds as the primary suspect for the corpse under the car."

I sipped coffee.

"Patterson is transmitting the Kovacs dental records right now. We'll know soon enough." He set down his dainty cup. "What aren't you saying?"

Even with the door open, the air in Dillard's office was still too tight. I shrugged.

"You aren't saying, Elstrom, who is the likeliest suspect for the murder of the man under the car."

I supposed he was looking for a couple of names. Maris's, for sure. Probably my own. I stood up.

"I'll be across the street from the Wal-Mart," I said.

Thirty-one

I'd already had my Wal-Doughnut and coffee when Dillard called at nine the next morning. Since there was nobody on the streets in West Haven, I got to the sheriff's building in ten minutes.

Dillard's office was almost misting with the smell of newly brewed blueberries. He'd set up a telephone on the middle of his desk, for a speaker call. After a sip of tea, he punched in a number, and a phone rang through the speaker.

"Lieutenant Dillard, Mr. Elstrom," Patterson greeted, from the other side of the Mississippi River.

"It's John Doe's teeth inside the charred skull lying on our medical examiner's table," Dillard said to the phone.

"Damn." Patterson said it with no conviction, and no surprise. I realized that he and Dillard had already talked and were making a show of going through things again so Dillard could watch my reactions and describe them later to Patterson.

"What was the cause of death?" I asked Dillard.

"Did you hear that, Sergeant?" Dillard asked the phone. "Elstrom here asked what was the cause of death."

"Good point for me?" I said, extra loud, for the phone. "Because not asking would imply I already knew?"

"Now, now, Mr. Elstrom," Patterson's voice said.

"You must admit, you didn't think to ask about cause yesterday." Dillard smiled across the table.

"I'm asking now: What is the cause of death?"

"Gunshots to the skull, exacerbated by fire."

"Popular cause of death, isn't it?" I asked the phone. "Gunshots followed by torching?"

The phone in the center of the desk was silent.

"Like what happened to your Officer Severs?" I went on.

Patterson cleared his throat. "Officer Severs was badly burned."

"Bad enough to require dental verification?"

"He was very badly burned, Mr. Elstrom," Patterson said.

"You hear back from the Windward Island police about those Kovacs photos? Did either the hostess at the Scupper or the woman at the *Gulf Watcher* identify either brother as the man who came around asking about Carolina Dare?"

From the phone came the sound of a chair scraping on a floor. There was no answer.

"Tell us, Sergeant Patterson, do you think Lieutenant Dillard here ought to take the Kovacs photos to Woodton, show them to the postmaster to see if it was one of the brothers who tried to get at Carolina's mail?"

"Why not?" Patterson asked.

"For openers, because you're finally getting around to thinking it might be somebody else."

"Come on, Elstrom," Patterson said.

"What bothers you the most about Officer Severs's death, Sergeant?"

"I suppose the fact that there was no motive for anyone—"

I cut him off. "Tell us again: How badly burned was Officer Severs's body?"

Dillard sipped tea, but his eyes, too, were on the phone at the center of the desk.

"Sergeant Patterson?" I asked.

"Very badly burned." Patterson's voice was faint.

The silence that followed got to Dillard after a minute. He turned to me. "What's going on here?"

I shrugged.

"Elstrom's shrugging," Dillard said to the phone.

"Sergeant Patterson knows he has to look beyond the Kovacs brothers," I said.

Dillard leaned toward the phone, as if it were hard of hearing. "Elstrom says you're going—"

"Damn it, Lieutenant," Patterson's voice cut in, stopping the parody.

"What game are you two playing?" Dillard snapped, glaring at me. "Neither of you is asking about Carolina Dare. She lived in that cottage. She could have killed the man, then torched the house to destroy the evidence."

"If so, she did it in self-defense," I said.

"I thought you didn't know her," Dillard said.

"I don't."

"What's her real name, Mr. Elstrom?" Patterson's voice was strong now.

"Carolina or Louise; Louise or Carolina," I said.

"Elstrom isn't smiling, but he wants to, serving up that bullshit," Dillard reported to the phone.

Patterson spoke, "Elstrom, you need to tell us—"

"Who's serving it up, Sergeant?" I said to the phone. "You're the one who's not being straight. You don't like a damned thing about the way Severs died."

Dillard's fist slammed down on the table, jarring the telephone. "You're protecting a woman who you think has skedaddled with over a million bucks, a woman who might share all that with you, once this charade is over."

I met his eyes. "Carolina or Louise, I don't know her."

"Like hell. You know she's a killer, Elstrom."

"You've got better suspects, Lieutenant."

Dillard leaned closer. "She killed before, Elstrom."

"I don't know—"

"One August, many years ago."

I stared at the teapot on the file cabinet and tried not to blink.

Dillard spoke softly. "A couple of old-time Rivertown cops remember you real well, back when you fought with a girl who disappeared right after her father was murdered."

"That has no bearing on what's going on here," I said.

"He's not grinning, Sergeant," Dillard said to the phone. Then he turned to look through my eyes, right into the center of my head.

"Maris Mays," he said.

Thirty-two

"No motive, no weapon," I said, for the fifth time.

The expression on Dillard's face didn't change. "A few years after Maris Mays disappears from Rivertown, a woman named Carolina Dare comes forth, full grown and apparently bereft of any childhood, including a record of her birth. Maris Mays is Carolina Dare is Louise Thomas."

"Find her. Ask her."

"She changed her identity because she killed her father," Dillard said again. He'd been saying it over and over for the last ten minutes. Throughout, Patterson had been so silent I wondered if he was even still on the phone.

"No motive," I said of that long-ago August. "And no weapon."

Dillard scowled. "You never wondered why the papers dropped the story of your girlfriend's disappearance so soon? Your Rivertown cops tipped them that young Maris might have caved in her old man's head. Back in those days, papers were real careful about printing stuff like that."

"Nobody found a motive, nor a weapon."

"Herman Mays was a whining, self-pitying, whoring son of a bitch, but there's plenty of men like that. The problem was, no one knew the family, father and daughter, well enough to say they weren't enjoying a cordial relationship." Dillard paused, then said, "Except you."

"Maris and I didn't talk about her father."

"Sure you didn't."

"What's your point?" I had a headache now, a real pounder from the blueberry fumes—and Dillard's mouth.

"Maris Mays killed before now," Dillard said.

"No motive, no—"

"She could have killed again."

"Like riding a bicycle, is it, Dillard? Kill once, it's easy to kill again?" I stood up, to see if he'd move to stop me. It would make sense for him to dummy up something to hold me as a material witness.

"We need to talk to her," he said from his chair.

I moved for the door. "She didn't have to kill to run with that bank money. We've come full circle."

"Lieutenant Dillard is right. We need to talk about Maris Mays," Patterson said, speaking at last. He must have heard my voice move away from the phone.

"You need to identify your burned men," I said, not turning around.

"You mean man," Dillard said. "There's only one."

"There are two. Patterson will explain."

I turned the knob on the door and walked out.

At three fifty-five in the afternoon of Thursday, August 10, I stopped to wait outside the florist's where Maris worked, like I'd done every working day that summer. She got off work at four, and if we walked quickly, we could have thirty-eight minutes alone in her apartment before I had to run for the evening shift at the laundry.

That day, four o'clock came and went. At four fifteen, I went inside.

The lady who owned the shop smiled as she shut the glass door on a refrigerated cabinet filled with pink and yellow flowers. "Maris is off sick today, Dek. She called this morning to say she wasn't feeling well."

I walked over to Thompson Avenue. At her street door, I was agonizing over whether to push the bell button or just try to call up through her open bedroom window, to see if she was all right, when I spotted her coming down the sidewalk from the other direction.

She stopped, still fifty feet away, when she saw me. Her face was strange, frozen looking. For a moment. I had the prickling sensation that she didn't know me, that she thought I was some nobody she'd caught staring at her. Then she smiled, a faint, worked-up smile, and hurried toward me.

"Dek." She reached to hug me. "Dek," she said again, into the fabric of my shirt.

She started sobbing.

I knew better than to leave town. My little showboat stunt of walking out on Dillard had bought me a little time, nothing more. That's what I needed, though—just a little time, to put some space between their questions and what I knew about Maris.

I drove to the motel, shut off the engine, and sat for a few minutes in the Jeep, watching the traffic roll by, up on the interstate. Being too cautious with Dillard and Patterson could cloud up everything around Maris and might start a manhunt for her. Being too straight about that August, when we were kids, could do the same thing. Either way could harm her.

More minutes passed. Nothing came clearer. All I could think to do was walk across the highway to the Wal-Mart.

I looked at knit shirts and electric razors, spray guns and screwdrivers and bug sprays. I studied labels for contents and uses, concentrating on anything but memories. After an hour, I was no smarter than I'd been when I entered the store, but I was considerably calmer. I bought Oreos and started back across the highway to the motel.

A blue SUV with a gold shield on its door was in the parking lot. Its engine was running.

"Care to go for a ride?" Dillard asked out the open window, as if he were giving me a choice.

"That would be peachy," I said, getting in. I offered him an Oreo, but he shook his head, probably rightfully; the chocolate and double cream filling would not marry well with the residue of blueberry that was sure to be sticking to everything inside his mouth.

He surprised me. Instead of heading north to the sheriff's department for more questions, he turned right, drove west, and then turned south.

"Did you have fun shopping at Wal-Mart?" he asked, after a couple of miles.

"Regrettably, they have everything I need," I said, clutching my Oreos and looking out the window at the white fields.

He nodded at the finality of that, and for another fifteen minutes, we said nothing. Then I began to recognize some landmarks I'd seen earlier.

"Woodton?" I asked.

"We're going to show the postmaster some pictures," he said, then said nothing more for the rest of the drive.

A clerk led us through the sorting room to a small office in back. The postmaster gave me the barest of nods, no doubt still weak from toting that tub of Carolina's mail, but he did reach up to shake Dillard's hand. Dillard and I sat down, across the nicked government-gray metal desk.

"We're seeking the identity of a body we found," Dillard said. "We think he tried to get at Carolina Dare's mail." He opened the envelope he'd brought, pulled out two pictures, and set them in front of the postmaster.

"Not him," the postmaster said, of Eddie Kovacs. "Not him, either," he said of the brother, Lance. He handed the pictures back across the desk.

Dillard pulled out another picture. The postmaster took it, held it up with its white back facing me, and stared at it for a long minute, frowning. At last he nodded. "That's your man," he said.

"He didn't give you a name?" Dillard asked.

The postmaster shook his head.

"It would have been an alias," Dillard said, taking the picture and sliding it back into his envelope. "No matter. We've identified him from dental records."

"Dead, you say?" the postmaster asked.

"Shot and burned," Dillard said.

I started to reach for the envelope in Dillard's hand. He shifted in his chair, moving it away from my reach.

Dillard tapped the envelope. "This man was in here in January, trying to get Carolina Dare's mail?"

The postmaster wiped a weary hand across his brow. "He was so insistent. I kept telling him he had to produce authorization. He kept saying, over and over, he was authorized, like that was enough." A small smile played at the edges of the postmaster's lips. Justice had been served. The man who'd tried to subvert the U.S. Postal Service was dead. Shot and burned.

We all stood up. Dillard and the postmaster shook hands again, and we left. In the car, Dillard put the envelope between us on the front seat and started the engine. As he pulled onto the street, I picked up the envelope and slid out the pictures. The familiar face was on top.

"Just like you figured," he said.

"John Reynolds," I said, but he knew that I knew better.

"Officer Randall Severs," Dillard said, "late of the Cedar Ridge, Iowa, police department."

Thirty-three

“Your dental records confirmed it: Our burned body is your Officer Severs,” Dillard said to the speakerphone on his desk. He spoke conversationally, with no hint of accusation in his voice.

“No doubt?” Patterson asked.

“The Woodton postmaster also verified it was Severs who was trying to get at Carolina Dare’s mail. Of course, our friend Elstrom here, identified Severs as well.”

“I appreciate your getting on it so quickly.” Patterson’s voice came through the phone flat, as if he were grateful that he had the Mississippi River to hide behind.

“Did you suspect right away, Patterson?” I said.

“I was troubled when we found the body in the police car. Severs was a careful man. But no, I didn’t begin to suspect anything until you brought me those letters. They linked Severs to the robbery, gave him reason to fake his own death and disappear, to hunt down the money.”

“How do we find out if it was one of the Kovacs brothers burned in that police car?” I asked the phone.

Dillard cut in before Patterson could fumble up an excuse. “It was that badly burned?” Cop to cop, Dillard was tossing Patterson a lifeline, an out for why the Cedar Ridge medical examiner blew the identification.

"Crispy critter," Patterson said.

"You won't exhume for identification?" I asked.

"Not possible, Mr. Elstrom," Patterson said. "Severs's closest kin, a cousin, authorized his cremation."

"So we will never know who was burned in that police car," I said to Dillard and the phone.

"Until we find the surviving brother," Dillard said.

"Lieutenant, did you recover any bullets from Severs's body?" Patterson asked.

"None yet, but we're still sifting dirt. The coroner thinks they came from a twenty-two."

"Not a thirty-eight?"

"Could be. With our coroner, often it's guesswork," Dillard said.

"There's going to be all kinds of hell to pay for this one," Patterson said. "I'll be in touch."

"Wait," I said, but Patterson clicked off.

Dillard replaced the handset on the phone. "How about some blueberry tea?" he asked.

I stared at him. "I can't stand the smell of it, can't stand the thought of it, can't understand why the hell anyone would drink it."

"It helps you think."

He swiveled around and filled his own cup, and another that had daisies on it, from the teapot behind him. Immediately, the stink of blueberries in the room intensified tenfold. He smiled as he reached across the desk to set down the daisy cup in front of me. "I always keep it warm."

"You hope that the tea will keep everybody here too stupored to rush out and catch criminals?"

The smile stayed on his face. "Nobody can stand the tea except me. But there's no doubting: It helps you think." He raised his cup and made a show of enjoying the aroma. "Take a taste, and tell me."

"Tell you what?"

"Take a taste, and tell me about the tea and where this case is."

The tea tasted like a funeral home smelled.

"It tastes like a funeral home smells," I said.

"All right, then just tell me about the case."

"The Kovacs brothers were the guys who entered the bank. Severs was either in on it from the beginning, or he found out that the Kovacs brothers were involved afterward, during the investigation. Either way, Severs was a partner, and the one who held the money. No one would think to suspect him."

Dillard nodded approvingly, as though it were the one sip of tea I'd taken that was firing my brain accurately.

"Then everybody sat back, to let the case cool," he said.

"Except Severs's stepdaughter discovered the money, sent it to Honestly Dearest. That got young Lucia killed."

"By Severs?"

"Him, or one of the Kovacs brothers," I said. "Lucia was a threat to them all."

"But now someone else knew: your girlfriend."

I looked at the teapot, let it go by.

Dillard set down his cup. "She got the money, Elstrom. She was involved."

When I still didn't respond, he went on. "Severs killed a Kovacs brother, faking his own death, and took off to find her."

"As the surviving Kovacs brother took off to find Severs," I said.

"But only Severs found his way to Rambling." He leaned back in his chair, as affable as a cracker rocking on a country store porch.

I knew where he was going. "No," I said anyway. "The Kovacs brother also found his way here. He's the only one left. He killed Severs."

"Maris Mays," he said, "your girlfriend."

"She'd left Rambling by the time he got here."

"Likely enough," he agreed. "Who's that leave, Elstrom?"

"I told you. The surviving Kovacs brother."

"I had a couple of men show Patterson's pictures around. Lots of people remember Severs, but nobody at a store, at a gas station, recollects seeing one of the Kovacs brothers."

He turned around then and busied himself with pouring more tea.

I waited him out.

He swiveled back and for a minute made a savoring face as he sipped his tea. "So who's left, Elstrom?"

I shook my head.

"Maris Mays had been running from cops her whole adult life," he went on. "Suddenly, a ton of money gets dropped in her lap, only now she's being hunted for that as well. By another cop, of all people. Now, I'm not saying she wasn't justified in wanting him dead. Hell, he'd killed his wife and his stepdaughter, then tracked your Maris down to Florida, and up here to Rambling. No doubt, he would kill her for that money."

"You think she faked her own disappearance, dribbled a little blood around the cottage, hid out for a few weeks, then came back to kill Severs? Have more tea, Dillard, or give it up altogether."

He smiled. "No, that's not what I think."

"A Kovacs brother killed Severs," I said.

"That's not what I think, either." His eyes were steady. "Your Maris had the money; she could run. But she'd always be looking over her shoulder for Severs. So she turned to the one person she could trust. You."

"You're wrong," I said, but the way my voice quivered, it sounded like a lie.

"Have her come in and the two of you can explain."

"I don't know where she is."

"You didn't help her before, either."

"Before?"

"That August, when you were kids. You didn't help her by keeping quiet about her secret. You could have spared her a life of running, given her a chance to rebuild her life, by tipping the police in Rivertown."

"Tipping them to what?"

"To what made her kill her father."

"No motive—"

"Yeah, and no murder weapon, either. I've been hearing you, Elstrom. You're not helping her now, like you didn't help her then."

"I'm free to go?"

"For now. I'll drive you back to your motel."

We stood up, but Dillard's door opened before I could reach for the knob. A young sheriff's deputy, not much older than I was when I knew Maris, stuck his head in.

"We've been digging up the dirt floor in the garage like you wanted, looking for bullets," the young cop said to Dillard.

Dillard had come up to stand next to me. "Yes?"

"They found another body."

Thirty-four

The young officer's words echoed off the hard walls like a palm slapping smooth skin. "She was buried in the dirt floor of the garage . . . wrapped in plastic . . . melted against her skin . . . estimating she's been dead longer, maybe a month more than the man."

"The woman who lived in the cottage?" Dillard's voice boomed, like a cannon.

"No reports of any other women missing," the young cop said.

Dillard's head turned, I think, to look at me. I was looking at nothing, a foot to the right of the young officer leaning against the doorjamb.

Dillard turned back to the young cop. "Any hope for a positive I.D.?"

"There's quite a bit of destruction from the fire, but the coroner says the dentals are usable, if we can get comparison records."

I made myself look at the young cop. "Does she have a slightly crooked eyetooth?"

"What?"

"A crooked eyetooth, left side?" My voice sounded so calm that I had the ludicrous suspicion that somebody else was manipulating my mouth, to make the words come out right.

The young cop moved to Dillard's desk, picked up the phone, and murmured something into it.

After a minute, he set down the receiver and turned to me. "Left front."

I asked if I could go then.

"No need for you to go to Rambling," Lieutenant Dillard said.

"No, I couldn't do that," my damned calm voice said.

"Absolutely nothing to look at out there," the young officer with life ahead of him added, lounging against Dillard's desk like nothing in the world was wrong.

I wanted to knock him down, shock that stupid, lazy look off his face, but I wouldn't have the strength.

"I'm done here," I said.

"You're sure about that crooked eyetooth?" Dillard asked.

"Maris Mays," I said.

I have no memory of being driven back to the motel, nor of walking up the outside stairs to my room to pack my few things in my duffel. I can only assume that I signed my credit card slip in a normal enough fashion. Perhaps, if asked, I might even have said that everything about my stay had been fine, thank you very much. I don't remember.

I do remember the snow. The sky, which had been gray all day, had given up and gone black by the time I crossed from Michigan into Indiana and began hurling down great, jagged flakes that rained into the beams of my headlights like ragged white shingles. I was grateful for that, grateful for the cover of the snow and the crawling speed that asked nothing of me except to follow the red taillights of the truck ahead. I shifted from second gear to third gear to second again, easy on the accelerator, easy on the clutch, thinking only with my ears, to keep the whine of the engine steady above the rhythmic pit-pat of my windshield wipers. Mile after mile, the snow blurred away the other cars and trucks, the exits and the trees and the lives that were still going on around me. Except for the red lights ahead, I was alone on that interstate expressway.

Several times my cell phone chirped, but there was nobody in the world who could tell me anything I wanted to hear, so I let it ring, until finally, somewhere around La Porte, perhaps, I thought to shut it off.

I got back to Rivertown sometime very late. Ten or twelve inches of snow had already fallen, and it was still coming down. Locking the Jeep, I looked up at the turret. It looked foreign, a dark oddity against the snow-blurred moon. It was not my place, not in the middle of that night. My place was somewhere else, in a spring and in a summer, long ago.

I started across the vacant spit of land. Snow jammed up, frigid and wet, between my skin and the legs of my jeans. It didn't matter.

No john-cars prowled Thompson Avenue. The tonks were dark, their neon signs cold. The good-time district had been hushed, made virginal, by the thick covering of snow. I cut onto a side street. I could only start there.

I walked slowly along the sidewalk, my footfalls dropping silent in the thick new snow. By now, my Nikes were soaked. It was proper. Boots would have been wrong for the walk I was taking. That day in August had been hot.

The wood-sided three-flat where my aunt had lived, where I'd been staying that August, was gone. It had been knocked down sometime in the years I'd been away, its lot graveled over for parking, pending development, I supposed, by some fool of an optimistic owner. So far, development hadn't come.

The florist's shop had been five blocks over. I used to hurry those blocks, that summer. Now there was no need.

The florist was gone. A cut-rate liquor store had taken over. I strained to see through the pull-down steel fence, through the windows, to where the counter and the refrigerated cabinets had been. It was too dark. The door was a putrid yellowish green in the light of the halogen security bulb. It had been pink that August, that last time I'd pushed it open, wondering why Maris was so late getting off work.

I left, followed our way from the florist's, turned onto Thompson, toward her apartment. My mind clicked off the fronts as they used to be: a shoe store, the Montgomery Ward catalog outlet, the Salvation Army resale store. The tonks, of course, dozens of them, then like now. Up ahead, the white ten pin light of the bowling alley flickered and went dark.

I stopped in front of her door, on that same piece of sidewalk I'd haunted as a boy. Next to me, the video arcade was dark, emptied for another night of its dealers and delinquents. With a hand shielding my eyes from the falling snow, I squinted down Thompson Avenue, trying to fix the place where she'd stopped, startled, before she'd put on a smile and hurried toward me.

Everything was blurry. I wiped at my wet eyes with the sleeve of my coat. It could have been the snow, running down my face.

"You're sure?"

She answered into my chest, something about a doctor and the middle of a second trimester. I said I didn't understand the words. She pushed away from my shirt, wet now from her sudden tears and my sweat in the August heat.

"I suppose we could get married," I said, instantly ashamed at the tentativeness of my words.

She wiped at her eyes and then cupped wet hands to the sides of my face. She smiled. But it wasn't Maris's smile; it belonged to an older woman, someone wiser than me, somebody I took to be condescending. "Dek, you're so stupid, so naive," she said, as though, I thought, to a child.

"I'll get a job, we'll get a place."

"I love you, Dek," she said—and laughed. Her face was wet, her nose was running, but she laughed. At my stupidity, I thought.

"Why are you laughing?" I screamed, furious at her mocking. "I can take care of you."

A couple, walking by, moved closer to the curb.

Maris looked at me, her reddened eyes wide at my sudden rage. And then she tugged at her door, ran inside, and slammed it behind her.

I never saw her again.

Thirty-five

For a day and a half, I moved slowly through the turret, numbed by images of Maris flashing nonstop, like an old newsreel, against the back of my brain. Over and over, I saw Leo and me walk her home, those first days of that distant January. I saw how, after hardly any time at all, Maris and I found excuses to hang back, too awkward to name why we wanted—no, needed—to be alone. Again and again, I saw Maris hurry to step in front of me, to stop me with a smile, and ask me to a dance. A hundred times I heard her laugh at the thrift store as she held up my floral necktie. And a hundred times I chafed anew in my itchy wool suit as we walked to the school. Over and over, I found the new softness of her lips in the dim light of a straw-shaded lamp in a two-flat basement and felt the urgency of all the afternoons that followed as we raced to her apartment.

The day of Lillian's funeral came again, lush and heavy with spring. Again I breathed in the mingling of newly cut grass and funeral wreaths, life and death, and later, the lighter scents of roses and Ivory soap on Maris's skin as we moved on her bed and her face changed from tears to a strange sort of acceptance to something I could not understand at all.

Once more I felt my lungs fill with relief as I watched Maris, stern-faced in concentration, cutting our initials onto Kutz's trailer, surrounding them with a heart and abating my guilt.

I again felt the heat of August and the wetness of her tears through my shirt before she ran, forever, from the stupid boy that I was.

I saw those things, and little else, as I moved through the turret. Gray daylight darkened into nightfall and lightened once again into gray, but I was barely aware. Time was passing as bundles of memories, separated only by such ragged little bits of oblivion as I could snatch, sleeping in the chair, on the bed, or on the floor. Always, though, the reality of the present jerked me awake, after but a few minutes, with the same oxygen-robbing sense of loss. There would be no more days and weeks and months and years of pretending that Maris was alive somewhere, and happy. Maris was dead.

I was aware, from time to time, of my cell phone ringing. Leo told me later that Amanda finally gave up calling and rousted him out of a meeting downtown at Sotheby's. He picked her up at the Art Institute, and together they drove out to the turret. He said they banged on the door for twenty minutes before I came down, and then only to open the door an inch.

"She's dead," Leo said I said, through the crack in the door before I slammed it shut.

"This is about old love?" Leo said Amanda asked, when they got back to the Art Institute. It was the first time she'd spoken since they left Rivertown.

"No," he'd said to Amanda. "This is about old guilt."

At six o'clock the next evening, I came out of it enough to fumble for my cell phone and listen to my messages. There were twelve: seven from Amanda, four from Leo, and one from Dina, the hostess at the Scupper on Windward Island. There were none from cops.

I grabbed clean clothes and my gym bag and went out to the Jeep. An ancient orange Ford Maverick with a bad muffler and a broken headlight followed me too closely to the health center, but it hung back in the darkness as I parked in my usual spot, next to the doorless Buick.

Farther back in the lot, the thumpers—petty criminals in training—were in their last hour of lounging by their cars. By eight, they had to turn the parking lot over to the drug dealers so that serious crime could commence. I made a show of leaving the door of the Jeep ajar so that even the dumbest of the thumpers wouldn't be tempted to cut the tape, or worse, the little remaining plastic on the side curtains. I even set the Discount Den radio up high and loose on the dash. There was no need for any of them to crack an unhealthy sweat looking for it in the cold air.

I ran four pounding miles, punishing my lungs and my legs and cultivating rage until I was sure I knew how to use it. Rage hones me sharper than does self-pity. Then I showered, put on fresh duds, and went to the Jeep. The Discount Den radio sat on the passenger seat, examined and rejected.

Leo put on a show of being delighted to see me when he answered his door.

"I seem to have picked up a tail," I said, gesturing toward the irregular rumble of badly tuned exhaust coming from the street.

Leo moved to the front window as I took off my coat. "Orange Ford Maverick with one headlight?" he asked, pulling aside the shade just enough to peek out.

"That's the one."

"Benny Fittle." He laughed, letting the shade fall back.

"That sallow-faced kid who rides around on a scooter, writing parking tickets?"

He smiled. "Amanda and I noticed him yesterday, parked down the street from the turret. You sure he's a tail? One headlight is awfully obvious."

I sat in one of the slipcovered chairs. "I'm a murder suspect."

Leo took it as a joke. "Not much of one, if the only surveillance you can attract is a meter man in a Maverick," he said, alliteratively. "Want a beer?"

I apologized when he came back with the Pilsner Urquells. "I'm sorry I laid it on you that way."

"I figured she was dead years ago," Leo said, although his eyes said different. He was ever my friend.

"She is now."

"And you'll never forgive her for it?"

"I wish she'd called, just once, after that August."

"You better call Amanda."

"I will, but first I need help from you."

Ma was at church, playing bingo, so we stayed in the front room, drinking beer and eating remnants of bridge mix from the previous night's film festival. Only the hard nuts, the petrified pellets sure to crack dentures, were left.

I told it to him sequentially, beginning with the fact that Reynolds, the blueberry watchman, was really Severs, the Iowa cop.

"A dead cop," I finished.

Leo took a long pull on the Urquell. "Severs killed Maris?"

"Dillard and Patterson might think so, but I have doubts. Severs stuck around at least a month after Maris disappeared. That's a long time to risk hanging around after killing somebody."

"Severs was a patient man. It took him until Christmas to track Maris to Rambling."

"True enough," I said.

"And he never did find the money."

"Not if he never did find that key."

"The key to nothing." Leo forced a small grin. "Then the last Kovacs caught up with Severs and killed him?"

"Unless it was me."

His eyebrows danced. "You weren't kidding? They really suspect you of killing Severs and of having the money?"

I pointed at the window shade.

"And that's why Benny Fittle is tailing you?" His lips broke into a wide grin. "Benny Fittle is going to crack this case? Benny Fittle?" He laughed then, louder and louder until he almost lost his beer, through his nose.

"They'll still send out bulletins on the Kovacs brothers."

Leo wiped his mouth with one of the cocktail napkins Ma set out on film nights. "With all that money missing, surely you deserve a greater effort than Benny Fittle."

"I'm figuring Dillard called Rivertown's finest, asked them to put an obvious tail on me. Benny Fittle is temporary, a shot across my bow to let me know they like me for killing Severs and grabbing the money. They'll get an order to search the turret, comb through all my assets."

"That won't take but half an hour."

I made the obligatory laugh, then said, "They don't really think I did it. They've got nobody else."

"There's that Kovacs brother, unaccounted for."

I wasn't ready yet to tell him why I'd come.

"I thought I was protecting her," I said.

"You were a kid," Leo said, raising the bottle to his lips.

"I knew she hadn't been abducted," I said.

"You hoped."

"I knew."

Always I'd pulled back from the whole of it. I'd never wanted to know how much he had guessed. Now he had to understand all of it.

"Even though my boss at the laundry vouched for my alibi," I said, "two detectives dragged me over to her apartment, to rub my nose in the scene. They were convinced I knew more than I was saying."

"Rivertown cops," Leo said.

"They were right. I did know more than I was saying."

Leo's eyebrows went still over the neck of his beer.

"They started me in the kitchen. By then, they'd carted Herman Mays away, but his blood was still all over the table, a big brown puddle, like spilled coffee. They made sure I saw that first.

"After a minute, they walked me through the front room, to Maris's bedroom. 'Ever been in here, son?' the biggest of them, a greasy son of a bitch, asked as he went to her closet. He kept his eyes on me as he started touching her skirts and her blouses with his filthy hands. He had dirt under his fingernails, probably from lunch—the pig—and I kept thinking I wanted to hit him, hit that slug for daring to touch her clothes with his dirty fingernails. He must have seen that on my face, because then he went to her dresser and began opening drawers, slowly, one by one, pulling out her bras and her panties, caressing them with his filthy fingers. Watching me with those fat eyes the whole time. I had to look away, at the wall."

"Jeez, Dek, don't tell me this stuff . . ."

"It was a good thing those were the days before DNA, because they might have found . . . my . . ." I stopped to concentrate on the blank television screen, and on taking slow breaths.

"It's over, Dek."

"It's not over."

"Fittle?" Leo asked, misunderstanding. "He's just a slap. He'll go away when the cops learn you don't have the money."

"Someone has to pay for Maris."

"Severs is dead, Dek."

"Maybe it wasn't Severs."

"That surviving Kovacs, then?"

"I still see her bedroom, back in high school. The curtains she'd made, white with a kind of pink piping; a tiny dresser crammed with girl bottles, perfume, a hairbrush, some cream. Not a lot of stuff, but girl stuff. Her stuff. There was a tiny nightstand with a Tinkerbell lamp her mother gave her when she was little. And the bed. Jesus, Leo, that narrow, lumpy, saggy bed with the white bedspread that she'd sewn piping onto to make it match the curtains." I tried to take a deep breath, but my chest was too tight to let it all the way in. "It was a crummy little bedroom in a crummy little apartment, but she made it special: white, with a little pink." I looked at him. "I still smell that bedroom, Leo."

He leaned forward, worry lined deep on his forehead. "Why are we doing this?"

"That fat cop was wasting his time, trying to unnerve me by touching her things. By then, all I was focusing on was making my face a mask. Because, right off, in the kitchen, I knew she hadn't been abducted."

"Come on, Dek—"

"I knew she hadn't been abducted when I saw the kitchen table."

Leo's thick eyebrows touched, confused. "The blood?"

"The typewriter."

"You knew right away that the typewriter was missing? The cops let you look in her closet?"

"No. She'd taken to leaving the typewriter out, on the kitchen table, all the time. No more hiding it, no more knuckling under to her father.

I hadn't known why, exactly. All she'd say was she'd told him she wasn't going to be stuck in some factory town her whole life. She was going to go to college and then become a famous novelist, she wasn't going to end up . . ."

"Like him?"

"She wanted to rub the bastard's nose in it, so she left the typewriter out, right there on the kitchen table."

"M. M.'s future machine." Leo smiled, the ghost of the memory flitting across his face.

"She was going to be somebody."

"If not a famous novelist, then a famous reporter, or a well-known playwright, all with that typewriter," Leo said. "I remember."

"When that miserable bastard came home at night, stinking of beer and sweat and whores, that typewriter was the last thing he'd see before he passed out at the kitchen table."

"She must have come a ways since that afternoon when we first brought the typewriter home. Remember how she was afraid Herman would discover it?"

"No more. At the end, she was using it to taunt him. In the middle of the night, when he roused himself awake, when he got up to come . . ." I took a sip of beer. It had gone warm. "That typewriter was the first thing he'd see," I finished.

Leo looked at me, not understanding.

"The typewriter wasn't there, Leo."

Leo set down his beer. "You said that. And that told you she hadn't been abducted."

I watched his eyes saying nothing, letting him work it.

"And from that, Holmes, you deduced, being such a smart young man, that she used the typewriter to smash the head of the miserable Herman as he slept at the kitchen table?"

"Yes."

"It's too much of a reach. We know she took the typewriter, because you found it in Rambling, but to think that she used it to murder her father . . . too big a reach. Where's the motive?"

"She was pregnant."

He stared at me, blank-faced. Then he said, "You poor bastard."

"It's what we were arguing about on the sidewalk, that last time."

"Jeez," he said, "old Herman found out, there was a row, and she killed him."

"That day on the sidewalk, she'd just gotten it confirmed by the doctor. She hung on to me, sobbing, saying stuff I didn't understand. But one thing I remember: The doctor said she was well into her second trimester." I stopped, then went on. "All I could say was we'd get a place."

"You poor bastard."

"Damn it, no!"

Leo leaned back in his chair to give me some space.

"You remember my Aunt Lillian?"

"The nice one? She died just before we graduated, right?"

"End of May. Her funeral set me off, made me almost crazy with the fear of death. That was the day Maris and I . . . The only time," I finished.

The new thought clouded his face. He'd done the math in a second.

"You're sure she said second trimester?" His voice was a whisper.

"I didn't know what that meant. Not for a long time did I think to wonder what that meant."

"Working backward from August 10, assuming she was at least four months pregnant, brings you to . . ."

"Early April, at least six weeks before Lillian died." I looked at him. "If only I'd listened, out there on the sidewalk. If only I'd listened."

His words came out clipped. "You heard 'pregnant' on that sidewalk that day. It's the loudest word in a young man's world; it drowns out everything else."

I went on, in a hurry now to get it all out of my gut. "That last day, she put her hands on the sides of my face and told me I was naive. If only I'd listened, I would have understood, really understood, why she'd taken to leaving that typewriter on the kitchen table. She wanted to make sure Herman saw it when he woke up in the middle of the night . . ."

"All horned up?" Leo's eyes raged.

"She wasn't going to let him break her dream."

Leo got to his feet and started pacing. "That miserable prick. It wasn't enough that he had her vacuuming and doing his laundry, he had to—" He stopped pacing and looked at me with eyes full of pain. "I wish he was alive, so I could kill him."

"I was so blind right after she disappeared. I thought I'd caused it all. It wasn't until I did the arithmetic, worked it backward, that I dared to believe it couldn't have been me, not from that one time in late May."

He came back and slumped in his chair. "What's the point now, Dek? Even if you had figured it out, right away, and told the cops, they would have heard the words 'motive' and 'weapon' the way you heard the word 'pregnant.' They would have launched a manhunt for her that would have ended with her in jail, maybe for life."

"Perhaps."

"They might have even implicated you, at least until they found out you weren't the one who got her pregnant." He shook his head. "No sir, you left them with no motive, and no weapon. You protected Maris. You left her free to run."

He started to reach for a mummified almond, thought better of it, and sat back to appraise me from his chair. "It's not over, is it? There's still the matter of the missing money. More important, there's still the matter of who killed Maris."

"That's why I'm here."

I pulled out my cell phone, punched the buttons for message replay, and handed it to him.

The corners of his eyes tightened as he listened.

Dina had left the message toward the end of my thrashing through the fog.

"Dek? A police officer stopped by the Scupper the day before yesterday, showing around a couple of photographs. He didn't say what it was about. None of us recognized either of the two men, and I didn't think much more about it. But today, a very rough-looking man came by, asking if anyone knew where Carolina Dare had moved. He said she'd inherited something, and he'd been hired to make sure she received it. He wasn't that kind of man, Dek. He was one of the men in the photographs."

"The surviving Kovacs brother, at last." Leo handed back my phone.

"Somehow he learned enough to track Severs to Florida."

"Does that mean he doesn't know Maris was killed in Rambling?"

"No. He could have killed Maris, then Severs, and then begun backtracking her movements to find the money."

"He just doesn't know about you, and that key."

"Not yet."

"What the hell does that mean?"

"Dina told Kovacs she'd look for a forwarding address, and to come back today."

"No cops? Why would she do that?"

"I've had an inspiration," I said.

Thirty-six

Aggert returned my call at ten the next morning, just as I was leaving the turret to meet Leo. Down the side street, the one-eyed orange Maverick sputtered and wheezed to life.

"You got your body now, Elstrom; two of them, in fact." He cracked a mint. "I just got a visit from Lieutenant Dillard at the Sheriff's Department. He told me they just found Louise's—excuse me, Carolina's—body, and wanted to know how I was told of her death."

Dillard hadn't even told him Carolina's real name. "That must have been a fast conversation," I said, high-stepping through the snow across the spit of land.

Fifty yards to my left, the orange in my peripheral vision that was Benny Fittle's Maverick was sputtering. He would need time to catch up. I stopped when I got to Thompson Avenue and acted like I was admiring the view of the tonks.

"Fast conversation; you got that right," Aggert said. "I told him the house and car keys had been slipped through my mail slot and a message left on my machine."

The Maverick's engine was smoothing, and a break in traffic big enough for both of us was coming. "Things are heating up," I said as I crossed Thompson Avenue.

Aggert sighed. "Our concern is only with the estate. Did you call with news of the key?"

Benny Fittle, subtle surveillance man, had pulled to a stop across the street and was staring at me through the side window of the Maverick. I stopped on the sidewalk. I didn't want him to know where I was going.

"Forget the key. I called to warn you that you might get a visitor. Someone's backtracking Carolina's trail, and that might lead to you."

"Why me?" he said quickly.

"You were her lawyer. People who don't know much think lawyers know everything."

The mint clattered against his teeth, unoffended. "I only held her will and notified her executor."

"I just called to warn you."

"That damned key, Elstrom. It comes down to that damned key."

"You can call Dillard, ask him to protect you. Or you can go away for a couple of weeks. I'll call you when things cool down."

"You've got to find that lockbox, Elstrom. I've called every damned bank in the state, as Louise Thomas's lawyer. They'll only talk to her executor. You find that lockbox. I'll escrow the money for the Feds. Then your killer will have nothing to go after."

"I'm going to give the key to Dillard."

"Are you crazy? No one will believe you just gave it up. That key keeps us safe."

"Carolina bet on that, too. It got her dead."

"It's our only bargaining chip."

"Whoever is hunting the money doesn't bargain; he kills. The key goes to Dillard."

His voice sagged. "When are you going to see Dillard? Today?"

"I've got stuff to do first. Next couple of days."

"You're screwing with our lives."

"I called to warn you. Get out of town for a while, Mr. Aggert." I thumbed him off of my cell phone. There was no time.

I was tempted to wave at Benny, but he was eating something round—a doughnut, maybe, or a bagel—and I worried that when he saw his cover was blown, his embarrassment might cause him to spit up all over what was surely the last Maverick running. So I gave him no hint he'd been spotted as I went into the liquor store. Inside, I hurried past the display of two-dollar pints and went out the back door. The owner kept it unlocked during business hours, as a service to those customers who lived in the alley. I ran to a building three doors down and climbed the exposed wood stairs to the second floor.

"What's Benny eating?" Leo asked when I opened the door. He was at the double window facing Thompson Avenue, washing years of grime off the glass in the tiny kitchenette apartment.

"A doughnut or a bagel. It ought to keep him occupied until I come back out."

Leo had moved fast. First thing that morning, he called a banker who knew a landlord who'd been happy to take a fast three hundred for a few days' use of the place above the shuttered hardware store. Leo had the keys by ten o'clock.

The room had been painted pale blue, then layered with cooking grease, cigarette smoke, and despair. The decor didn't matter; we were after the view. The double windows looked across Thompson Avenue and the little spit of vacant land to the timbered door of the turret.

"It's going to be a while before I can pay you the whole rent on this." I'd brought one hundred and eighty dollars, all that remained of Maris's seven hundred.

"I'm doing this for Maris, not you."

I moved closer to the window.

"Not too close, Dek. This won't work if you're spotted here."

I stepped back.

The paper towel squeaked on the glass. "You sure we've got forty-eight hours?" he asked.

I couldn't see his face, but there was no mistaking the nervousness in his voice.

"Dina called me right before I came over here. She said the Kovacs brother just left the Scupper with my card. He was driving an old heap with Indiana plates. That means no rental car, no flying." I checked my watch. It was ten thirty. "Assuming no breakdowns, he'll arrive sometime tomorrow. My guess is he'll wait until dark, tomorrow night, to come at me."

He stopped rubbing on the window. "I still don't understand why you didn't ask Dillard to have the surveillance start now."

"Our county sheriff doesn't have jurisdiction." I pointed at the window. "The surveillance would get passed to Rivertown's finest. When they find out it involves the turret and me, they'll tell Benny to stock up on more doughnuts because he's going to be working late. Dillard said he can get a one-shot accommodation from the Cook County sheriff. Two coppers will be waiting for your call, starting tomorrow night. You alert them, they're here in five minutes to nab Kovacs."

"He'll come tomorrow night, for sure?"

"For the key to a lockbox that holds over a million dollars? You bet."

I bent to look at the long lens camera he'd mounted on a tripod.

"Good enough to pick out the wood grain on your front door at night, so long as you don't jiggle the camera," he said. "With luck, I'll be able to give them a license plate number along with the description of the car." He set the Windex on the floor beneath the window and turned to look at me. "What if he doesn't come tomorrow evening?"

"Then the next night, or the one after. We've got the key to over a million dollars."

Benny Fittle chugged away at nine thirty-five that evening. He might have been convinced I was tucked in for the night. More likely, he was out of doughnuts. Either way, we could now set things up. Leo hoofed it across Thompson Avenue to the turret.

He'd insisted that we fine-tune the view through the long lens by maximizing the lighting that would fall outside the turret. After we each got something to eat, I was to watch from the kitchenette and report improvements as he adjusted lights on the first, second, and third floors. Then we would switch locations. He would come to the kitchenette, to satisfy himself that the lighting on the timbered door was the best we could get.

"This is a waste of time," I said as he stomped the snow off his boots outside my door.

"Dare I bring up the last time you did night surveillance with a long-lens camera?" he asked, coming in. He was referring to a night when I'd staked out a Dumpster.

"I was looking for something that wasn't there."

"You fell asleep."

"Allegedly. And that had nothing to do with lighting."

"We make sure everything's right tonight." Leo fluttered his fingers at the floor of the turret. "Want to take some sawdust to breathe so you'll feel at home?"

I fluttered a finger of my own, told him I'd call him at eleven, and headed over to what used to be a Dog 'n Suds drive-in. Nowadays, nobody drove in; they mostly staggered up, exhausting ninety-proof fumes. Still, the hamburgers were decent enough, if only for the truly undiscriminating, and they were fast. I got two, wrapped in foil to minimize their flammability, and hustled back to the shiny walls of the kitchenette.

At ten fifteen, as I was finishing my first hamburger, a rusty red Honda Civic pulled up to the front of the turret. I trained the long lens on it to see a kid in a red shirt and matching ball cap get out. Leo had said he ordered one of his grunge pizzas from Mama Pasta's, a fogged-window joint that had been hardening arteries in Rivertown since before I was born. Through the camera, I watched Leo comically smack his lips as he paid for the pizza—his usual abomination of pineapple, spinach, and double Polish sausage—and wave off the change.

I finished the second hamburger at ten thirty. Then, for a time, I played the long lens up and down Thompson Avenue, looking at the cars and the girls and the johns.

At eleven, I called Leo's cell phone, as we'd agreed. I was going to begin by complaining that I could smell his pizza through my window.

He didn't answer. After five rings, his cell cut over to voice mail. I clicked off and squinted through the long lens. Lights burned brightly through the slit windows on the first and second floors. They were too narrow to see through, but I supposed he was in my office, where I kept my four-inch television and the electric blue La-Z-Boy.

I tried his cell again. Still no answer.

I called my landline, which rings in my office. It rang five times and then switched over to my machine.

I swung the long lens down to the first floor, focused on the timbered door, but thought he'd stepped outside.

A faint sliver of light ran down the opening edge of the timbered door. It was slightly ajar. I moved the lens down the sliver of light.

Something lay at the bottom, at the threshold.

It was a hand, fingers splayed. Not moving.

I ran down the stairs.

Thirty-seven

At six o'clock the next morning, they moved Leo out of intensive care, to a bed by the window in a semiprivate room. The guy in the bed by the door looked to be eighty pounds and dying of cancer, but he seemed in better spirits than Ma and Endora when they saw me come past the curtain. They gave me the kind of look nuns give to child molesters and turned back to whispering to Leo. I backed out of the curtained area, leaned against the doorjamb, and started chatting with the cancer patient. By unspoken agreement, we kept the conversation away from plans either of us had for the future.

After an hour, Ma and Endora left to get coffee. Neither looked at me as they walked out. The cancer patient noticed, and shrugged as best he could with tubes running into his veins.

"*C'est la vie,*" I said.

"What?"

"*Vie*: that's French, for 'life'. I just said 'that's life,' in French."

I think he laughed. "I'm about out of *vie*."

I walked around the curtain.

"You look horrible," I said to Leo—and he did. His pale body, all one hundred and forty pounds of it, had been beaten into shades of greenish yellow, purply blue, and, for brightness, a few spots of vivid red that had not yet dried to maroon. Still, there was but one tube running into his arm, and only two white bandages on his skull where he'd been stitched. Then again, I was desperate to see positives.

He motioned with his untethered hand for me to come closer. "You should see the other guy," Leo slurred, through bruised and swollen lips.

"You saw the other guy?"

"Nah."

"Hear anything?"

"Just your voice, afterward, saying you were sorry you've always been such a jerk."

Screaming at 911 in my cell phone, I'd run, as best I could, across the high snow on the spit of land and my own little street to drop to my knees at the timbered door. I'd been too afraid to lift his head out of the blood on the snow, so I held his hand and prayed to every God I'd ever heard of, until the ambulance came. Then I'd prayed in the Jeep on the way to the hospital.

Now he pinched my arm with his fingers, tugging me closer.

"You called that cop in Iowa?"

"Right after they wheeled you in. I called Dillard in Michigan, too."

"A couple of Rivertown coppers, by the names of Malloy and Cruck, stopped by with photos of Mother Kovacs's sons."

"I talked to them in the hall."

"I'll bet they were impressed by your planning, how you laid this super trap to catch the missing bank robber. They probably begged you to join their department."

"They love me like Ma and Endora do."

"I heard. It sounded like ice hardening." His lips twitched. He was trying to smile.

"Listen, Leo . . ."

He attempted to lift his head, gave it up after an inch, and sank back into his pillow, somehow smaller.

"Don't," he whispered.

I didn't. "Tell me," I said instead.

"I'd ordered nourishment, my special concoction—"

"I recognized the pizza guy by the clothespin clipped to his nose."

"It was magnificent, but I was only halfway through when I heard a rustling sound from down below. I thought it was you, come to share the gourmet experience, so I left the pizza and went downstairs. And then, nothing."

"Nothing?"

"Almost nothing. The guy uttered, 'Shit,' and then coldcocked me from the side as I got close to the bottom step."

"That was it? Just the one word?"

"Your man Kovacs isn't much for discourse. The fact that he continued beating me, though, after I lost consciousness means he was expressing disappointment that I wasn't you."

"You saw nothing?"

"I'd turned on the lights downstairs, as we'd planned, and slipped a hundred-watt bulb in the outside light. Like I told the cops, the guy came at me from under the stairs."

"I don't know that those guys will do much, Leo."

"Malloy and Cruck?" This time he made a whole smile with his damaged lips. His teeth were pink with blood. "They'll go have coffee cake. They were humoring your Michigan cop's request, bringing by those pictures. We can forget them. Word is, they do their own breaking and entering, on city time. They don't have time for anybody else's B and E."

I'd heard the same rumors. The Rivertown squad was not known as crime stoppers.

Leo mumbled something.

"What?" I asked.

"Was the guy there to kill you, or was he looking for that numbered key?" he murmured.

"Looking for the key. He took a chance, coming in when somebody was there."

"Dek?" He was fading, his voice becoming inaudible. "You said that Kovacs was driving up."

"He couldn't have made it that fast in a car. He must have taken a flight."

"He didn't get his key," Leo said. "You should get out of Rivertown for a few nights. Go stay with Amanda in her armored condominium."

"She's not returning my calls."

"Bring wine, bang on her door."

Ma and Endora loomed at the edge of the curtain.

I started to turn to leave.

Leo motioned with his good arm. I bent back down.

"I told the cops that, as greasy as those Kovacs brothers looked in the police photos, with their oily hair, and boils and pimples, jeez . . ." He stopped, searching for the word. "He smelled fresh. That's it: fresh. That's it," he said, his voice barely audible now. "There was something fresh about the bastard, like spring."

"What do you mean, fresh?"

"Tired," he murmured, and then he closed his eyes and went to sleep.

The dumbest man on the planet took a long time to straighten all the way up. His head was suddenly, and hugely, heavy with all the wrong assumptions he'd made. He concentrated on making his feet work as he stepped around the gloom that was Ma and Endora. The cancer man said something, but the dumbest man on the planet didn't want to hear anything above the clacking of his shoes on the glossy tile floor.

He knew the smart play: Call Dillard in Michigan, Patterson in Iowa, tell them of the man from Michigan, the brother from Iowa. Have the two cops conference in federal authorities to dispatch manpower and make arrests. Then sit back. The wise plan was obvious.

But the wise plan would do nothing for the furies in the dumb man's heart. It would do nothing for the memory of the woman, haunted and hunted, fleeing to Michigan, only to be murdered and burned. And it did nothing for the pain of the good, trusting fellow who lay beaten on a hospital bed, trying to wisecrack his way through a body full of pain.

The wise plan did nothing for revenge.

The dumbest man on the planet checked his watch. It was eight o'clock. There was barely any time at all, and the dumbest man on the planet had a lot to do.

Thirty-eight

East Chicago, Indiana, was only an hour from the turret. It was all the time I could afford, but it was enough. East Chicago was plausible, little more than ninety minutes from Rambling.

I stopped at a men's clothing store, bought a shirt, a pair of suspenders, and an extra-large golf hat that rode too low on my head. Then I pulled into the first bank I saw.

The Workman's Bank of East Chicago was an old two-story building that was missing mortar from its rows of red bricks. Inside, the oak transaction tables, the granite-topped teller line, and the roll-top desk visible through the president's open office door were old, too.

The safety deposit box vault was in the basement. The slender lady in the floral dress might have been younger than the bank, but only by a few hours. She wore glasses with thick lenses.

She peered at me. "You said the largest we have?"

"Yes, ma'am. I need to lock up a lot of stuff."

"That'll be a hundred and twenty-five dollars, for the one year's rental."

She cleared her throat politely. A careful woman, she wanted to see the money first. I paid with most of the rest of Maris's cash. I hoped it was appropriate.

The slender lady fussed behind the short counter riser and slid a signature card through the opening.

I started to write, then said, "Darn."

"Something wrong, young man?"

"I wrote my name illegibly. May I have another?" I moved the original card aside.

"Of course." She handed me a second card. I printed the name, then wrote the signature as I remembered it, from studying it in the Jeep five minutes before. I slid the card back.

"Thank you, young man." She filled out the four-part rental agreement and handed it to me.

"Bottom copy mine?" I asked.

"Yes."

I printed and signed again, made a show of separating the pink bottom copy because I was a helpful young man, and handed back the remaining three copies, still attached.

She handed me a small blue envelope. "Two keys inside, young man. Twenty-five-dollar charge if you lose one key, fifty if you lose both and we have to drill the box."

I opened the small envelope. The keys were old, and ridged; not like the numbered key Maris had left.

"What if I only want one key?" I asked.

"Two keys is the policy. Folks who don't want the second key put it in the box and leave it there."

"Yes, ma'am."

I checked the clock on the wall. At least eight hours remained until dusk. I was back to expecting that my visitor driving up from Florida wouldn't show up until after dark.

"One more thing, ma'am?" I smiled.

"Yes?"

"I want to make double sure I don't lose these keys. May I have a letter envelope and a sheet of paper to wrap your little key packet in?"

She smiled at my caution—someday I would make a fine senior citizen—and gave me the envelope and a piece of stationery. Both had the bank's name and logo on them.

"Perfect," I said.

The folks upstairs were just as nice, more than willing to let me used the old Selectric typewriter abandoned on a vacant desk in the corner. I fed in my newly acquired sheet of letterhead and, on behalf of the entire staff of the Workman's Bank of East Chicago, Indiana, typed a letter to its newest lockbox renter, welcoming him to Workman's family of happy customers. I added that everyone hoped he would stop in again. I typed the matching envelope, folded in the letter, and stuck it with a postage stamp from my wallet. I mailed it outside.

I called Aggert's cell phone from the Jeep. He didn't answer, of course, but he'd still be checking for messages.

"A friend of mine got beat up last night, by someone looking for that lockbox key. I'm done working for Louise Thomas's estate. This is all too risky. I've just mailed you the key. You give it to Dillard." It would keep him in West Haven, waiting for the mail.

I started the Jeep, then called Dillard. He was in.

"False alarm," I said. "That Kovacs brother that's supposedly headed up here hasn't left Florida yet."

"Where exactly did you get that information to begin with?" he asked. I'd been brief and vague when I'd first called him, but he'd gone along. Now he was not happy.

I revved the Jeep's engine, mumbled something about losing the cell signal, and clicked him away. He'd phone his contacts at the Cook County Sheriff's Department, call off the alert. There would be no coppers standing by, to come to the turret that night. It was what I needed.

I threw away one of the new lockbox keys in Indiana and tossed the other out the window as I entered Illinois. I changed out of the new suspenders and checked shirt and threw them away with the hat at a gas station in Chicago.

Arnold Duddits was an artist, though instead of chalks and paints, he worked with rubber stamps, a computer, and the same kinds of papers, fonts, and inks that banks used. His forgeries of canceled checks and bank statements were excellent. Certainly they'd been good enough to ruin me.

Two years before, I had testified for the defense in a municipal corruption trial. The case had drawn a lot of media attention because it involved allegations of insurance skimming by a popular west suburban mayor. I'm no document examiner—I leave that to experts like Leo—but I can chase down a paper trail of deposits, cashed checks, and bank balances, and that's what I did for the defense. I testified that their documents did not show any wrongdoing on the part of the mayor.

I'd been played. The documents were fakes, created by Arnold Duddits for an ally of the mayor's. And when it was reported that the duped expert witness for the defense was the son-in-law of Wendell Phelps, one of the movers and shakers of what moved and shook in Chicago, the case took over page one of both the *Chicago Tribune* and the *Chicago Sun-Times*. Duddits made me a front page fool, and that tanked my research business, because demand for fact-checkers who get facts wrong is always zero.

I set to drinking, a common enough recourse for failures. Common enough, too, was my need to find someone to blame for my downfall. I chose Amanda. She was innocent of any involvement in the case, she loved me, and she was handy. Most important, she was Wendell Phelps's daughter—something that, in my stupor, I took as the root cause of the publicity and therefore all my troubles.

Of course, Amanda divorced me. That slid me, on my dumb ass, the rest of the way downhill. I stopped only when I slammed into the turret. Unheated, uncleaned, it had been unoccupied by anything but vermin since 1929. Fittingly built of big stones, it literally was rock bottom.

Through my whole decline, I hated Arnold Duddits, and I did it publicly. Within hearing distance of several reporters hanging around outside the courthouse, I told Duddits I'd kill him. It was ninety-proof nonsense, but it made for an appropriate last sidebar on the front pages, before I disappeared into my stone cylinder in Rivertown.

Duddits worked in a depressed district of warehouses, in a tiny sham of a stationery store that could never have prospered enough to support his lifestyle of fast cars and slow women. It didn't. Duddits made his real money with his stamps and computers and papers and inks.

Distaste curled his upper lip as I walked in. "Is this some kind of damned joke?"

"Do you see me laughing, Arnold?"

"Out, Elstrom. Out." He pointed to the door.

I set the envelope on the counter.

"Out," he said.

"Look inside."

"I don't want to see what's inside."

"Look inside."

I like to think it was my skill with words, coupled with my boyish charm, that persuaded him. Realistically, though, it was probably the way my pounding heart made the vein in my sweating forehead pulse as I leaned across the counter.

"I'll kill you if you don't look inside that envelope, Arnold."

He picked it up and took a half step back. Then he fingered it open with his forefinger and thumb, as if he were expecting anthrax.

"Money and papers," he said, after taking the scantest of peeks.

"Forty-seven dollars. It's all the cash I've got. I'm paying you so I'll be complicit."

"What?" Still holding the envelope with his two tweezing fingers, he pressed back against the shelves of dusty papers. I leaned farther over the counter. He had no more room for retreat.

"Complicit. Paying you makes me a co-criminal. You don't need to worry that I'm setting you up."

He shot a glance at the front door. "Out," he said, hut his voicc was weakcning. His eyes came back and locked onto my pulsing vein.

"You know you ruined me, don't you, Arnold? Made me a chump? Sent my business tumbling, and me to the booze? That it got me divorced and tossed onto the street, and now I'm living in an unheated pile of limestone that's going to cripple me with arthritis?"

Pressed against the back shelves, he tried a smirk. "I wasn't charged with anything."

"That pisses me off, too, Arnold."

He shrugged, still working that smirk.

"I hate you, Arnold." I strained to get my forehead another inch across the counter.

"Tough."

"I've got nothing." I paused to breathe in, and to give him yet another second to admire my pulsing vein. "Except a gun, Arnold. I've got a gun."

His smirk trembled but didn't shrink.

"I'll kill you if you don't do what I want."

"You wouldn't dare. You made front page news when you said that the last time."

"I chiseled the numbers off the gun, and I've got somebody who'll give me an alibi."

The smirk went away.

I backed off the counter, named the sequence of states Maris could have followed, driving north. "Four different banks. You choose three. The last bank is in East Chicago. You don't have to be perfect, you just have to be reasonable. Make photocopies, and copy those again. You can destroy the originals, anything with your fingerprints on it. I just need the photocopies."

"I'll think about—"

I told him the dates and the amount that had to appear on the documents. "You'll remember them?"

"Maybe."

I looked at my watch. "I'll be back at three thirty."

I had work lights, the ones that have shiny bowl shades and spring clips. I had extension cords. I didn't have motion sensors. I stopped at a hardware store and bought the kind that have an outlet for a lamp cord. It took less than an hour to set them up—one on the first floor; two on the second, for the kitchen and my office; and one, which I hoped would not be triggered, for the otherwise empty third floor, where I slept.

I hoped they would appear to be a reasonable, and easily defeated, security system.

. . .

Duddits's window was dark at three twenty. I banged on the door. There was no answer. I banged some more until a light flicked on at the back of the shop. A shape moved through the gloom, unbolted the steel door. Duddits's hair was shiny. He was sweating.

"Busy day, Arnold?" I asked affably.

He turned without saying anything, and I followed him to the counter. He switched on the overhead fluorescents, disappeared into a back room, and reappeared in less than a minute, wearing thin surgical gloves. The flap on the envelope he was carrying was unsealed. Carefully, he bowed the envelope open and let the documents inside slide onto the glass counter. He folded the envelope three times and put it in his back pocket. Even though he was wearing gloves, his fingers had not once touched any of the photocopies inside the envelope.

I slipped on my own gloves, grabbed from a box in Leo's hospital room, and spread out Duddits's work. The papers were flyspecked from being copied, and copied again. The first three were from banks in Georgia, Ohio, and Michigan. They showed the transfer in, and then out, of one million two hundred and seventy-six thousand dollars—the exact amount stolen in Ida, Iowa—as Louise Thomas worked her way north. I had no idea where Duddits got the names and logos, but I knew he'd been careful enough to have used real banks.

The last of the photocopies were of the very real signature card and rental agreement for the lockbox at the Workman's Bank of East Chicago, Indiana. Duddits had forged the signature exactly as it had been written on the witness line on Louise Thomas's will.

I slid the photocopies into the envelope I'd brought.

"See you around, Duddits," I said at the door.

"In hell, Elstrom."

I parked the Jeep a mile away, on one of the side streets on the other side of Thompson Avenue, and walked to the turret.

To wait.

Thirty-nine

I sat, shivering, against the stone wall on the fifth floor of the turret. A wisp of frigid air blew in through the slit window above my head. I'd cracked it open to keep me alert. And to hear.

It was almost midnight. I'd been waiting since dusk.

Outside, a truck lumbered up the overpass, and the railroad signal began to clang as another late freight rolled through. Across the spit of land, the jukeboxes in the tonks pulsed out rock and roll music made fifty years before. It was a regular night in Rivertown. Except that I was hiding, waiting for someone with a gun to come for me. Someone different than the night before.

I heard a car clattering off Thompson Avenue. I stood up, careful to step around the ladder I'd pulled up after me. The top slice of the turret, the fifth floor, is gotten to only by a trapdoor. There is another trapdoor, in the ceiling, that leads to the roof.

I eased to the edge of the window, worried that I'd see Maverick orange sputtering back under the streetlamp. Benny Fittle had left at nine forty-eight, convinced, I hoped, that the absence of my Jeep and the dark turret meant that I was gone for the night. I didn't need Benny around to clutter up my plan.

There was something else I didn't need: a dead cell phone. A couple of hours past sunset, out of nervousness, I'd thumbed open my phone to check the charge. It didn't light up. My first reaction was to open the trapdoor, drop the ladder, and run down for the charger. My second reaction was that would be too risky. I might have chosen the exact moment my visitor arrived, and that could get me killed. I told myself it was better to stay where I was, atop a heavy, bolted trapdoor, sitting beside my largest kitchen knife, the handle of a baseball bat I'd found floating in the Willahock, and a flashlight. That conversation with myself wasn't entirely effective. Every minute or so, I started shivering. I tried telling myself that was from the cold. That didn't work much, either.

It was a sedan down below, an old clunker, black, or perhaps blue. It had turned off the side street and onto the stub of road that passed the turret on its way to city hall. The sedan cut its lights fifty yards away and coasted into a dark patch well behind the glow from the streetlight. Its engine went silent.

There was no moon. I kept watching the dark place where the car was but could see nothing. Lovers, perhaps, come to watch the Willahock.

A car door creaked open and, after a long few seconds, closed. There'd been no flash of an interior light. It was him, then.

Another car door opened, and closed just as quickly.

There were two of them.

I'd never considered that two would come.

One I could fight, if I had to. Even against a man with a gun, I had odds with the knife and the bat handle. They were lousy odds, but odds nonetheless. Against two men though, I had nothing. There were no odds against two men, not two men with guns.

I reached down to the floor. I needed to feel, again, the reassuring thickness of the lock bolt on the trapdoor. I'd oiled it that afternoon, so I could slide it all the way home. My fingers closed on the bolt. It was tight, locked solid.

I straightened up, edged to the window. Five stories below, the ground around the turret was black in the moonless night, too dark to see someone approaching the timbered door. When he—they—picked the lock and came in, the first-floor motion detector would trip the work lights I'd hung high on the beamed ceiling. Proof that I was gone, and enough light for them to find what I'd left behind.

But two of them had come.

I pressed against the cold limestone, straining to hear through the opened window. Only the sounds of a truck and a couple of drunks came back. A shiver prickled across my scalp.

Suddenly, a great, distorted rectangle of white light blazed across the snow. They'd opened the front door, tripped the first-floor lights. Other, thinner strips lay around the rectangle, bright spears thrown to the ground. Light from the slit windows.

They were in.

The long white rectangle narrowed and then disappeared. They hadn't panicked at the sudden light; they hadn't rushed to slam the door. They'd shut it almost leisurely. The turret was isolated on a deserted street, well removed from Thompson Avenue. No need to worry, not for two men with guns.

I watched the snow, imagining them moving through the first floor. They'd quickly see there was only a table saw and a white plastic chair. I'd left nothing for them on the ground floor.

A minute passed, then another, and then more white shafts of light lit the snow; these were farther out, spears thrown harder. I hadn't heard them on the circular stairs. They'd padded up, taking care not to ring the metal.

That was the plan. They were following my plan.

I stepped back from the window. The second floor would take the time. They'd have to work through the kitchen, to make sure that there were only cabinets and lumber and tools, that no one was hiding, waiting for them. Then they'd cross to my office.

I'd left the file folder open on the card table. It was labeled CAROLINA DARE/LOUISE THOMAS ESTATE in laundry marker letters too thick to miss. Setting it up, a few hours before, I thought of that file as cheese in a mousetrap, set to trigger a delayed-action kill spring.

Except now there were two mice. The kill spring suddenly looked weak.

I'd figured it would take no time at all to see how Louise Thomas moved the money through Duddits's banks in Georgia and Ohio and into Michigan and to understand how Louise's lawyer got control after she died. The will in the file was almost identical to the one I had. Except that Duddits had removed my name as executor and inserted the name of that fresh-smelling bastard who'd killed Maris and beaten up Leo.

Duddits's last bits of fiction showed Aggert's withdrawal of one million two hundred and seventy-six thousand dollars from Louise's last bank account, in Michigan, and the documents he filled out to rent a large lockbox at the Workman's Bank of East Chicago, Indiana.

They were good documents, my fear whispered to the needles dancing on my scalp.

New lights flashed outside. More spears now lay on the snow, farther still from the second-floor beams. I stared at them, not believing. The men had climbed up to the third floor.

There was nothing for them on the third floor. The trail to the money was in a file folder on the second floor, in plain sight.

It was caution; they were making sure no one was in the turret. Let them check the third floor, see the bed, the clothes piled on the chair, the fiberglass shower temporarily installed. There was nothing else there. Let them come up to the fourth floor, even. The stairs ended there. There was nothing at all on the fourth floor, not even the ladder, now.

Outside, some drunken fool shouted across the spit of land. I pulled at the casement window, carefully drawing it closed to shut out the noise. What I needed to hear was inside, on the third floor.

I knelt to feel the slide bolt again. Certainly it was solid enough to hold the heavy trapdoor in place no matter what they hit it with. The whole floor was strong, made of tight planking milled close to a century before and cut thick enough to stop bullets. I pressed my ear to the fine gap between the trapdoor and the floor.

A sliver of light wavered faintly, just in front of my eye. I turned away quickly, blinked my eyes swiftly to regain my night vision. I'd installed no motion lights on the fourth floor; they'd come up silently and were examining the seams in the trapdoor with a flashlight. My mind flirted with lunacy: I wanted to scream down through the wood, tell the fools that everything they needed was lying on my card table. I made no sound, of course. I held my breath and looked away from the light faintly outlining the trapdoor.

Something began scratching at the underside of the trapdoor, as if testing the wood, probing it. The scratching stopped. Something hit the trapdoor, hard. It hit it again, just as solidly. A man's voice swore, faint, muffled by the thick wood.

They'd taken a two-by-four from downstairs, used it to ram the trap door. That it was bolted shut told them someone was on the fifth floor.

My mind flashed ahead. They'd think of my tools, scattered in the kitchen. They'd choose the electric circular saw; I had nothing else that could cut through thick wood. They'd know it would take them a long time to cut through the floor, even wielding a circular saw, but they were figuring they had at least four or five hours until sunrise.

I had those hours, too.

I rolled off the trapdoor and quietly stood up. I had the knife, the baseball bat handle, and the flashlight.

I opened the slit window facing the spit of land. I could yell out, wave the flashlight beam, and hope someone on Thompson Avenue would hear. The window, though, was narrow, and with the first three floors lit up by my work lights, a flashlight beaming from the fifth floor might be hard to spot. It would be better if I went up to the roof. I could wave the flashlight up there like a beacon.

Footfalls pounded the circular stairs below. They were running down to the kitchen for my tools.

I moved the ladder under the trapdoor to the roof. Once outside, I'd pull the ladder up behind me and use it to wedge the trapdoor shut. Then, in my pea coat and knit hat, I could dance myself crazy to stay warm as I shouted and waved my flashlight signal into the sky. Sooner or later, some late-night denizen would focus foggy eyes on me long enough to yell for the cops.

The metal stairs rang again. They were charging back up to the fourth floor. I had plenty of time. They'd soon learn it would take hours to cut through the planking to get to the fifth floor. Then they'd think they'd have to do it again, to get to the roof. Except that was impossible. The roof timbers were over a foot thick, impossible to cut with a circular saw. I would be absolutely safe, up on the roof.

I climbed the first rungs of the ladder. Halfway up, my fingers grazed the heavy braided pull rope for tugging the roof door closed. I climbed five more rungs and reached for the first of the twin side bolts. I'd greased them in October, the last time I'd been up on the roof. The first bolt slid back as if it had been buttered. The second slide bolt was tougher but loosened on the third tug.

They started pounding beneath the floor below. For a moment, I paused, confused, as metal thudded against wood, clanging every third or fourth blow. I guessed they were swinging my crowbar at the heads of the metal bolts that fastened the hinges through the oak. Let them swing. The old carriage bolts were blacksmith hardened; a week's worth of beating wouldn't crack them loose.

Twin side bolts undone, I reached up and pushed against the trapdoor. It didn't move.

Down below, the pounding stopped.

They were thinking. They'd have to use that circular saw. I had plenty of time to work the roof door loose.

The pounding started again.

I moved up another rung, got better leverage, pushed up with flat palms. The trapdoor did not budge. Bile worked up the back of my throat: The roof was new, thick and well insulated. The kind of roof designed to keep heat trapped in the turret, where it couldn't melt away the twenty-four inches of snow that had fallen since December.

Furious at my cockiness, at my stupidity, I ducked my head, lunged up with my shoulder. Once, twice, and again. The trapdoor didn't flex an inch. It was frozen to my new roof under a winter's worth of snow and ice.

The pounding stopped.

I gave the roof door a last push. Nothing. I started down the ladder.

The slit window facing Thompson Avenue would have to do. Yell and wave my flashlight; somebody would notice. If not now, then later, when the lizards and the city hall staffers passed by on their way to work. The floor was thick; there was time. I jumped off the ladder while I was still two rungs up. No need to worry about noise.

Excited laughter came from down below. Laugh, you bastards, I thought as I moved to the window.

I pushed the window all the way open. And stopped.

New spears of light lay on the snow down below, farther out from those cast by the first three floors. They were from the fourth floor, just below me—but these weren't white from incandescent bulbs. These were orange . . . and flickering.

I looked down at the floor, not believing. Faint threads of orange light danced in the gap around the trapdoor. I dropped to my knees, pressed my nose against the crack.

Fire.

I jumped up and ran to close the window that would turn the turret into a gigantic flue, sucking the flames up toward me. The Kovacs brothers could stay down on the lower floors and wait in safety. For me to come to them.

They laughed, down below, crazed men, excited by the spectacle.

Die of smoke. Die of burns. Die of gunshots or of beatings.

Don't die suffocating, waiting to choose.

I grabbed the knife, slid back the locking bolt. I tugged open the trapdoor—and jumped.

Forty

A bone in my ankle snapped as I hit the floor, crumpling me forward, to my knees, screaming from the pain.

They laughed, dropped the flaming papers they'd been waving to make the smoke and the fire, and slugged the back of my head, to drop me, unconscious, like a swatted fly.

A wave of glacier water shocked me awake, running frozen between the tape on my mouth and the tape over my eyes, into my nose and my ear. I tried to roll to my side, to sneeze it away, to breathe, but they'd taped my arms and my ankles, too. I couldn't get the momentum to roll over. I fought panic, focused on breathing through my nose. Air came, but it was ragged and exaggeratedly slow, like gasps from a dying man.

The toe of a shoe nudged at the side of my head. "You awake?" The voice was flat, midwestern.

It was good that he was talking. I made a noise into the tape across my mouth.

"What's that?" a different voice asked. "You hear that, Butch? Piss-head grunted. Think he expects us to understand?"

"Sure as shit, Sundance. Grunted like a pig."

Butch and Sundance. They were playing with cowboy names from an old movie. At least it wasn't Starsky and Hutch. I couldn't have stood it if it was Starsky and Hutch.

Butch giggled a noise. Then the toe came again, from the direction of his voice. Not hard. Not yet.

"We don't speak pig," Sundance said. "We're going to take the tape off your mouth, so you can answer real polite. Got it?"

I made frightened noises into the tape a second before he ripped at my mouth. It wasn't a reach.

"Where's the money?" Butch said.

"There's a file—"

The toe kicked the front of my ear, snapping my head sideways. "The money, asshole." The tip of the boot came back, to play with the pain.

I made myself see Maris, trapped inside her Rambling house as the wind howled outside and she fought to not cry.

"Indiana—" I gasped.

He kicked me again, not as bad as the first time.

"We seen the file," Butch said.

"Then you saw it all. He put the money in a bank in Indiana."

"How'd he get it?"

"She came to him scared, probably because she found Severs poking around. She said she knew something about a bank robbery, maybe even said something about having the money. Aggert convinced her to appoint him executor of her will, in case something happened. That gave him access to everything she owned. Then he killed her."

"I told you, Eddie." Sundance's voice was shrill. "No way Randall would have killed her, not without knowing where the money was."

"Shut up, damn it." Lance Kovacs's boot came back to my ear. "Go on."

"Aggert used that legal authority to contact banks until he found out where she parked the money. He withdrew it."

"And put it in that lockbox in Indiana?"

"The Workman's Bank, in East Chicago."

"We'll kill you if you're lying."

"Aggert's hanging around his law office in Michigan. He'll leave the money alone until things die down."

"How come you know this?"

"Aggert was setting me up. He hired me to nose around about the woman's death, being real public about it, when all the time he'd already killed her. He was going to get me blamed for the murder, then for taking the money—and for killing Severs, too," I added, as if I believed Aggert had killed the blueberry cop. "I put that file together to give to the cops, show them Aggert's the one."

"The money is in East Chicago?"

"I want Aggert dead."

It was the truest thing I could say. My eyes were wet beneath the tape, from anger, frustration, and from stupidity that went back decades. I saw Maris smile, that first time we walked home together. I saw, too, a life with Amanda that would never be. It was all welling up in my eyes, all the waste.

Sundance's boot pounded a step or two next to my head. He kicked me, and I blacked out.

Sometime later, perhaps ten minutes, perhaps an hour, I came to. I was on my belly. Something stickier than water was working its way down the side of my head.

I strained to sense any change in the air, any sound in the room that meant they were still there. Outside, a truck with a bad muffler vibrated one of the slit windows. I could hear nothing else.

My arms, taped behind me, were numb. My shoulders throbbed as if they were being pulled from their sockets. I counted to ten as slowly as I could manage and lunged into a roll to my right. My shoulders ripped, and for a second, I thought I would faint. But I teetered, and held, and gradually some of the pain passed as I settled onto my right side.

I worked my left shoulder, up an inch, down an inch. The tape at my wrists tore at my skin, unyielding, but then it moved a little. Then, ludicrously, it came completely off my left wrist. I tore it from my hands, my eyes, my ankles.

My throat caught at the magnificence of it. They'd used my duct tape, the cheap, no-name stuff I'd bought at the Discount Den one day when I'd been killing time, watching Leo agonize over which dumb luau shirt to buy. I'd ended up buying two rolls of the silver tape, to keep the slashes in the Jeep's side curtains closed. The cuts kept opening anyway. The tape was crap. The adhesive dissolved when exposed to water. Or sweat.

I stood up and hobbled on duckling legs to the slit window. The old sedan was gone. In the east, the sun was coming up.

They would have taken the file, to slap him with.

With luck, I'd just committed murder.

I put my palms on the stone sill, to steady myself as I looked out—and for a time, I cried, like a child, for things I didn't understand, and for things I did, and for a blond girl with a boy's name, who would never again see a sunrise.

Forty-one

"This is crazy," Leo whispered.

It was the first week of April. Though it was one o'clock in the morning, the night was warm. The moon was cooperating, too, casting just enough light to work.

"This is restorative," I said in a normal voice.

"Crazy," he whispered.

"You don't need to whisper," I whispered. "No one can see us, down here in the dark, and the trucks on the overpass will drown out what we're doing."

He scraped in silence for a moment and dropped another piece into his plastic bag.

"Couldn't you have found something else to obsess about while I was recuperating?" he asked.

"Like what?"

"Like being straight with that Michigan cop, Dillard. You could have told him that Aggert killed Maris, that the Kovacs brothers killed Severs. You could have thrown in that it was Aggert who beat me up."

I shifted onto my good leg. I'd been lucky. The break in my ankle had been clean. Even with a walking cast, though, it still hurt.

"Could you identify Aggert from a photograph?" I asked, dropping a particularly fine piece into my own bag. "Do you think they'd pick him up, based on your recollection that your assailant smelled fresh, and my assurance that Aggert's a known breath mint user?"

"What about the Kovacs brothers?"

"Same thing. I can't identify them. My eyes were taped shut."

"You know what I mean." Another piece fell into his plastic bag.

"You know what I mean, too. I don't just want Aggert picked up. And I don't just want him tried."

"It's been days, Dek. You've heard nothing."

"Work." I peeled away another sheet.

"Aggert could come back at you," Leo said, which was what he'd really been talking about the whole time. "He broke into the turret a couple of times before that night he beat me up."

"It's worth the risk. Besides, he thinks I mailed him that key."

"By now he knows better. He knows you set the Kovacs brothers on him. He's got to want to kill you."

"Maybe he thinks I've already tipped the cops."

"Maybe Aggert's been too busy fleeing the Kovacs brothers."

I turned toward his place in the dark. "I want Aggert to run, like Maris ran. I want him to know fear, to jump at every little whisper in the night, like she must have, for all those years."

"For most of her life, Maris was running from Rivertown."

I leaned against the old wood, to give my ankle a rest. "Maris trusted Aggert, and he killed her. For that, I want him to run from the Kovacs brothers. Then I want them to catch him."

Even now, well after the Kovacs brothers had kicked me into a week's recovery, spent thinking, in bed, I startled myself by how certain I sounded, saying I wanted a man dead.

"How much of this is about punishing Herman Mays?"

I didn't answer because I didn't know.

Leo stopped scraping. "You can't always put everything right, Dek."

"We're putting something right, this very minute."

His breath quickened beside me, and I knew he was fighting a laugh. "Well, yes, there's this . . ." He lost it then and laughed the longest he'd laughed since Aggert had beaten him.

"Why can't Rivertown, tank town though it may be, have its inviolate monuments, like Chicago and New York and"—I paused, grasping—"Pittsburgh?"

"But this, this is only—"

"Shush," I said, not for the noise, but for the disrespect.

"Pittsburgh? Name a monument in Pittsburgh."

"Don't have to," I said, working the broad, dull blade. The garbage bag next to me crinkled as I felt for the opening to drop another piece in. "The point is, every town's got its monuments, places that must be maintained and cherished."

"We're defacing."

"We're restoring."

"Speaking of restoring—"

"One project at a time," I said, cutting him off.

"Have you talked?"

"Only after you called her to tell her I'd been roughed up. She wanted to come right over. I, being a hero, said my wounds were superficial. She said she was thinking of going to Paris, get a head start on an art book she was researching. I said she should go."

"And?"

"I told her I loved her, as an adult."

"And?"

"She said to call when I was ready to bury Maris." I leaned into my work, and a piece the size of a road map lifted away. "I can feel your lips smiling. Keep scraping."

We worked, then, in silence. By four in the morning, the touch of our fingers told us it was done. We dragged the garbage bags, heavy from the rubber content, over to the trash receptacles and were gone.

We'd agreed we'd wait until noon, but he was outside the turret, in the Porsche, idling, at quarter to eleven. I knew him well enough to know he'd show up an hour early. He knew me well enough to know I'd be ready and waiting. Juvenile minds, no matter what their ages, often think in perfect synchrony.

Word had traveled fast. The dirt and gravel lot under the overpass was filled, and cars were parked all the way back up the road. We left the Porsche a half mile away and hobbled down.

I counted twenty-eight people ahead of us in line, chirping like larks at the wonder in front of them.

"Six hot dogs, one cheese fries, and two lates," Leo said an hour later, when we finally got to the window.

"Not lates, jerk weed; it's lah-tays," Kutz snarled from behind the little opening.

"Whatever, Mr. Kutz."

Kutz bent down to the window. "You shits are here awful early." Lack of a formal education had never inhibited Kutz from communicating clearly and directly.

"We heard you were renovating," Leo said, without a hint of a smile. "Looks so much better."

Kutz's ferretlike eyes glistened, but that could have been from the grease.

Both Leo and I stepped back a foot to make a show of admiring the old wood trailer. It was once again its peeling, graying white, except for the hundreds of bits of purple latex that still clung to the wood like lavender corn plasters pasted on old skin. I hoped the wind would blow them off soon, so that the restoration would be complete.

Kutz pushed the plastic tray through the opening. Leo frowned at the not-steaming coffee and took a sip.

"Careful of that; it's lukewarm," Kutz said, through the window.

"This is your regular coffee, Kutz," Leo said. "Weak and burned as always."

"That whip cream shit was too expensive; I cut it out. It's still a lah-tay, just without the cream."

"You charged us eight bucks for two cups of your same old dish-water?"

"I figure you shits are just after the caffeine, being as you might not have gotten much sleep last night." His beady eyes moved from Leo's face to mine. "And I figure you want everything the way it used to be, right down to the lousy coffee."

Leo gave him the barest of smiles and took the tray from the counter.

The picnic tables around back were full. Fifty more people were eating standing up, like guests at a large garden party. It might have been my need for self-congratulation, but they all looked like they were enjoying a world once again made right.

We found an open place by the back of the trailer, set our tray on the ground—genetically imprinted to survive, most ants seem to avoid Kutz's hot dogs—and began to eat. Ten feet away, a dozen shiny black garbage bags, the exact kind I use, sat neatly twisted shut next to the oil barrel garbage cans. A thirteenth bag had been opened by some disbeliever, its contents made visible. For a time, we enjoyed the expressions of the people who stopped by the open bag as they were leaving, to smile and sometimes finger the torn sheets of rubberized lavender paint that should never have been applied to such a landmark.

I took the last bite of my hot dog. Finally, I let my eyes find the familiar spot on the back of the trailer, visible now, once again.

And saw.

I brushed at my eyes with the back of my free hand, worked my throat to swallow the last of a hot dog instantly turned to a greasy lump.

"Leo."

He moved closer, to look where I was looking.

"Your heart, another reason why this edifice should never have been painted—" He stopped then, seeing everything. Then he pointed, his voice now hushed. "Wasn't there just the one . . . ?" He let the question die, because he knew the answer—and the meaning. He dropped his hand.

I moved my fingertips to touch the heart she'd cut in the wood that August day, enclosing her initials and mine. For forever, we'd said, when wonder was new.

But there was a new carving now, cut deeper and much later, too much later. It was a larger heart, surrounding, as though protecting, the outline of the old.

"She was here," Leo said.

I saw her in my mind, the ghost of a girl on a winter's day, standing in the snow, cutting with the point of a key, or maybe, like the last time, with an ivory-handled knife that she'd brought along.

I looked away when my imagination began drawing another picture of her, standing outside the turret, thinking, wondering, if she should knock on the door.

She hadn't. She'd gone away. Like the last time.

Forty-two

I can see the First Bank of Rivertown from the roof of the turret. It is a squat, triangular-shaped stucco building, set on an oblique plot where two crooked roads meet just off Thompson Avenue.

Its name, First Bank, is unnecessarily distinguishing, for there has never been, and probably never will be, a second bank in Rivertown. The lizards who run the town have no need for another. The First Bank has never advertised for new customers, never given away toasters or coasters or calendars. It serves as an appliance of city hall, that municipal black hole, to suds away any such fingerprints and palm grease as might have stuck to cash payments for zoning changes, building permits, and business licenses.

I was up on the roof at six that morning, sipping coffee, looking at that bank. It was later in April, and it was good to be on the roof, riding the webbed lawn chair that I keep up there for nights when I cannot sleep. The roof is where I think best, when everything is closed and the only sounds come from the trucks and the trains hurrying past Rivertown.

That morning, though, I wasn't up there thinking. I was done thinking, done wondering. It was time.

Lieutenant Dillard had called four days before. "I've got Sergeant Patterson conferenced in with us, Elstrom."

Dillard went on before I could ask what he'd been doing. Or not. "There was a little shootout this morning, in the northern part of our wonderful state. Seems one of the local constables up there came across two boys named Kovacs, digging holes on a hobby farm. Being neighborly, and knowing that the owner of that hobby farm was a lawyer named Aggert, the officer inquired as to why they were digging holes on Mr. Aggert's land. Neither of the Kovacs brothers thought to respond verbally. Instead, they drew handguns. The constable, himself a hunter and marksman, shot them both, several times. Since the brothers are no longer able to answer questions, the constable called the state lab team. After some digging, they discovered Mr. Aggert, buried in a field of recently dug holes."

"The brothers were looking for the bank proceeds," I said, because it was reasonable to say.

"No doubt," Dillard said. "It's a fair guess that Aggert was not forthcoming about whatever he knew, so the brothers killed him and began digging up the property."

"What did Aggert know?" Again, I was being reasonable.

"We're not completely sure, but we have uncovered some tantalizing leads."

"Wonderful," I said.

"You hear that, Sergeant Patterson? I told you he'd be ecstatic."

Dillard paused, to let Patterson express his own delight. When Patterson didn't, Dillard went on. "The Kovacs brothers had been living in their automobile for some time. First off, we learned they discovered that Severs was living in an inexpensive motel in Benton Harbor."

"How did they learn that?"

"We're guessing through some mutual contact back in Iowa, but we'll never know. Anyway, we got to that motel too late; the manager said he'd thrown away all of Severs's stuff. We think it likely that the Kovacs brothers, from information they either beat out of Severs or found in his motel room, traced his activities backward, to Florida."

"Florida," I said.

"The very same Florida you mentioned, Elstrom, just days ago. Remember when you called to say the Kovacs brothers were on their way up from there, and asked my help in alerting your local county sheriff, to be ready to come save your sorry ass?"

"I do recall that, Lieutenant."

"You were vague as to how the Kovacs brothers knew to come after you."

"I told you I'd gone down there, looking for Carolina's trail. I handed out my cards to several people who'd known her. One of them called me, to say someone else had come looking for Carolina."

"That woman, Dina, who worked with Carolina?"

"Yes. She was trying to be helpful, so she gave the man my card. I began to worry that it might have been a Kovacs brother and called you for help."

"But you canceled the alert."

"I got to thinking that I was in no danger. I knew nothing. And I was right. No one came to Rivertown, Lieutenant."

"Except that person who beat up your friend, at your residence, the very same night you were expecting a visitor from Florida."

Dillard had talked to the Rivertown cops. "Coincidence. My local police think that was a random home invasion."

"This whole thing is a puzzle, Elstrom," Dillard continued. "Especially the lockbox."

I moved the phone away from my cheek, afraid he might hear my breathing quicken. I was almost certain that I had never mentioned the existence of Maris's flat key to either Patterson or Dillard—but the meanings of "almost" and "certain" are miles apart. It was one of the things I'd been rethinking, mornings up on the roof.

"Lockbox?" I asked, after too long.

"The Kovacs brothers had bank documents that show the movement of a considerable amount of money up from Florida through Georgia and Ohio and into Michigan. That money appears to have ended up in a lockbox in East Chicago, Indiana."

"I know nothing of that."

"We went to East Chicago," Dillard said. "The lady that runs the safety box vault is quite elderly. She wears thick glasses. She's not sure she'd be able to identify the man who rented the box, but she is positive that he wore a checkered shirt and suspenders. And she is certain that he never came back after renting it."

"Aggert," I said.

"So it would appear." Dillard said. "That would explain all the holes on his farm. The Kovacs brothers were digging for the key to that lockbox."

"The insurance people will want to see if they can drill that lockbox," Patterson said, speaking for the first time. "Unless, of course, Mr. Elstrom, you can think of something else?"

"There is one thing," I said. "Since both Kovacs brothers survived Iowa, whose body was torched in Severs's car? Another robber?"

"Or some itinerant," Patterson said quickly. "We'll never know."

I'd touched a nerve. "Damned shame, not knowing," I said.

"Like the fact that, without a positive identification that it was Aggert who rented that lockbox, it might take years to get at what's inside, and then only if the annual rental goes unpaid." Patterson was indeed having a foul day.

"Damned shame, not knowing that as well," I said.

"There's another thing, Elstrom," Dillard said.

"Yes?"

"The Kovacs brothers had a copy of Louise Thomas's will. It names Aggert as her executor, not you."

When I didn't respond, he said, "Elstrom?"

I'd showed the Louise Thomas will to too many bankers and post office employees to lie. "I can only guess that the Kovacs copy was a forgery, to get Aggert involved." Word for word, it was true enough.

"Damned shame, not knowing," Dillard mimicked. Then he told me I could come up to claim Maris's remains.

The safety deposit vault was in the basement. I fingered the flat key in my pocket as I walked down the short corridor.

"I believe I have to sign an access card," I said to the middle-aged woman, "for a box rented a few weeks ago."

"Name?"

"Elstrom. Vlodek Elstrom." I showed her my driver's license.